Spirits Unleashed

The first book in the Spirit Wars series

Thomas Pierce

Prologue

"This one will do nicely to send a message," a man in formal black garb stated.

"But sir, are you sure that this one is necessary? The amount of damage it can do once let loose could be catastrophic," a second man with similar attire responded.

The first man snapped back, "Do not question me rookie. Release 349, end of discussion".

"As you wish," the second man stated, his features growing pale as to what was about to unfold as he reached for his radio. "Lift all containment protocols on captive 349, code is 3582, under authority of Agent 6".

In the distant desert near the mostly underground metal fortress, a pair of men in dusty jeans and worn jackets laid on an overlooking hill with a radio scanner lying nearby. One man turned to the other "349? Captive? What have they been doing in there?"

The second responded, "I don't know, but with how one of the agents sounded things might get really ugly really quick."

As if responding to the man's statement, an unearthly shriek erupted from the facility that could only be described as demonic. Following the sound was the most horrific looking entity the pair had ever seen.

A creature wrapped in gray and black smoke jetted out from the building, ghastly wings seemingly oozing shadows as it unfurled its wingspan to reveal a skeletal form similar to a hawk; if one were to grow 15 feet long and was born in the pits of hell. When the falling smoke touched the desert flora, flowers seemed to harden and grow spines as cacti fired their needles in every direction like a biological shrapnel grenade.

The two men quickly scrambled to their feet and bolted in the direction of their black truck as the creature shrieked once more before it shot off into the clouds, sending off a ripple of booming energy as it shattered the sound barrier.

"What is that thing???" one man stated to the other, gasping to regain his breathe.

"I don't know," responded the second before he continued, "but we have to warn the others...who knows what that thing is capable of."

Chapter 1: Project Binding

Luke quickly scrambled notes down as his chemistry professor lectured through another class of chemical bonding. Luke's notes, however, were not about the lecture. His mind racing, he rushed to get his thoughts on paper before they flew out of his head like a steady breeze.

Brushing his dark brown hair from his eyes, Luke wrote line after line of equations and descriptors for variables. Finally, he wrote and circled a short phrase: *energy retainment.* With every thought now written down, he dropped his pen before leaning back and inhaling deeply.

"And following this lecture, as is custom for Fridays, a short quiz on what we have learned this week" the professor stated from the bottom of the lecture hall.

"Shit," Luke muttered as he exhaled. He had missed the entire week's lectures in an attempt to find a breakthrough on his little side project. In doing so, he had doomed himself to another failing week. If things continued at this rate, he would fail the only class left needed to graduate.

Luke grabbed a quiz from the stack as it was handed to him, before then handing off the rest of the stack and quickly attempting to answer the questions. Questions he had completely ignored the lectures on and would have to guess through the entire quiz.

Once finished with the best guess answers he could muster, Luke strode from the lecture hall to meet up with his friend John. John Olsen was a burly type in contrast to Luke Connor's slimmer but athletic physique. Towering well over 6 feet tall and built like a bull, John had long dirty blonde hair, a matching beard, and deep blue eyes. He looked like a Viking, and one would assume he threw axes and chugged entire casks of ale on his weekends.

His physique was balanced, however, by a lackluster intelligence. While Luke could swim in equations and come out with a fish, John would simply sink like the rock he is.

"Man, whoever decided math needed letters in it needs to be executed," John exclaimed. "I'd be lucky to get more than a C in this class."

"At least you will pass," Luke responded with a sigh. "I spent yet another class scribbling, so at this rate I might as well just sign up for my class again next semester."

John pointed down to the notebook in Luke's hand in response. "Speaking of which, figure out your little problem yet in your book of symbols?"

To this, Luke opened his notebook to the page he was working on in class. "I think I may have finally cracked the code." Luke then pointed to one of the equations he jotted down, "This should give the proper distribution of electricity through a device based upon its size to capture and contain a spirits energy." "And this," Luke continued as he pointed to another equation, "hopefully gives us the proper angles of reflection needed to contain the energy. Assuming of course we can find a way to shape a crystal to meet these parameters."

Luke closed his notebook as John shook his head, "Man, I can't make anything of that mumbo jumbo you wrote down. But if you say it should work now then why not give it a try?".

"Well, I would," Luke started before he paused for a moment. "However, I used the last of my quartz on my previous attempt." Luke's memory shot back to the crystal shattering in his dorm room minilab from a flaw in one of the earlier equations.

"However," Luke stopped walking and paused again. "I do know where I might be able to get one." He then quickly turned around, sprinting back in the direction of the science building.

"Hey, wait up!" John yelled to Luke as he did his best to follow his eager friend.

Luke slowed down as he reached a closed door near the center of the science hall's ground flow. "Geology 101" Luke read; the writing printed on a plaque near the top of the door. He then reached for the doorknob, knocking as he slowly opened the door and peered into the empty classroom.

"Come in," a young woman called out to the sound. A welcoming smile spread across her face soon after as she saw who it was. "Oh, Luke! How can I help you today?"

Sabrina Grier was a graduate student roughly one year older than Luke... and assistant to about half the geology department at their university. While Luke spent his energy on science fiction style projects, Sabrina spent hers learning everything she possibly can within her field.

Similarly built to Luke, she had a thinner athletic physique and darker hair. Her eyes and drive were where she detoured from Luke's own, however. While Luke's dark brown eyes formulated equations to solve problems his personal project created, Sabrina's eyes seemingly soaked in every inch of her surroundings like a pair of hazel sponges. Luke had achieved a perfect ability to block out everything around him during research, while her focus was more on discovering every little detail in her surroundings.

"Good evening, Sabrina!" Luke replied, barely containing his excitement for the project that led him into this room. "Is there any chance that you may know where I can find a chunk of quartz about this big?" Luke then motioned his two hands together as if he was smoothing out a snowball fit to be fired from a cannon.

Sabrina looked for a moment, before switching her gaze towards the ceiling in thought. She then returned her gaze down to Luke's eyes before replying, "As a matter of fact I do! As luck would have it, I found one about that size while out for a hike the other day. If you follow me to my dorm, I can retrieve it for you." Without waiting for a reply, Sabrina brushed past Luke and made her way towards the exit of the science building.

Not to be left behind, Luke quickly turned and kept pace with her.

John, having just entered the building, saw the two of them walking back out of the room. With a roll of his eyes, he fell in line with the pair. "So, I take it you found what you were looking for Luke?" John asked, knowing the answer already from the excitement that seemed to drip from Luke's body.

"I hope so!" he replied concisely.

Sabrina laughed before questioning Luke, "Let me guess, this is for your little ghost hunting project isn't it?"

Luke's face immediately shifted from excitement to a beet red before he answered with a slight nod.

"Oh, don't be embarrassed," Sabrina stated with a reassuring smile. "If your project can prove the existence of ghosts and an ability to capture them in one go, then that would be the discovery of a lifetime!"

Normality washed back over Luke's face as he acknowledged the statement with a nod; his excitement quickly returning to the forefront. Moments later, the group reached Sabrina's dorm building and walked the hall to her room.

After Sabrina unlocked the door, she moved to her desk where various shapes and sizes of minerals sit. In one quick motion, she grabbed a crystal around the size that Luke requested and handed it to him. "So, does this mean you have another breakthrough on your device?" Sabrina asked with a slight tilt of her head.

"I hope so," Luke responded. "If I can shape this crystal just right, it should allow me to capture certain frequencies of energies. More specifically, the exact frequencies that give ghost hunters the knowledge that spirits are nearby. Of course, there's no telling until I can finally put it to the test."

Sabrina nodded, "That's great then! Let me know if it doesn't blow up in your face and I'll join you for the field test!"

Luke smiled to her gratefully as he replied. "Thank you, I will be sure to let you know first what the outcome is of this test!"

With that, Sabrina waved goodbye and closed her door. Leaving an ecstatic Luke and an amused John to head back to their own dormitory room. Unfortunately for the pair of them, their housing lay on the opposite side of the campus.

"So, Luke. If this crystal doesn't shatter when you shock it, how do you plan to actually test if it works?" John asked his friend.

Luke rubbed his chin as he pondered the question for a few moments. "Well, there's that old house a mile or so away from campus. The abandoned one with that horror movie look. We could test it there. Measuring the EMF readings in the house both before as well as after bringing the crystal with to see if there is any difference between the two."

At this, John stopped walking and began to laugh uncontrollably.

"What?" Luke asked frustrated before continuing his explanation "the house has even showed up on multiple ghost hunting shows. Many of which were even able to confirm that something is there!"

John continued to laugh for a moment before finally wiping the tears from his face and clearing his throat. "Your idea makes perfect sense, and I've seen those shows. Which is exactly why I'm laughing. There is no way in hell that you're going to get me into that house. Fuck that spooky shit."

Luke and John continued walking while Luke considered this last statement. He didn't take John for the type to fear a run in with a ghost. After all, what's the worst a spirit could possibly do?

"Agent 6, 349 has just flown over a secluded tribal island in the Pacific", A man in business casual attire sitting behind a computer stated.

"Good, send a recon team to record any changes in the island and contain them," Agent 6 replied.

The man at the computer nodded before turning back and typing commands into his computer. Across the display, the words *Recon Team 12 Bravo reassigned* flashed for a moment. The screen then switched back to the radar view, where a large dot moving quickly to the west could be seen with each pulse of the signal.

On the coast of California, a secluded warehouse style building bustled with energy as a team of eight men and women in unmarked black uniforms skittered about. Helmets were slapped on, rifles snatched up, and backpacks were loaded full of ammunition and other supplies in their preparations. The chopping of a helicopter's blades could be heard from outside as it made its landing right on the concrete slab beyond the exit doors.

"Quit fucking around you lazy slobs and get to the ride! We have a mission to complete, and we need to do it quickly with no errors!" The leader yelled out to the other seven in the team as they strapped on their packs and entered the helicopter one at a time.

The pilot called back as the leader embarked, to which the commanding officer waved a wordless response to lift off. The team then found their seats and looked to the leader; expecting the typical briefing that followed at this point. The leader flipped open a folder as he prepared to address the team.

"We are to scope out a small island approximately 300 miles out. Inhabiting the island is a small tribe that has had no contact with the outside world. We sneak in, check on the tribe, and report their condition to HQ. In addition, we are to watch out for any aggressive flora or fauna while completing our objective. The helicopter will drop us off, refuel, and return to pick us up. Given the quick turnaround, we have a short window to find the tribe and send our report via satellite before pickup. Understood?"

The rest of the team responded with a unified "Yes Sir!" Everyone except for one member, who now sat with a confused expression on his face.

"Sir did I mishear you?" the man asked with a bit of shock. "We are to watch out for aggressive... plants?"

The leader's eyes bore into the member as he responded, "You heard correct, and I don't question the orders given to me. Do you think to question the orders I am giving to you?"

"No Sir!" the member responded before falling silent; a look of worry hidden on his masked face.

Once the helicopter landed on the sandy beach of the island, the team disembarked one by one. With rifles in hand and eyes open for any threats. Up ahead, a clear path through the trees could be seen; the ground worn down into a makeshift trail from constant foot traffic.

The leader pointed to the path as he turned to command the men and women once more. "This must be a trail used by the tribe. We will use it to quickly reach them to ensure mission success. If any tribal members are seen on the trail, incapacitate them so as to not alert the rest of the group to our presence. Understood?"

"Yes sir," the group replied in a hushed tone as they entered the covered trail in pairs of two. The leader assumed the front while the questioning team member paired off in the back; where he constantly scanned his surroundings for what the briefing had mysteriously warned against.

As the team made their way down the trail, they noticed an eerie silence. The lack of tribal sounds made sense since nothing was well known about the tribe and its mannerisms. So, what would the squad expect to hear?

No. The eerie silence was in fact the vegetation.

A slight breeze carried the salt of the ocean through the air. However, nothing in their surroundings bent to the wind. Every tree, every bush, every bit of life by the trail seemed to stand rigid in defiance against the natural order. In addition, every bit of plant life had transformed into more hellish versions of themselves everywhere the expedition looked.

Every bush seemed to be covered in thorns that had their fill of blood with the crimson hue that permeated them. And the trees. The towering palm trees looked as though they were covered in a layer of granite; grayed "bark" that you would have to take a sledgehammer to make any reasonable progress in splitting it.

As the team took in their surroundings, they grew increasingly on edge by the malevolence of it all. The trail seemed more like a dungeon with each step taken. Stoic trees seeming to watch their every step, and bushes waited for someone to carelessly wander off the beaten path. Even the flowers looked menacing. For instead of bright petals welcoming you to explore their various smells or attract insects for pollination, these ones had pitch black petals. From the center of every individual flower was a single protruding spike, stained the same crimson color as the thorns on the bushes.

The team cautiously trekked further down the trail, moving with a renewed sense of urgency to get the mission done and get out.

While they progressed down the trail, the team members noticed their path had begun to widen. Ahead, the bright sunlight of the day could be seen flooding through the opening in the haunted forest. Relief flooded over them as they made their way out of the menacing woods, however the relief quickly burned away at the sight in the clearing before them.

The rough dirt of the path ahead was stained an increasingly ominous shade of brownish red; presumably from the blood of the various corpses lying on and around the trail. The team had seen many deaths on their missions, as well as having caused quite a few themselves. But nothing could have prepared these people for something as horrific as this.

Limbs were severed in the most brutish of ways. As if they were aggressively ripped off during the attack. Screams were frozen in shriveled mouths as eyeless sockets peered onward, with hands frozen partway towards a feeble attempt at protecting their faces. The various poses also showed signs of the tribal members being caught unaware, as if the assault happened instantaneously from an unexpected threat.

Even more concerning than the torturous deaths was the state the bodies were left in. This attack could not have happened more than 24 hours ago, yet every single body now lay shriveled like oversized pieces of jerky; The blood seemingly drained from them in the moment of their collective demise.

The leader of the team shook his head clear and started signaling to set up a perimeter, to which members moved out and secured the area in every direction. Whatever had attacked the tribe seemed to be far gone now as they went through the typical steps of securing their location. Once everything was finalized, a singular squad member stepped forward to address their commanding officer.

"Sir, the location is secured and ready for us to send our report back. In addition, we spotted the actual village about 100 yards out. However, the only thing we have been able to see from this location is the structures. There are no recognizable signs of life left within our vision."

The leader replied, now wearing a grim expression. "Well with an attack like this I doubt they would be out and about anyway. We will send our report in, sync our body cams to the sat link, and then proceed to clear the village before returning to our extraction point."

The team member nodded to acknowledge the command as he rejoined the perimeter they had set up.

The leader then approached the area now cleared of corpses. He produced a black laptop from within his own pack and set it up on a makeshift table. From the laptop's side, a satellite transmitter stuck out angled upwards towards the sky.

12 Bravo report of arrival

The forest itself seems to hold a menacing aura about it as we walked a trail we could only assume was used by the tribe. Flowers and bushes seem to be armed in a way that makes them unidentifiable. Palm trees are heavily armored.

First contact with the tribe was grim. Bodies ripped apart and drained of all fluids. Pictures of the scene will be uploaded with this report. Body cam footage will be livestreamed via the satellite link of a village up ahead as we search for any survivors.

The leader quickly attached photos taken of the scene they discovered to the report and sent it all in. Following this, he activated a receiver on the sat link.

After he stood back up, the leader pointed to two of the team members. "Smith and Holloway, you are to guard the sat link and ensure proper footage is sent to HQ. The rest of you pair up and turn your body cams on! We will approach the village from the trail. You two circle left, while you two circle right." The officer directed everyone into pairs as he spoke, before assigning the last man as his own partner.

"We will enter from the main entrance. Cover each other's positions and fire upon any signs of aggression we may come across."

Once he finished barking out their orders, various tones of "yes sir" could be heard in response. As soon as everyone was in position and the satellite footage was linked, they began making their way to the village proper.

Smith, who had previously questioned the aggressive plants, was now on guard for communications. With his mind filled with a sense of fear, he turned to his partner in an attempt to calm his nerves.

"So, Liz. We have a forest straight from a horror movie, and a pile of bodies that look like they were turned to jerky in a matter of hours. What do you make of it all?"

Liz turned to the frightened member, expressionless through her equipment. "Well first of all Adam, we are on guard. Therefore, this isn't the time for chit chat. To answer your question though, I think the sooner we get off this island the better. If nothing else, than for the sake of my sanity."

Adam nodded as the pair returned their gazes to the fields surrounding them.

When a few minutes passed and nothing appeared to jump out at them, Adam cleared his throat and continued speaking his thoughts. "You know, the most unnerving thing to me should be the bodies. How they were mangled and drained. But the thing I can't clear from my mind is the flowers. They almost looked like weapons, ready to fire. Defenses set up for an unexpecting victim to fall into a trap they would never escape from."

This time, a visible shudder could be seen from Liz as she turned her head to face Adam. "Could you shut up about the damn plants?! I would rather get this done and get out before whatever did this to the tribe comes back."

Adam sighed in reply to her outburst as he resumed his duties of keeping lookout over their equipment.

Once the leader of the troop approached what could only be the village entrance, he noticed how empty and untouched it appeared. Huts lined with stripped bark from the palms and grassy roofs seemed about as well kept as they could be.

There were no signs of a siege on the structures, nor signs of any victims of death here. In fact, there weren't even any signs that people have lived here for a while. No hurriedly abandoned food, no lingering fires. Not even signs of a struggle as objects such as makeshift bowls seemed to be stored away properly. It was as if they had been attacked in the dead of night, and no one had time to even sound the alarm.

The leader made a mental note to expand their search to the surrounding fields if they had time prior to extraction. He then signaled the other two units to begin their sweep of the perimeter with a slice of his arm through the air. Moments later, he and his partner joined the search: Cautiously stepping forward into the village proper.

Rifles swiveled in every direction as the three teams cleared corners around huts, tables, and anything else that might hide a hidden threat. The leader, now finished with clearing the near side of the first hut, signaled his partner to take position on the opposite side of the entrance. With a pause, the pair switched on flashlights attached to their helmets.

The leader then nodded, and the two of them swung inward synchronized; rifles and lights peering into the darkness of the hut.

As their lights burned away the darkness, they were greeted with a peculiar sight. Even the inside of the hut was tidy. There was no blood, and nothing was toppled. It was as if nothing ever happened inside, and the space within laid perfectly untouched.

With the first hut cleared, the team continued to the next hut in line. As the leader and his partner made their way to the next structure, the perimeter teams finished their sweep and entered the village from the opposite side. Once again, the leader and his partner moved into position, nodded, and swung their lights inward.

The lights then struck a demonic figure, and a raspy screech pierced the air.

Chapter 2: Sabrina's Secret

"Carefully now," Luke muttered to himself, alone in his and John's dorm room. Notebooks laid scattered across his desk depicting notes, equations, and diagrams. Front and center sat a notebook with a quick sketch of his new and hopefully, last, attempt at a containment crystal.

Slowly and carefully he grinded away the edges of the crystal given to him by Sabrina the day before. He had originally planned on shaping and conducting the initial tests once he got back to his dorm room. However, he was struck by a relentless hunger that took wave upon wave of food to quell. Furthermore, once he was sated, he plopped down onto his bed and passed out until around midday.

John was absent from the dorm room when Luke had woken up, however his roommate often went out to town on Saturdays for who knows what, so it came as no surprise to him.

The hum of the grinder and the vibrating buzz of the crystal being molded into shape were the only sounds that filled the room. Sunlight glinted through the open window sitting over Luke's desk as he paused on his work to check the progress of his design.

The sketch he had drawn showed a cylindrical shape with six faces; The ends of which each pinched down into a conical point. The crystal, however, was currently in a state between cannonball and rod. Luke decided he would shape the crystal one half at a time, taking measurements along the way to make sure everything was perfect. By completing one side first, he also gave himself a guide for the second half.

The side molded into a rod was close to where it needed to be, and after being satisfied with the current measurements, Luke proceeded to grind the first flat face into the rod.

Luke worked through the better part of the day grinding and shaping the crystal. The sun had started to set on Luke, which reminded him to check the time.

"Its past eight already???" Luke asked the empty room around him, before finally noticing the dryness in his throat. Inhaling dust all afternoon without even a sip of water had left his throat grinding like two sheets of sandpaper.

He walked over to his bed and grabbed the water bottle from the stand next to it. Slowly he sipped the water, feeling the moisture return to his throat before he chugged the rest of the bottle. Once he sated his thirst, Luke checked his phone to see he had missed a few notifications throughout the day. The first of which was from John.

Apparently, John was going home for the week, and thus wouldn't be back until the following Sunday. Following this Luke cleared various email notifications until all that was left was another text, this time from Sabrina.

He opened the text which read: *Hey Luke! I was wondering how your project was coming along. I was hoping to drop by and see your progress now that I'm back on campus.*

Luke let out a small laugh before his eyes shot wide and he scanned quickly for the time stamp.

"Phew, it was sent ten minutes ago," Luke stated with a sigh of relief. While he and Sabrina were by no means romantic with each other, Luke had a secret attraction for her. Because of this, he made a point to never put her off or give her any reason to assume the wrong impression... Not that he would get the nerve up to ask her out regardless.

It's coming along well! Sorry I just looked at my phone, head over anytime you want! Luke sent in reply.

A few moments later a text reading *See you soon!* flashed at the top of the screen.

He then pocketed his phone and returned to the desk to resume operation crystal dust, with a filled water bottle in hand this time around.

About 15 minutes passed of seemingly endless grinding before Luke heard a quick double knock at his door. He quickly brushed the dust off his hands as he stood up to see who was there.

Luke smiled as he swung the door open for a casually dressed Sabrina. Wearing what looked like a T-shirt used to paint a house and a worn-out pair of jeans. Spotting the relaxed outfit, Luke froze and looked down to notice he was wearing the exact same jeans and black tee as yesterday. Except this time, they glittered with crystal dust.

"Uhh looks like I forgot to change," Luke stated sheepishly with an awkward grin on his face. "Come on in though, John won't be back all week so you can use his chair." Luke quickly moved John's chair from his desk to the crystal dusty nightmare that was Luke's workspace.

Sabrina peered at Luke, then at the desk, before bursting out laughing. "So, are you working on your crystal project or were you throwing a glitter rave?" she asked teasingly.

"A rave obviously," Luke announced before quickly wiping some of the crystal dust off the desk and onto the sleeve of Sabrina's shirt. "There, now you've been officially invited!" he stated mischievously.

Sabrina looked down at her shirt in mock horror before laughing again and sitting at the desk. "So, how is your crystal coming along?" She inquired.

"Pretty well considering I haven't really moved from this spot most of the day," Luke answered. He lifted the crystal up with the six sides finished, but the ends still resembled rods more than cones. Luke then pointed to the sketch of the crystal in the notebook on his desk. "I only really need to bring the ends down into this cone shape and it will be done."

Sabrina inspected the drawing, and then the partially finished crystal. "Interesting. Well finish up so we can see how it looks then!" she encouraged.

Luke nodded in response before he resumed his task of grinding the crystal.

Roughly another hour passed as Luke finished grinding the ends of the crystal into the desired shape; confirming along the way that they still matched up with his measurements as he worked. Once the ends were finally done, he proceeded to polish the crystal to a mirror-like finish. With the invention finally completed, he handed it to Sabrina to inspect while he took a sip of water.

"It looks more like a gem than a cage," she pondered. "So, how do you plan on testing it now?" she continued as she handed the crystal back to Luke.

"Well, the first test I will be doing here," he responded as he pulled out a battery with wires attached to the terminals. Luke set the crystal down before placing the simple device against the tips of the crystal's cones.

After a few moments, he removed the wires and took a reading of the crystal. "Hmmm, well it didn't explode this time. And the readings, if accurate, show it's holding the proper charge. The only thing left to do now would be to test if it can contain the energies often attributed to a spirit's presence. Which for that test I've been meaning to ask you, would you like to come join me at the haunted house nearby tomorrow? There's no reason to wait for John to get back since he's apparently afraid of ghosts, and I could use the company."

Sabrina let out a small chuckle, "Wow I never thought a big guy like him would fear ghosts, but sure! I have no plans and I'm curious if it works. That house they keep showing on all the ghost shows right?"

Luke nodded, "Yep that's the one. I figured if there was anywhere I could test both the existence of ghosts as well as if the crystal works it would be there."

Sabrina stood up and gave Luke a quick hug, which he reciprocated. "Sounds good. I will drop by in the morning so we can head down there. In the meantime, you should wash the glitter off and sleep normally tonight."

Luke looked from her teasing grin to his sparkling T-shirt and laughed "yea yea ok, have a good night, Sabrina."

"You as well," she responded before shutting the door behind her.

Once Sabrina had left the room, Luke gathered a towel and wrapped it around himself. He then walked down the hall to take a steaming hot shower in his dorm's communal shower room; making sure that no remnant of 'glitter' clung to him. Once finished with his task, he returned to his room and ate a sandwich he saved in his mini fridge just in case he forgot to eat again. Which honestly, happened often when he had a breakthrough on his project.

Following this, Luke plopped down onto his bed before starting a stream on his laptop of a random ghost hunting show. As the sounds of their hunt filled the room, Luke let his mind wander off into eventual sleep.

When Luke woke up the following morning, he hurriedly threw on some jeans as well as a dark gray shirt and a maroon light jacket. Pocketing the crystal he had shaped the day before, he left the warmth of his dorm building for the brisk springtime air.

While Luke began his walk across the campus to Sabrina's dorm, he made note of his surroundings. A light flurry of snow had apparently drifted down overnight, with a slight cold front setting in.

So long as the wind didn't pick up though, the jacket he grabbed would be plenty warm enough for the short walk to the abandoned house. The sidewalks were void of foot traffic this morning, which was normal considering Sundays were either catch up days for homework, or one last chance to go out before the next week of classes started. So, most students living on campus were tucked away in various areas of study or relaxation.

Luke entered the dorm building on the far side of campus, shook off the chill in the air, and proceeded to Sabrina's door. Her door was about halfway down the hall on the second floor, and he tapped a melody of knocks upon her door upon reaching it.

Moments later, the door was opened by a yawning pajama-clad woman.

"Wakey wakey Sabrina," Luke teasingly stated as she wiped the sleep from her eyes.

"Good morning you pain," was returned with an unfocused grin creeping across her lips. "Let me get dressed and we can head out." Sabrina closed the door again, leaving Luke to lean against a wall and contemplate how he was going to test the crystal once he got to the house.

He had checked the crystal before leaving his dorm, and the electrical charge was still intact. So, everything was going perfectly up until this point. As the door opened back up again about ten minutes into Luke's brainstorm, he shook away his thoughts to acknowledge the person on the other side.

A now more awake Sabrina stood in the doorway, wearing a fitted red sweater and some black jeans. She closed the door behind her before letting out another big yawn and turning to Luke. "Someone really is in a hurry to test their little project."

Luke replied, clearly showing his excitement throughout his body. "Well of course I am! This is the furthest I've ever gotten to actually succeeding."

The pair then walked out of the dormitory building and started their journey off campus in the direction of the haunted house.

"So, have you thought about a name for this project of yours?" Sabrina asked as they walked across the street separating the campus from the city proper.

"As a matter of fact, I have. I have been calling it Project Binding. Seeing as the whole idea of it is to...well, bind a spirit to this crystal" Luke held up the crystal from his pocket as he finished his statement.

"You sure you don't want to call it something like ghostbinder?" Sabrina cheekily replied, as Luke rolled his eyes at the suggestion.

"No, but I did think to call it spooky ball at one point." The two of them laughed at this before they crossed the street and entered the neighborhood beyond the campus.

The houses on this side of the city were spaced an increasing distance apart due to this side of the campus being close to city limits. Bare trees powdered with the overnight snowfall lined both sides of the road. The layer of white grew denser as the houses they passed became sparser.

"Only about half a mile until we reach the house," Luke observed as his gaze wandered over the densely wooded roadside. The trees gave off an eerie haunting vibe, as if they were part of the next Halloween special on TV. At this thought Luke let out a slight chuckle before he shook his head at Sabrina's look of confusion and continued along the road.

The rest of the walk was uneventful as the two students eventually reached the house. The structure certainly fit the look of a haunted building, with columns supporting the overhanging roof over a worn and rotted wooden porch. The door clung barely on by its bottom hinge; angled as if something forced its way through the top to escape into the world.

Windows stood unwashed, and between the weathered wood layering the walls and the chilling emptiness beyond them, one would expect to see a shadowy figure walk across the portal at any given moment. As if to accent the creepy look of the dilapidated house, a chilling breeze had recently begun blowing through; now that there were no woods barricading it away from the current party.

"Curse this wind, the walk back is going to be a lot colder than the walk here at this rate" Luke muttered to himself.

Sabrina nodding in agreement. "Well, hopefully it dies down as quickly as it came before we leave. Although we should have better protection from it as we get closer to the campus again anyway."

Luke then pulled the crystal out as they approached the front door of the house.

"Do you have any idea how you intend on capturing anything we might find here?" Sabrina questioned, which Luke had thought about and gave a quick reply.

"To be honest, I have no idea. I guess we will just have to find out when we find one of the hot spots." Luke then grabbed the upper edge of the door and pulled slightly. Wood scraped against wood and hinges shrieked as the door slowly opened.

The two of them slid through the doorway into the stale darkness once the entrance was wide enough, and Sabrina turned a flashlight on using her phone.

"Where do we go from here?" Sabrina asked Luke as she scanned the cobweb coated furnishings left behind by the previous owners.

"Well, the story goes that the last family that lived here met an untimely demise as their oldest son was seemingly possessed by a demon. One evening while they all sat together in the living room, he came in with a knife and stabbed each of them through the back of the neck. Starting from the outer edge of the room so as to not get caught by the others before his task was complete. Given that all the reported hauntings stem from that event as well as the living room being considered the epicenter of energy, I think we should start there."

Luke started to walk down the hallway as Sabrina lit the way with her phone. Once the two of them approached the turn off into the nightmare room, Luke's hands began to shake. Upon entering the room, his hands began to shake even more violently.

"Are you ok?" Sabrina asked, with a worried expression on her face.

"Yes actually, to be honest I don't even know why my hands are... wait a minute!" Luke opened his hands to reveal that in fact the crystal he brought to test was causing the commotion. The further Luke walked into the room, the more violently the crystal shook.

This gave Luke an idea, and he lifted the crystal with one hand to expose it as much to the room as possible without letting it go. In response, the crystal started to spin like a cyclone between his fingers. The speed of the object continued to increase, before slowing down and finally coming to a halt. When Luke pulled the crystal down to look it over, a dim red light radiated from the center.

"Holy shit," he breathed. "I think that pretty much confirms that the crystal works." Before Sabrina could respond, however, a banging noise was heard coming from the hallway. Luke quickly spun around defensively as he spat out a quick comment. "What was that!?"

Sabrina turned her gaze away from the noise and back to Luke as she replied. "I don't know, but assuming you already caught the spirit haunting this house, it might be someone that needs our help."

Luke considered Sabrina's words for a moment before making his way into the hallway in search of the source. From a door just under the staircase, a second bang could be heard from the other side. Luke swung the door open to peer into a curved staircase leading down into what looked like the house's basement. He took a deep breath, looked to make sure Sabrina was at his side, and made his way down the staircase.

Upon reaching the concrete floor of the basement, Luke stumbled through the room with his hand outstretched as he felt for a light switch. Once he unknowingly made his way into the center of the room, a click was heard, and the room filled with a blinding light.

Luke blinked away the glare as his eyes adjusted, and then jumped slightly when he spotted a man with a clean-shaven face and black suit sitting in a chair only a few feet away.

The man grinned as he opened his mouth to speak. "It's a pleasure to finally meet you Luke Connor. We have been keeping track of you and your little project for quite some time now."

As the man stated this, Luke looked to Sabrina. Her hand ended up upon his shoulder to comfort him. Partnered with this gesture, was a knowing, guilty look painted on her face.

Chapter 3: Repercussions

Chaos erupted as the team leader and his partner opened fire upon the horror within the hut. A humanoid figure covered from head to toe in semi-translucent skin stood within the dwelling. Needle-like teeth could be spotted from within its gaping mouth as it let out another shriek.

Moments later, a rain of bullets pierced the monster's skin from the two operatives in the doorway. Black tar-like blood slowly oozed from the creature as it lunged at the team leader. In a singular swipe, its dagger length claws separated the leader's head from his body. An onslaught of bullets continued, as the partner was able to fill the creature with enough rounds to drop it before it could strike again.

The blood-soaked man took one look in the creature's sunken black eyes, before he gifted a final bullet right between them.

The lapse in action was extremely brief, however. For once that final shot was fired, shrieks could be heard from all the remaining huts. The man spun around to see teams two and three were being swarmed by at least twenty of the creatures sprinting from the huts.

The former leader's partner reloaded his magazine, but before he could start firing into the crowd the other teams were finished. Screams filled the air as limbs were ripped from their bodies; the blood pouring from every wound being lapped up hungrily by the creatures as if they had not had a drink in months.

Seeing that they had already lost, he decided to silently backpedal out of the village entrance towards the base camp while the creatures were busy consuming his team.

Liz and Adam unshouldered their rifles and pointed them in the direction of the village, visibly shaking as screams, shrieks, and gunfire rang through the air.

Adam spotted a single figure and fumbled to grab his binoculars. "It's Jake," he stated to Liz as he slid his gaze down the trail to the village. Upon seeing the mass of gray, he whispered a shaken "What the fuck" as he dropped his binoculars.

"What is it?" Liz turned to him and asked, the barrel of her gun shaking, still in the direction of the village.

"I... I have no idea. But whatever it is, Jake is the only survivor."

Icy silence clung to the air for a few moments as Jake finally reached the base camp. "Go! Now!" he yelled as he continued running. Liz and Adam looked at each other before shouldering their rifles and joining Jake on a retreat down the forest trail.

"What the hell happened in there???" Liz barked to Jake.

"Everyone is dead. Something happened to the villagers, they all have been transformed into some kind of demonic alien. They tore everyone to pieces. I only escaped because they were too busy devouring the others to notice me away from the group."

The color drained from Liz and Adam as they tried to process what Jake was saying.

Moments later, light could be seen from the beach side of the trail where they had been dropped off. Relief washed over the party as their escape was close by. The momentary reprieve was cut short however, as one of the darkened flowers fired its spike and narrowly missed Adam. The three survivors practically sprinted now as the flower drew the spike back into its petals with a long red vine.

Soon after, spikes began shooting through the air from every direction; the party now having to duck and dodge around the organic projectiles.

A spike grazed Liz and she let out a cry of pain, stumbled, then regained her footing and continued running. "It burns so fucking bad," she stated. Her healthy arm now grabbing her shoulder where the spike cut a thin line through her skin. "I think there is some sort of acid in those spikes, don't get hit," she managed through gritted teeth.

Seconds later, a spike hit its mark... as one shot straight through Jake's knee in a cruel irony. He cried out and collapsed to the ground instantly from the pain as his leg gave out. Jake moved to yank it out, however the spike shot open like a grappling hook and latched on to the back of his knee.

A searing pain filled his entire leg as the other two could only watch in horror as spike after spike grappled into his free limbs. The flowers all then began to pull their spikes back, dragging Jake to the side of the trail.

Liz moved to help, only for Adam to grab her arm and pull her back. "You can't help, you'll only join him" Adam stated coldly, clearly in shock at the events.

They both turned back to Jake to see him pulled into one of the thorn-covered bushes. His screams were quickly stifled as thousands of thorns pierced his skin and drained every last drop of his blood out, before dropping the lifeless husk on the ground with a heavy thud.

Liz's jaw dropped open as Adam tugged on her arm again, snapping her out of her daze. The pair bolted the rest of the way out of the forest and back onto the beach. "12 Bravo requesting immediate extraction", Adam practically yelled into his radio.

The two remaining squad members stood alert, with rifles pointed at the trailhead as if at any moment monsters and plants would burst through to finish them off.

Finally, after what seemed like an eternity, the helicopter arrived to carry them far away from the hellish island. Liz and Adam practically vaulted onto the vehicle before it even touched the ground. They sat back, panting as they began the voyage home.

Adam turned to Liz and spoke up once he had recovered enough of his breath. "I don't know what the fuck happened on that island... but thank God it was isolated. Could you imagine if an outbreak like that hit the mainland?"

A room full of professionals sat in silence, taking in everything that happened on the various body cam feeds displayed across the room. As the chaos ensued in the village, they watched as one by one cameras fell to the ground, screams filling the air as blood splattered over the screens. Then, the cameras all slowly went dark. Multiple displays showed *Connection lost... attempting to reestablish.* Eventually, the only cameras left functioning showed the inside of the helicopter as it made its way back to the warehouse.

While some people took notes on the events for research purposes, Agent 6 turned to the man sitting behind the computer which still showed tracking information for 349.

"Where is the creature now?" he asked calmly.

"Sir, it seems to be on a direct course for Japan. It will reach the island within 8 hours if it keeps up its current course."

Agent 6 nodded in confirmation before he walked out of the room. As he made his way down the hall, the Agent punched numbers into his phone before holding it up to his ear. Two rings, followed by a voice slightly irritated.

"Yes Agent 6? We are currently in an observation of captive 187. Make it quick."

"Apologies Director," the Agent replied with a pause before continuing his report. "But we might have a problem. 349's free roam has already provided us with information as to the power of the creature. I am sending you the footage now."

Silence crossed the phone line, with the faint sounds of the horrors previously viewed coming through to the Agent's end of the call.

After the Director had finished watching, the line sat silent for a few more moments before he finally spoke up. "How did the creature accomplish this?"

Agent 6 cleared his throat, "Well sir, that's the issue. It didn't seem to direct the transformations at all. It appears its presence near the island was all that was needed to turn the members of the tribe. As if it gave off some form of aura; everything in the area was morphed simply by being in its vicinity. We don't know if it can direct any of its powers or if they simply infect everything around it, but even the waters surrounding the island seem tainted now. There are reports from our satellites indicating a spreading mass of tendrils where the ocean vegetation around the island used to be. And what's more, the creature is now heading straight for Japan. If it reaches the island, this infection is sure to spread across the entire landmass. Japan will be lost in a matter of weeks."

"I see. Well, consider this observation a success. We now know what the creature is capable of, so return it to its cell before we lose an ally in the pacific."

Agent 6 paused for a moment, before stuttering out his next reply. "Well, Director. There seems to be one issue with that. We have already tried to recall it... however it seems that the collar we placed on it was damaged when it went supersonic leaving the facility. We just found the collar shattered on the ground in the desert. Sir... we have lost all control of the experiment. The Phantom Hawk is now unleashed on the world."

A moment of silence followed before the Director finally spoke "I see. That will be all then Agent 6." Following this, the Director promptly ended the phone call with his agent.

He then turned to the researchers that were observing captive 187 in the room with him. "End the observation. 349 has escaped its bindings. Top priority is to now discover a way to imprison it before it destroys the world. If you can't find a way to imprison it, find a way to destroy it. I'm leaving, for I have an agent to reprimand."

With that, the Director left the room. A sliding metal door shut behind him as realizations settled in amongst the researchers left behind. This may be the end of the world.

Back in the housing area of Area 51's Paranormal Division, Agent 6 sat in his room. Hours had passed since his call to Director Johnson, and dread had slowly settled in. The night was getting pretty late, so to try to calm his mind he went to the bathroom, undressed, and stepped into the shower.

While in the shower, flashes of the horrors he witnessed leapt through his mind. Even as the warm water flowed over the agent, chills wracked his body, as he still heard echoes of the screams from the attack. What was to become of the world now? What had he done? Soon the creature may make its way back to the facility. And if it does, will he be one of the ones turned? Or will he be one of the survivors, forced to try to overcome the very land itself. This wasn't something any amount of training could have prepared him for.

As Agent 6 stepped out of the shower and dried off, he heard a knock at his door. The agent quickly got dressed before opening it, to see two other agents and the Director standing outside. "Good. Evening. Director," he managed to stammer out, unsure of what this late-night visit had meant.

"I'm sorry agent," the Director replied curtly. "However, we cannot allow this kind of failure to permeate our operations. Consider yourself discharged." And with that, the Director walked off. Leaving the two agents that flanked him behind in the doorway.

Handguns then promptly rose from beneath their suit jackets and the message was now clear to Agent 6. As the Director walked away, two gunshots quickly filled the air as a solid thud echoed through the hall.

Agent 6 quickly pulled the stacked bodies of the other two agents into his room and shut the door. Thank God even with his frayed nerves, he still had a quicker draw than the others. The second one luckily even faltered at the sound of the first gunshot, before quickly collapsing onto the first body as Agent 6's second shot struck true.

With the halls now empty, Agent 6 clutched at the grip of his handgun he now hid under his suit jacket and made his way down the corridor. The agent turned a few corners before he breathed a sigh of relief. No one had come out to check on the commotion. They probably assumed that if they had witnessed the event, they would be next.

The agent made his way through the corridors until he finally reached the open air outside. He then walked the short remaining distance to his car, before turning it on and quickly but calmly driving his way out of the checkpoint. Luckily, it seemed that no one had known about his current situation; as the gate guard let him out without further incident.

Agent 6 drove down the road leading away from the facility in the dark of night. The bodies wouldn't be found until the cleaning crew was directed to retrieve his own corpse in the morning, so he would be able to get a decent head start in his escape. Which left his mind free to plan his future. He had to go into hiding after this, as they definitely would be hunting him now. But where would he go? What would he do? The Director had connections all over the globe.

Not to mention leaving the country would only lead him onto a closer path to the Phantom Hawk.

While planning his life on the run, Agent 6 failed to notice the cactus his headlights shone onto: A charred black color with crimson tinted spines. It began to inflate once the headlights hit it, as if a trap was laid in anticipation of a midnight traveler. A mostly silent pop then sounded as it exploded. A split-second later, a rain of hardened needles shattered the Agents windshield.

The surprise caused him to spin the wheel as he swerved trying
to avoid this unknown assailant. However, he spun his car a bit too
far; causing it to flip over five or six times before it finally came to a
halt off the side of the road. Luckily though, the car managed to
upright itself on the last flip.

Agent 6 clutched his head, which was throbbing from the jolts of
the crash, as he opened his door and stood up. He then reoriented
himself, shaking off the minor pains and aches as he pulled out a
flashlight to inspect the surroundings. The moment he clicked it on,
he spotted another charred looking cactus expanding a few feet in
front of him.

Before the agent could react the cactus popped, sending
hardened crimson needles in every direction. Agent 6 stiffened up,
before his body crashed down backwards; hundreds of needle holes
mutilating every inch of his body before implanting into the side of
the car behind him.

Agent 6 laid motionless on the desert terrain. A wide-eyed look
of fear was painted on his face as his empty gaze stared into the sky.
The body would not be found until the next perimeter patrol did
their rounds later in the night.

Chapter 4: The Truth

"Wait, what's going on? Who are you?" Luke inquired, his eyes finally adjusting to the sudden difference in lighting. He looked around the room as he asked his question. The man was clearly out of place amongst the dirty and disheveled basement.

"My name is Lewis Williams. I lead a group of people that watch out for the... let's say supernatural. I will explain more later. For now, though, we must go somewhere a little more secure." With that, the man stood up and made his way up the stairs.

"If it helps at all, I have been part of this group for a few years. They are good people and can be trusted," Sabrina stated in an attempt to calm Luke's nerves.

"Can I even trust you though?" Luke replied, clearly on edge still over the sudden turn of events.

"Just... please listen to what they have to say, we can talk more about my involvement afterwards," Sabrina replied as Luke made his way up the stairs behind Lewis. She sighed as he reacted coldly to this revelation, before following the others up the stairs and out of the rundown house.

Luke peered across the street towards where Lewis headed and noticed a black painted cargo van parked against the curb. The sliding door of the vehicle opened as Lewis approached. He then proceeded to climb into it and sat down on a bench seat across from the door before he beckoned Luke and Sabrina to come join him.

Luke sat within the vehicle and noticed a pair of men in the front seats of the van. As soon as everyone filed in, the two men quickly got up, shut the door, and returned to their seats to start the vehicle. Moments later, the van roared to life and proceeded to make its way down the road.

With the car making the journey towards an unknown location and nothing of interest being discussed, Luke took the moment to look around his new surroundings. Mounted near the roof on the opposite side of the van from the bench was a screen which currently showed the news. The back of the van had a shelf filled with random tools and objects, as well as a shelf full of nothing but quartz.

Luke had to do a double take when he saw the crystals. What did these people want with the crystal? He looked towards Sabrina as she gave him an awkward smile, which pretty much confirmed to him that she had been spying on his project this whole time.

"We have quite a distance to travel, and the van is secure enough from others trying to listen in, so let me explain who we are." Lewis stated with a short pause before he continued. "We are a secret organization called the Duskwatchers. Our singular purpose in this world is to keep an eye on the supernatural. We mostly are left to observational tasks, however on occasion we have had to step in and take a more active role in some events."

Lewis paused again to make sure Luke was absorbing this information before he continued his explanation.

"Recently though, we came across a discovery that puts the entire world in danger. Once we saw this, we knew we had to act fast. Our entire organization was mobilized, and Sabrina was approached to join; for she had known someone with possibly the only drive and skillset needed to contain this problem safely." Lewis looked towards Sabrina for a moment before gazing back at Luke during the last part of his statement.

Luke sighed as his anger with Sabrina calmed down a bit. At least she didn't enter his life solely to spy on him.

As he processed the information given to him, Luke only ended up with additional questions in his mind. One question in particular stuck out to him more than any of the others. Lewis mentioned a problem, but he didn't state what it was. Is Luke being kept in the dark, or is this some form of poor buildup to a large reveal?

"Wait, so what is the problem and how am I involved? I assume it has something to do with my crystal invention, but what could be so apocalyptic that also involves ghosts? They're pretty much harmless."

As Luke finished his statement, Lewis replied with a simple finger raised, pointed at the TV. Sabrina grabbed a remote and turned up the volume as Luke turned his head back to see what could possibly interrupt this conversation. The news, however, seemed to have answers to the questions he had.

Breaking News

Reports have been coming in from all over Asia of an unknown object heading straight for Japan. Radar indicates possibly a military aircraft, while reports from fishing vessels indicate it may be some sort of animal. Although these reports could be untrustworthy, as they indicate a giant bird with shadows that seem to envelop the beast. No photos or video evidence could be obtained regarding the event.

Japan has issued a statement to all foreign countries that it will not be threatened by a military show of force. If the unidentified object is indeed a foreign military vessel, they will be shot down and the approach taken as an act of war. Their military is currently mobilizing, and a handful of their allies have already vowed financial and military support. If this is an assaulting force, we may be witnessing the start of the next World War.

The news continued with interviews of diplomats and military analysts. Everyone seemed to be guessing at anything from a spy plane scouting out the location, to a new kind of jet capable of dropping a possibly unknown weapon of mass destruction.

Luke spoke up without averting his gaze from the screen. "So uh, I assume this is not a plane, and somehow related to spirits."

Lewis replied calmly "Oh, it's not related to spirits. That thing IS a spirit."

Luke's head spun to face Lewis so fast that you thought it might pop off. "Hold on, how can people see it?! How can it be tracked?! All of a sudden out of nowhere spirits are not only confirmed to be real, but also that they are tangible in the world?"

As Luke pelted him with the endless barrage of questions, Lewis remained quiet and listened until he finished. This mysterious man then leaned forward onto his knuckles, as he turned towards Luke with a serious expression.

"You see Luke, that is the problem I mentioned."

Following a short pause, Lewis continued to explain the situation to Luke. "A few months ago, we received word from one of our contacts stationed in Area 51 that the researchers there had discovered a portal linking our world to an alternate dimension. Or at least, a mirror dimension. For it was actually a shadowed version of our own reality. A team was sent in through the portal to recon the area, but they were unable to return. Short range communication indicated that the team made it about a mile into the portal before they were brutally murdered by something within."

Lewis continued, "A robot was sent in next, which was able to gather a few samples of the surroundings; including an altered portion of one of the team members muscle tissues. Pictures were also sent back showing the team was ripped apart and bleeding what can only be described as physical shadows. It was as if the world itself was changing them the moment they were injured."

Lewis paused for a moment to let Luke process this information before he once more continued with his briefing of recent events.

"The samples of the soil and plant life indicated that this alternate dimension was extremely hostile, and living matter seemed to act more like single cell organisms. The stronger plants and animals would drain the energy and nutrients out of the weaker ones, creating an ecosystem based off a perfect transfer of energy. As opposed to our reality, where only about 10% of the energy we consume is used."

"This has led to a drastic evolution in the mirror dimension where humanity would fall somewhere on the lower end of the food chain so to speak, with many beasts way more powerful above them. What is more important however, is the bottom of this food chain. Whereas we have simple living organisms at the bottom of ours, the bottom of the mirror realm's food chain is pure spiritual energy that has bled through the barrier between our worlds. When something dies in our world, its spirit bleeds over into the mirror world. This spiritual energy then proceeds to meld with and feed an ecosystem that has spent billions of years evolving with an infinitely created energy source."

Luke sat back and rubbed his eyes. This was a ton of information to take in at once. Not only is there an afterlife, but it's essentially just their energies feeding another world? Like some sort of parasitic bond where we are the nutrient being leeched? Luke processed this all as much as he could before a realization shook him to his core.

"Wait, so did the creature on the news come from this other world?"

Lewis nodded as he replied. "We had some of our men scouting Area 51 and listening in on radio communications. The researchers at the facility found a way to contain and capture some of these creatures. The creature on the news was Captive 349, also known as the Phantom Hawk. It was released for a field test; however, our intelligence indicates that the collar they used to control it shattered. This thing has been freed within our world, and I believe the only way we can stop it is with your help. We want you to join us, acting as the leader of our related operations in the field. We can provide you with the materials and resources needed to craft and perfect your invention, so that we may use it to contain this threat to our world, as well as possible threats in the future."

"So, Luke Connor, would you be willing to aid us?"

Luke looked between Sabrina, Lewis, and the TV. This was not how he thought his day would go at all. Somehow his ghost capture test turned into a ghost world reveal complete with an impending apocalypse. How lovely. But it looked like he would have to step up from college student to warrior, for the sake of all of humanity.

After a few more moments passed, Luke cleared his throat. "Yea, you can count on my help. What are we going to do first?"

Lewis nodded and replied "First, we get a team together for you to set out for an island the spirit has already hit. We need to know what this thing is capable of."

Chapter 5: The Island

The van pulled up to a field in the woods with what looked like a small hunting lodge standing in the middle of the clearing. Luke, Sabrina, and Lewis all exited the vehicle as Lewis led the way to the lodge. The two men that drove secured the van's doors before they joined the flank of the group.

Luke peered up at the tree line where the sun was attempting to shine through the thick foliage. It appeared that they had driven all night to some unknown location. Upon reaching the door, Lewis opened it and held it while the others walked in.

Luke's gaze panned across the interior of the structure to discover it was in fact just a simple hunting lodge. A fireplace made from stone sat across from a few simple chairs. Around the corner, a small kitchenette could be seen furnished with a plain wooden table and another couple of chairs. Across from the kitchenette was a wood stove for keeping the place warm in the winter. The only hint of technology that could be spotted was a small black camera that sat in the upper corner of the cabin; angled to be able to see the entire room.

As the door shut behind the party of five, Lewis moved back to the front of the group and made his way to the fireplace. He picked up one of the iron pokers that sat in a stand next to it, before he placed the sharp end into a crack in the fireplace and turned it. The stone wall of the fireplace started to shake, and moments later it swung open to reveal a hidden spiral staircase that led down underneath the lodge.

As the group made their way down the staircase, there was a buildup of sound that stood out against the hollow footsteps of the party. Once they made their way to the bottom, Luke's jaw nearly fell off as the room at the bottom of the staircase came into view.

Computers and monitors lined the walls; with cameras that watched everything from random streets to secluded looking parts of woods and deserts. A few of the monitors had the news open on multiple stations, as people discussed the "fighter jet" that seemed to disappear hours earlier right before it was going to fly over Japan.

There were two doors on the far end of the spacious room that sat ajar. However, hallways turned immediately within, so the contents of these hallways were blocked from being easily viewed.

In the middle of the room the group currently stood in, some sort of command station sat. Upon the station's table stood an exact digital replica of Japan. The model even moved and reacted in real time to events that went on in the country; as cars, people, and even lighting seemed to shift slowly on it.

"This is our command center," Lewis said. "Your things are currently being moved to your private quarters, which Sabrina can show you upon your return. As time is of the essence to collect what we can on info about the Phantom Hawk, I'm afraid you will have to catch up on any sleep you've missed on the boat ride out."

Lewis walked over to the map of Japan as Luke and Sabrina followed. He pushed a few digital buttons and punched in some coordinates, and the map phased out and shifted to a view of a small island. The island was very exotic looking even on this display. For instead of the typical lush greenery you would expect, everything seemed to be painted in dark shades of black, gray, and red. Lewis pointed to a clear beach on one side of the island where small people could be seen setting up tents and barricades, and armed guards patrolled the perimeter.

"You will be taking a chopper to a platform in the Pacific Ocean. Upon your landing, a boat will be waiting for you to take you to this outpost that is currently being set up on the island. Jake is our commanding field officer at the outpost and will brief you with further details of your expedition upon arrival. Do you have any questions?"

Luke stared at the island for a moment before he spoke up. "Yes actually. The color of Japan seemed so realistic, yet the colors on this model look mostly washed out. Are you unable to get a clearer image of the land here because of how secluded it is?"

Lewis smirked before he replied. "Oh, no. This image is just as clear as the one you saw of Japan. What you are seeing is the effect the Phantom Hawk has had on the land. Be careful down there, even the plants seem to want to kill you now."

Luke looked at Lewis wide eyed as Lewis turned back away from the party at his side to focus more on the outpost being set up.

What had Luke gotten himself into?

"Oh, it's about time you got here. These people told me you needed my help with something to save humanity, not that I was told much more than that."

Luke looked up to the familiar voice and saw John approaching him. "John?! You're a part of this as well?!" Luke was shocked, as he didn't take John as the secret agent type. Sabrina could very well keep her secrets, but John was always the first to blab at anything new he learned.

"Well, a part of this as in they said I would be a great help for you on the physical side of things. I'm about as new to this secret group thing as you are" John replied before he let out an awkward laugh. "There I was just leaving for my weeklong trip home, when some guys approached me and told me they needed my help. I agreed and they filled me in on the trip out here as to what that meant."

Luke chuckled as a thought had occurred to him. "Wait... so you signed up to hunt a spirit? Aren't you afraid of ghosts?"

The color seemed to drain from John's face as Luke made his statement.

Once his appearance returned to a more normal shade, John opened his mouth in reply. "Well, for one thing they didn't tell me *what* we were following until much later. For another thing though, I couldn't possibly let you wander into this alone. I'd be worried sick the whole time."

Luke laughed at this, before Lewis spoke up.

"Apologies for interrupting this reunion, however as I said time is of the essence. Your ride has just landed outside to take you to the Pacific. I wish you all the best of luck on the mission. Come back with whatever information you can gather... and come back safely. You're no use for the rest of this if you're dead."

With that, the three friends left Lewis by his command table.

Sabrina led the way back up the staircase as her comfort with the location showed. Once she reset the wall, everything upstairs returned to the look of a plain, old hunter's lodge. No one would be able to suspect that there was some high-tech underground base with how it looked now.

As they left the lodge behind, the blades of a helicopter could be heard chopping through the air. A man jumped out of the waiting ride and ushered the three students into their seats. Luke had never been on a helicopter before, so excitement filled his veins as it took off from the field.

While they climbed into the air, Luke peered down at the ground below him. They were indeed in the middle of the woods. Trees stretched on endlessly in all directions, with the occasional road that winded through it all. Obviously the more scenic route some people took when they traveled through the area; seeing as there was nothing close by that resembled civilization.

As the helicopter flew, however, the trees were slowly replaced with small towns and larger roads. Eventually highways filled the scene as the ground below them shifted into different areas. Luke took this moment to turn to Sabrina, his curiosity now getting the better of him as he asked "So, why all the secrets?"

Sabrina turned back to him, and with a slightly awkward tone gave him a reply. "Well, first I'm sorry. To be honest I wanted to tell you sooner, but the organization wanted to be sure you had the ability to create what they were hoping for. And once you had succeeded in finishing your invention, Lewis wanted to be there to personally invite you to the organization."

Luke took her words in before he nodded in understanding. "I guess that's ok, since no harm was actually done. Now that I am apparently part of your secret organization though, no more secrets or we are gonna go rounds."

Luke smiled to accent his point as Sabrina laughed, "No more secrets."

With this out of the way, Luke returned his view to the passing land below.

Slowly, a shoreline appeared in the distance. It grew larger and larger until all that could be seen was the crashing waves below. Ripples covered the surface of the ocean, with Luke still staring down at it as a small dot could be seen in the distance. As they flew closer, the dot continued to grow larger. A helicopter platform with a small structure next to it materialized where the dot was, floating in the middle of the ocean. This was clearly the platform previously mentioned since the helicopter started to make its descent once the structure was close enough.

The party of three disembarked from the helicopter and were quickly guided to a small boat off the edge of the platform. Once they were seated in their new ride, the boat left its dock and began to make its the journey across the rippling waves. The excitement of the previous day and this morning seemed to catch up to Luke however as he closed his eyes in exhaustion. The waves of the ocean rocked the boat, and the motion lulled him into finally giving his body the rest he didn't realize it craved.

A hand shook Luke's shoulder, which caused him to shoot up straight in his seat. His groggy eyes blinked the sleep out, as Sabrina laughed for a moment at his reaction.

"We're here Luke, time to wake up."

He rubbed his eyes and blinked a few times to clear his vision while looking around to take in his surroundings.

Before him was the beach he had seen on the command table. The sand seemed to be a slight grey, while off in the distance you could see the palm trees surrounding a trail which led into the forest.

The view, however, was slightly blocked by the sharp barricades that had been set up around a camp. Tents were set up in two rows within the defensive barrier. Smaller tents that seemed to be for sleeping sat closer to the water, while a larger tent sat towards the front of the area by the barricades. The larger tent was probably to serve as their staging point for any expeditions.

Luke's stomach grumbled as the next thing he noticed was a table set up with everything from roasted chicken to sandwiches to various vegetables and carbohydrates. Luke's eyes suddenly honed in on the table, which luckily the group seemed to walk in the direction of.

"Sabrina," a man stated as he nodded in her direction. "And I assume you two are Luke and John," he continued while he directed his gaze to everyone upon stating their names.

The man then continued. "My name is Jake. I am the officer you are to rendezvous with upon arrival. However, given the length of your journey, that can wait a moment as I assume you are all famished. Luckily for you, the organization feeds its members well." With this last statement, Jake waved his hand over the table Luke was hyper focused on. Jake then finished his statement with the best words Luke could hear at this given moment. "Dig in, afterwards we will discuss our plans for the expedition."

Luke didn't need to be told twice as his hand reached out and grabbed a plate and a fork. First, he just *had* to grab a cut of the roasted chicken, since the smell of garlic and herbs wafted into the air towards his nose from the perfectly cooked meat. His mouth watered the moment he smelled the chicken, so that was priority number one. Following this, he filled the rest of his plate with asparagus, some buttered rice, and some fried potatoes. Luke had no idea how they were able to bring such enticing food out this far from civilization, but he was not about to question it.

Once he finished filling his plate, Luke went ahead and took a seat at a nearby table. Sabrina and John shortly followed, taking up seats next to and across from him, respectively. Hungry as ever, Luke stabbed the chicken with his fork and took a large bite out. It was even better than he expected. The chicken's juices flowed over his tongue, which made him moan as the taste of garlic and rosemary coated his tongue.

He didn't even realize that John and Sabrina stared at him with amused faces until he finished the chicken and looked up. "What?" He managed around a mouthful of chicken, which caused the other two to laugh at him before they shook their heads and dug into their own plates of food.

After the three were finished with their meal, Jake beckoned them over from within the large tent next to the barricades.

"Now that you three are fed, it's time to brief you on the expedition. Before we start, know that you will see some horrors you couldn't have possibly dreamed of."

John shivered at this, as Luke looked over to the forest. A high-pitched scream could be heard from the forest trail. As if in reply to Jake's words, something ran straight out of the tree line and towards the camp.

Chapter 6: Lesson Learned

Luke froze for a moment as the grotesque creature sprinted for the camp. Semi-translucent skin made it possible to see every organ in the creature's body in the light of day, although none of them seemed to be moving. It was as if this creature was some kind of animated corpse. Like a zombie, but much more horrific looking.

Where eyes should have been, there was nothing more than sunken black pits. They didn't look empty, but simply as if actual living darkness and shadows filled the sockets instead. It let out another high-pitched screech as it charged the camp, which revealed rows of sharp needle-like teeth. Its arms swayed in rhythm with its stride, and where its fingertips on its hands should have been, it instead had massive dagger-like talons.

As the creature bolted towards the camp at an impressive speed, a team of gunmen took post behind the barricades. The creature made it to about 10 feet from the barricades before the team was able to aim and fire. Within moments the creature was struck by a hail of bullets, and with a final screech it crumbled and fell to the ground.

Luke, mesmerized by his thirst for knowledge on this supernatural creature, started to approach its new resting place against the soil. Jake motioned for two of the gunmen to fall in line behind himself as the three of them followed to ensure Luke's safety.

John, now frozen in terror, stood in the tent as Sabrina brought up the rear of the party to inspect the creature's body.

As Luke got close to it, a pool had already started to form of what looked like black tar-like blood. This hellish fluid had already begun to ooze out from the many bullet holes that filled the creature's body. The black pits in its eye sockets were indeed literal darkness, as the last wisps of shadows seemed to evaporate from them. The creature's mouth still gaped open from its last screech, which revealed the teeth to be more like a mix of hardened flesh and enamel. It appeared that this thing's gums had melted down over its teeth before they hardened, which created a sharpened and armored shell around what could have possibly been human teeth.

Up close, it was clear that the talons on its hands were made of bone. The arms of the creature were much thinner than you would expect from a human, as most of its bone mass had somehow pierced through its fingertips into sharpened blades, dyed crimson by what one could only assume was blood.

"Well, it seems that the locals wanted to introduce themselves to you instead" Jake spoke calmly, as he looked down at the body.

Luke quickly swung his head to face Jake. "Wait, the locals?"

Jake nodded before he replied. "This island was once home to a small tribe, uncontacted by the outside world. When the Phantom Hawk flew over, everything on this island was corrupted. The trees are armored now, and the flowers will attempt to shoot and trap anything they deem as prey. Even the local tribe succumbed to the corruption, which created what you now see in front of you."

Luke stood silent for a moment before he turned back to the creature. He now noticed why some of the features stood out the way they did. The creature's teeth *were* in fact a person's flesh melted and rehardened, and the talons *were* in fact bone that had been liquified and stretched to puncture through the skin. It was then rehardened into the weaponized state it was now in; stained by the blood of every bit of tissue it tore through on its forceful exit out.

Luke shuddered at this thought, with extra focus in the back of his mind on how his fingertips felt in particular. He began to rub his hands together in an attempt to calm the tingling sensation that came with his thoughts. The transformation this person went through had to of been extremely painful.

Jake gave him a moment to finish processing what had happened before he motioned for Luke to join him back at the tent for the briefing. "Our goal on this island is to study the effects the Phantom Hawk has had. This is for two key reasons. First, we need to see if we can find a way to reverse the effects the spirit's corruption has on people. Second, we need to see if there is a way for us to protect ourselves from the corruption when it is time to face the Phantom Hawk itself."

Jake leaned forward over the table in the center of the tent as he continued the briefing. "A team of ten gunmen will join you and Sabrina in the field. I would say John as well, however he seems to be in no state of mind to join you currently."

Following this statement, everyone looked up at John. John had been staring blankly down at the ground in front of the tent throughout the briefing. His face was bleached of all color, as white as a fresh snowfall. Luke couldn't blame him though, for he himself was horrified at the events of the creature's attack. However, Luke's thirst for knowledge on something so extraordinary kept him calm in the moment.

Jake continued to speak as the two stable members' gazes returned to him. "Our first expedition today will be to study the plant life by the trail itself. We will then return to camp, rest for the night, and make our way to the village to study the creatures from a distance in the morning. Our men will be armed and protect you from all angles. In the case of an attack, you two will break off from the main group with an escort back to camp while the rest cover your retreat. The remainder of the group will return once the immediate threat has been neutralized. Are we clear on our roles here?"

To that, Sabrina and Luke nodded.

Following this, Jake called over a group of armed men who had been preparing weapons and gear next to the barricade. Luke took a deep breath and exhaled, as he and Sabrina walked towards the entrance of the forest, flanked on all sides by people armed with assault rifles. A pistol holstered on each person's right thigh, and knives sheathed on the left.

The group proceeded to walk into the forest cautiously. Luke made note of the palm trees, which indeed seemed armored now. What used to be bark was now hardened into a sort of carapace, almost like a beetle's shell. The model showed the trees as more gray back at headquarters. Was the model off? Or could the trees have simply become more corrupted as time went on?

The flowers that lined the trail were completely black, with a single crimson spike that stuck out of the center of the void-like petals. Completing the triad of hostile vegetation were the bushes which sat over the flowers. Branches and leaves melded together into a darkened web of foliage, as crimson thorns lined every exposed inch of these plants as well. Even the air itself felt unnatural. For although there was a breeze, not a single plant stirred in the forest. Every inch of the area seemed ready to leap at a moment's notice, and this feeling quickly put the entire party on edge.

Once the last of the group passed through the entrance between the trees, the calm was quickly broken; for a flower to the party's front suddenly shot the spike out from between its petals and quickly pierced through the leg of the man in front. He yelled out in pain as the spike opened into the shape of a grappling hook to secure itself in place. A thin red line connected the spike to the flower, which had a jarring, flesh-like appearance.

The moment the grappling hook shaped object had seated into place, it promptly began to tug on the man's leg. He tripped over from the unexpected jerk, which caused him to land straight onto one of the bushes.

The moment the thorns penetrated his flesh, you could see the life begin to escape his body. His skin shriveled and shrunk against bone and muscle. Every drop of blood was quickly absorbed by the bush, as if it had some vampiric craving that would never be sated.

Within moments the man was limp, his husk discarded to the ground by the bush once nothing was left for it to drain.

The rest of the group froze on high alert but were unable to think of an action to take after the horror they had just witnessed.

Luke, as if on instinct, looked to his right next to the trail. Lined up perfectly with his position was a flower twitching. As if on autopilot, he quickly jumped backwards when the spike shot from this flower as well. It barely grazed his leg, however the burning that came with it felt as if the entire leg had been cut off.

The spike shot straight through his pocket, expanded, and grappled onto the quartz crystal he had captured the ghost in back home.

Luke gritted his teeth in pain as he felt a vibration over his leg. He looked down at his torn pocket and noticed the crystal was shaking. Red and black shadows seemed to bleed out of the spike that grappled around the crystal as they were absorbed straight into the spiritual prison.

A few moments passed, and the whole group watched as the flower slowly turned back into a withered, wilted version of its original form; no deadlier than a tulip you would find in a field. The trauma of the transformation seemed to take its toll. For as the last of the corruption seeped out of the flower and into the crystal, the plant crumbled into a pile of dried petals and leaves.

In a moment of ingenuity, Luke quickly grabbed his crystal and placed it against the cut on his leg, which instantly stopped burning. It had seemed that the burning wasn't from the cut itself, but from the corruption that had seeped into the wound. He took a moment to calm down, as he looked up at the rest of the group.

"Guys" he started before pausing to catch his breath. "I may have found a solution to our plant problem."

With this, he tossed the crystal into the bush that had recently fed on a member of their escort. Everyone watched as the crystal absorbed the corruption out of the bush in the same manner it had done with the flower. The leaves returned to a flexible, albeit browned form. Branches seemed to soften up as they snapped off. Slowly but surely, the entire bush returned to a more normal appearance; although it quickly crumbled as the corruption that powered it was removed.

It was now confirmed that the corruption could be reversed. But what it left behind was a husk of the living thing it took over. Did this mean that the corruption tainted the energy itself? Or maybe it simply replaced it with a darker source of power? Whatever had happened though, one thing was clear. There was no reversing the process if it went too far.

In fact, who knows what would've happened to Luke had he been unable to remove the corruption from his leg.

The group continued even more slowly down the trail a bit, as Luke gorged his crystal on corrupt energy. They had made it past twenty or thirty plants before the crystal seemed unable to absorb any more power. With this, they decided they had plenty to study, and made their way back to camp to rest and prepare for tomorrow's trip into the village.

...And back at the military warehouse on the west coast of the United States, Liz hunched over in pain as the cut her arm received continued its torturous burning.

Chapter 7: Outbreak

As soon as Adam and Liz landed back at the military warehouse, Adam was taken to debrief the mission as Liz was escorted to the infirmary. The burning pain grew and grew, and the more time that had passed the more the pain spread within her body. It had started just in her upper arm, but by the time the helicopter had landed back at base it burned from her fingertips through the right side of her chest.

"What happened?" the medical personnel asked her, as she recounted the event on the island with the flower. A blood sample was drawn and taken to the lab, but results would not be available for a few hours.

The pain continued to spread, however. As she sat on a bed in the infirmary and waited, Liz couldn't take it anymore. She stood up to find a doctor for some pain meds, but quickly crumbled to the ground. The pain had reached her heart, and the moment it did it seemed to spread through every inch of her body.

The color of her skin began to fade away as her skin took on an almost transparent sheen. She screamed as she could feel her gums melt away, her jaw dislocating in the process as the flesh from her gums rehardened around her teeth. Reinforcing them into a sharp, needle-like elongated form.

The next scream was more haunted, as she watched her arms collapse. Under her horrified gaze, she observed her bones begin to shed away layers of mass. This liquified bone then began to move slowly through her arms and into her hands. As the mass reached her fingertips, she screamed again as the bone began to reform, slicing through her fingers and ripping every strip of tissue that got in its way as it sharpened and hardened into blade like appendages.

She drew one more breath in to scream, however it was cut short. Instead, what came out was a ghastly shriek as her eyes melted away into the shadows. The only thing left on her mind was a strong aggressive craving for blood.

In a medical lab on the other side of the facility, a sample of blood slowly darkened into a black tar. The glass vial that contained it fell at this sudden redistribution of weight and shattered against a vent. It then split into millions of airborne particles as it was sucked straight down the shaft to the building's air conditioning unit.

■■■

Luke, John, and Sabrina all sat around a table within one of the tents. They debriefed Jake on their mission a few hours ago, before they had a quick meal and retired to a research tent to study the crystal. The quartz prison sat in the middle of the table, secured upright with a makeshift stand of rocks. It now glowed a mix of red and black, fully sated to its limit by the corrupted energies in the area.

Upon hearing about how the crystal had cleared away a portion of the corruption, Jake sent an update to headquarters. In response, headquarters decided to put off the village expedition, and sent what they said was a "gift" to Luke. This way, he could work more on his project in the field.

Luke opened the box that had been flown in, and his excitement almost burst out of his body. Inside was a belt, with various pouches and holsters that lined it. He counted six holsters capable of holding more of the larger shaped crystals. A few of the pouches also looked perfect for handfuls of dice sized crystals, which would be perfect since Luke figured he could use a smaller version of his design to target plants without having to retrieve it after each throw. This would be a much safer option in clearing out the vegetative corruption.

The remaining holsters had a device for measuring electro-magnetic frequencies, as well as ports to hook up cables to conduct electrical charge testing. The last of the holsters contained a solar powered grinder, with a diamond encrusted grinding wheel to craft more binding crystals in the field. A small strap to hook a field notes journal completed the design of the belt. Luke threw the gift around his waist and clasped it in place. His excitement reached its peak when he once again looked inside the box. There were probably around a hundred chunks of quartz in various sizes scattered along the bottom.

The three friends sat around the table and tested the filled quartz crystal. EMF levels were pretty much through the roof, however the electrical charge the crystal had was gone.

"It seems as though the pure electricity that filled the crystal was used as a sort of conduit for the spiritual energy nearby, so every time the corruption or the ghost back home was absorbed, the electrical current in the crystal shifted. It was probably then fully pushed out once the crystal was full of corruption, acting as a sort of seal to the entire device." Luke exclaimed excitedly, as Sabrina nodded and listened to his discovery.

John, however, just gave him a blank stare. "Yea, what you said. I'll just assume that means it worked as intended", he stated before laughing and returning to his drink. His nerves were now fully calmed after about his third glass of whiskey. Apparently, the expedition had a supply of liquor hidden away somewhere.

Luke would have to ask about this once they were ready to leave the island, as he himself could use a drink as well now.

Shortly after the crystal's observation session, John left to sleep off the buzz he had been feeling from his self-medication. With a promise that he would join the next expedition now that he had come to terms with the reality that ghosts are not only real, but also extremely dangerous.

Sabrina watched Luke work, as he scribbled a new smaller crystal design for clearing a way through the forest. Once his design was finished, he pulled a chunk of quartz out of the box that sat next to him. He started preparing it by carving the chunk into a stack of small cubes using a cutting wheel attachment that came with his new fancy grinder. He then proceeded to shape these cubes one by one into miniature versions of his larger crystal.

Sabrina yawned "I think I'm ready for bed. Good luck with your design, I shall see you in the morning Luke!" She patted him on the shoulder before she left for her tent.

Luke finished cutting the crystals into shape before he tossed them into the pouch on his new belt. With this, he leaned back to admire the results of his work. As he looked over his notes, he realized that now that his invention was proven, he was going to need to create a real name for the trap itself. *Project Binding* simply wasn't going to cut it.

Luke stared thoughtfully at his notes for a few moments before he picked up a pen and wrote *Dusktrap* by the sketch of his design; in reference to the shadows it seemed to capture when used on a corrupted "living" thing. With this completed, he left the original Dusktrap on the table, and took himself and his new gear belt to his own tent to rest up. With the work he put in tonight, they would be able to continue their expedition to the village tomorrow.

As Luke's head hit his pillow however, it quickly shot back up once a screech pierced the air. As he threw his clothes back on, he rushed out of his tent to the sound of someone's stifled scream. Standing just inside the barricade was Jake. Where once he had normal hands, there now protruded long talons currently pierced into one of the guards' throats. A short distance away from them was the dead man that everyone watched get sucked dry earlier that day. Only, he was alive and well, with his own talons shoved deep into another man's heart.

Panic filled the camp as Jake and the unnamed man were both gunned down. A strange rhythmic scream came out of Jake as he fell, different than the usual cries. It almost seemed as if he was calling someone or something with how the tones of his scream repeated.

Once what used to be Jake and the other man collapsed, their bodies returned to a shriveled husk state. It appeared that the husk state didn't mean they were truly dead, it just made them into a puppet. A puppet that waited for the corruption to pull its strings.

But when did Jake die? He didn't even go on the expedition with the rest of them.

This thought was quickly interrupted however, as the sound of a boat raced towards the shoreline. Luke swiveled his head back to the forest on the opposite side, as a cacophony of screeches could be heard. Sabrina and John ran to him before Sabrina spoke.

"What the hell is going on?!" She yelled over the sounds of screams and gunfire.

Before Luke could answer however, the two men that were meant to be their retreat escort arrived at the trio. "Go go go the boat is here for us! We gotta go now!" one barked at the friends.

The group of friends reactively sprinted towards the boat with their escort. As soon as they began their sprint to safety, a small army of creatures crashed through the barricade. Talons swung in every direction, ripping apart the guards as less and less gunshots could be heard in their defense.

As the group frantically leapt onto the boat, the vehicle left the dock and sped away from the island. Luke looked back and watched as the camp was overrun by creatures. Tents were fully destroyed, and the last remaining guards fell amidst the creature's screeches. Moments later, the island fell silent. The creatures could be seen in the shadows of sporadic campfires hunched over the corpses. Moving in ways that could only mean they were taking their fill of the bloody feast left behind in their victory.

"I... I forgot my filled dusktrap," Luke stammered, clearly upset at his first successful invention being lost to the onslaught. For although the tent that surrounded the table it stood on collapsed, the crystal still sat on the table in plain sight. Its red glow was like a beacon to the carnage the island had just witnessed.

The three friends looked back towards the beacon somberly, when one final gunshot rang through the air from a hiding guard finally attempting to defend himself.

His shot missed however, and instead struck the abandoned crystal. As soon as the crystal shattered, a rolling red and black smoke carpeted the ground, before a banshee like creature shot up into the air. The group slammed their hands against their ears as the new spirit spread its arms and let out a painfully sharp shriek. The specter then turned its attention to the feasting creatures below it and quickly dove down.

The creature's screams filled the air as the demonic banshee ripped through the crowd. The monsters fell as the ghast flew through them; their bodies exploding one after the other. Soon, not a single creature was left except the banshee, which floated in the air above the camp as if to admire its work.

That is, until it noticed the boat that was speeding off. To which the banshee turned and began a flight straight for the survivors.

"Faster! Go Faster!" Sabrina yelled to the captain. Who, confused at the urgency of her tone, turned to see what the commotion was about.

As his eyes set on the banshee, he frantically shifted the boat into the fastest speed it could manage. The watercraft now bounced against wave after wave as the spirit slowly moved further out of sight. Falling behind in its chase, until it finally gave up and returned to the island.

Everyone breathed a sigh of relief as they made their escape. Luke's mind raced once they were clear of any immediate danger as he processed what had happened. He had a theory, but it would have to wait for them to get somewhere safe. For now, the group just needed to get back to headquarters. Things on the island took a horrible turn.

However, they had no idea what news was currently awaiting them back home.

Chapter 8: Shadows Fall

The three friends arrived back at the hunting lodge via helicopter, which took off again only moments after it had landed.

The sun had just started to peak over the trees as they arrived shortly after dawn. Once they made their way back down into headquarters, the group was greeted by a room full of chaos.

Cameras shifted a monitor at a time to various locations in an area dominated by eastern themed buildings. Personnel could be seen running back and forth around the room; some on various calls as they moved about. A few of the monitors showed dead silence on the cameras, while others displayed crowds screaming and fleeing as the same creatures from the island chased close behind.

The creatures ripped and tore at anyone that fell behind or tripped, which filled the streets with a river of blood as more and more of the civilians fell.

Luke stood as if in a trance at the bottom of the staircase. Sabrina and John shared his look of horror as Lewis approached the group.

"I hope you have some good intel for us, because things took a turn while you were gone," he stated calmly amidst the frantic room.

"Wait, what is going on?" Luke asked, his eyes still glued to the screen.

Lewis looked at the monitor before he turned back to Luke. "Officially? Tokyo has gone dark. No one has had any communications returned in the past four hours. But as you can see..." Lewis trailed off as he waved his hand towards the monitors, as if the carnage displayed finished his statement for him.

"Our recon team in the area alerted us right before the outage. The Phantom Hawk rose in the dead of night over Tokyo, where it is currently still located. From its newly found territory deep within the city, its corruption is spreading in every direction. We have lost contact with our team, but it can be all but confirmed that the city is lost. Hundreds of thousands of people have been turned into whatever the hell you can call those monsters, with millions more either dead or soon to be."

Lewis paused for a moment to let the group of friends process this information before he continued. "In addition, we just intercepted communications that the Japanese military is considering this a virus outbreak. The city is under quarantine, and soldiers have been given orders to shoot anyone that attempts to break through the blockades."

Luke turned his gaze to Lewis fully now, as a question rose in his mind. "Wait, but if this happened only a few hours ago, why did you send us the boat? Our expedition for exploring the village wasn't expected to take off until today."

Lewis replied with a soft tone as to not share in the chaos of the room. "We sent the boat because of the islands commanding officer... You see, Jake was an undercover agent for us. He was chosen for this mission specifically because he had been to the island previously to observe the creature's effects on it. His squad, however, only had three surviving members. Himself, a woman named Liz, and a man named Adam. That is, until we intercepted Adams debriefing report. The report stated that the only two to survive were himself and Liz. Jake was reportedly killed during their escape. Drained of all blood and left as a husk by the plant life alongside the trail towards extraction."

Once he processed this new bit of information, Luke finally put the pieces together as to what had happened on the island.

"Wait! The same thing happened with a man on our trip. He and Jake attacked the camp last night, and when killed returned to husks. I think that the corruption that was on the island took over their bodies like puppets; not converting them until it felt the moment was right."

Lewis nodded as he listened to this before he inquired, "And what about the expedition?"

Luke dropped his head somberly at this question.

"The second expedition never happened. Your boat had arrived just in time, and only five of us made it off the island. What's more, my invention seemed to work well in containing the corruption. However, the first one I made was shattered by stray gunfire when we were leaving the island. It seems that the spirit I had trapped previously inside of it was morphed by the corruption I collected while cleansing the forest. Instead of a random unseen spirit, something akin to a banshee flew out. It killed everything on the island before it attempted to catch our boat. Luckily, we were able to speed away fast enough for it to give up its chase."

"Hmm. I see." Lewis replied, deep in thought. He pondered this for a moment before he continued. "So, it would seem that the spirit had no loyalty to the corrupted creatures, even though it was also morphed by the same source. That could possibly help us in dealing with these things. And you said you cleared some of the plants of their corruption? What happened to the plants after?"

Luke hesitated for a moment due to the nature of his report. "Well, bad news is they didn't survive. It seems that once the corruption spreads far enough, whatever it has taken over is pushed past the point of recovery. The moment the corruption was withdrawn, the plants instantly wilted and perished."

Luke paused again as he remembered the cut he had received from the plants assault.

"However, if the corruption is caught quick enough, I think it can be reversed. One of the plants grazed me with a launched spike when we entered the forest. Luckily though, my crystal seemed to withdraw the corruption from the wound. I was harmed the same time one of the turned men was, and the burning pain from the cut went from feeling like my leg was on fire to a dull throb pretty much instantly."

Lewis nodded along as he listened to this, only to freeze at the last part. "Oh no" he muttered, before he turned to one of the personnel close to him and barked an order. "I need intel on the Area 51 recon facility in California. Now!"

The person replied with a quick "yes sir" before they strode to a nearby computer and started to type furiously into the keyboard.

Luke had a quizzical look on his face at the sudden change in urgency, so Lewis explained the circumstances.

"Well, you see, in Adam's report only two people made it off the island. He himself had made it out without a scratch, however his partner Liz. Well, she was as the report put it: *grazed by a stray attack from one of the plants.* She was taken to the infirmary upon arrival with complaints about an intense burning pain."

Luke's stomach churned as he heard this. If his theory was correct, then- "Sir! We have camera feed of the facility!" The person interrupted Luke's thoughts as he found the source Lewis was looking for.

"Pull it up on monitor one" Lewis replied.

The group turned to the monitor and fell silent. Slowly the chaotic room calmed down, as everyone focused on the talon wielding creatures that walked through the rooms and halls of the building. Wandering in the hunt for some hidden prey.

"Rewind their camera feed, focus on the infirmary," Lewis ordered calmly.

The camera rolled back in high speed through the events of the day, as everyone watched pools of blood slowly recollect into people that went from mutilated piles of flesh to normal workers going about their shifts. When the carnage stopped, the cameras played back again at normal speed. Luke, as well as everyone else in the room watched in silent horror at what could only be this "Liz" person transformed into one of the creatures right before their eyes.

"Wait, what's that?" Luke inquired, as something seemed to go on in one of the facilities' other cameras with a label titled *Medical Lab*. At the same moment as the horrid transformation happened, a vial of blood darkened before it fell off the counter and shattered against a vent.

Lewis spoke, "That seems to be the cause of the outbreak. Pain like she described would have the wound observed, followed by a blood test for any irregularities. Her blood must have seeped into the HVAC system and created an airborne infection that turned anyone she had not already attacked. The only question is, why did the blood turn when she did?"

"I may know the answer actually," Luke stated with a short pause to gather his words before he continued. "Many ghost hunters believe that a spirit can be bound to virtually anything that remains of a person when they die. From DNA left behind in hair and skin cells, to even objects that were cherished by the person."

Lewis nodded "This is true, and we have confirmed it on multiple paranormal accounts in the past. How does this tie in with the corruption though?"

Luke quickly replied, "Well because the corruption isn't attacking the body. The corruption is attacking the spirit. It's acting like a supernatural virus and warping the person's energies. This in turn is causing the corrupted spirit to warp the body to fit its new image of itself. That also explains why once the corruption has spread, there would be no way to undue it. The corruption has destroyed the spirit, and the body has been warped on a cellular level beyond repair. Once thoroughly infected, it is no longer the same person, or plant or animal. It turns into a new creature completely. Removing the corruption then becomes like removing the heart of a person. You take a vital part of its anatomy out, and the entire thing dies."

Everyone's gaze slowly returned to the live feed cameras in Tokyo. Realization settled into the room as to the grim nature of what they saw turned for the worse. Not a single person that fell on those screens could ever be saved.

A minute or two passed before Lewis once more spoke up. "Well, does anyone have any suggestions for a new course of action? We aren't exactly prepared to take on the Phantom Hawk in our current state, and our resources are vast but in no way limitless."

Sabrina was the first to reply to him this time. "Well, I think the best course of action would be to control the outbreak in California. That military facility is on lock down. So, if we can clear the corruption from it, we may be able to prevent it from spreading through the US. In this way, maybe we can prevent a war on two fronts."

"Good idea. Focus on the smaller closer threat, and maybe we can learn more about the larger one over the horizon", Lewis replied thoughtfully.

"Or maybe, it would give us a method to test an idea I just had", Luke chimed in.

Everyone turned to look at him as his own gaze dropped to the notes he had just jotted down. "By any chance, do you have access to a weapons lab?"

Lewis pointed towards the right door at the opposite end of the room. "Well, that would be our experimental weapons facility through there. What did you have in mind though?"

Luke grinned, as he held up a diagram for an almost alien like gun. Shaped similar to a thick rifle, with two slanted rows of holes that ran down the top of the barrel with some smaller crystals sketched into the slots.

"Well, I was considering the problem with my original crystal. Which was that you had to physically touch it to the corrupted target for it to remove the corruption." Luke continued as he took out a few of the smaller crystals he formed on the island. "I had originally thought I would fix the issue with the plants by simply making individual crystals I could toss to each plant to cleanse it from a distance. The problem with this technique for the creatures, however, is that the purification isn't instant. Throwing one of them at a creature would probably annoy it for a moment as it bounced off. Not to mention that with how quickly they can move, you would probably miss your throw in the first place.

"However, this rifle design could possibly top feed rows of crystals into the chamber. The sharp end of the crystal would be fired with enough force to embed into the creature; giving it plenty of time to cleanse the corruption. A gas canister can be used as a propulsion force, which would also make ammunition easier to replace in the field. Since then, gunpowder wouldn't be needed."

As Luke finished stating his idea, Lewis called out to a woman nearby. "Please escort Luke to our weapons lab and pass along that they are to help make this experimental weapon."

Luke followed the woman towards the door on the right as Sabrina conversed with Lewis about an attack plan on the military facility. John, worn out entirely by his biggest fears becoming a living nightmare in front of his eyes, entered the left door instead. Making his way straight towards his room for some sleep after the mental exhaustion he had been through.

Luke walked down a long winding corridor before he was led through a metal sealed door. On the other side, was a multitude of stations. Design tables had diagrams of different weapon blueprints and ideas that would possibly lead to testing. Fabrication stations for both 3D printing parts as well as molding metal framework were then splayed around these design tables in an efficient manner.

Over to the right of the room was what looked like an ammunition crafting station, and on the opposite wall monitors were hanging. Lines of data about structural integrity, strength, and other aspects of the weapon ideas scrolled slowly up the screens. Hell, the back of the room even had a firing range for a final in-house test of the weapon before it went out for field testing.

As he was introduced to the design team, Luke handed over his diagram of the new rifle. Once the team understood the purpose of this weapon, they set to work fine tuning it. Luke watched them sketch out a more streamlined version, as he explained to the ammunitions team the necessary shape and angles for the crystals to be used for ammunition.

With the design finalized and checked over, it was agreed upon that 3D printed weapons would be the best path to take. The plastic shell would be overall lighter than a metal one, which would allow for easier extended use. With compressed gas for propulsion over gunpowder, damage to the weapon itself would be minimal anyway.

Once the weapon parts were printed and pieced together, the rifle was handed to Luke. "Your design, so it's only fair you get to be the first to try it," a man stated with a wink.

"But uh... I haven't ever actually fired a gun", Luke replied sheepishly.

To this, the man took Luke to the range and explained basic gun safety and trigger control. As Luke held the firearm, he noted to himself that it was relatively light for its size. The black and silver weapon was also easy to wield with two hands; due to the way they shaped the barrel and grip. Luke mentally commended the teams for the amazing work that they had done.

As he loaded the crystals into the row of holes on top, the extra weight from the crystals pressed the weapon downward into his hands. Which made it even easier to hold the gun while giving it some much needed heft.

Luke aimed the rifle towards a gel dummy down range and pulled the trigger. A simple lever system opened the gas canister for a split second, letting out enough pressure to jettison a crystal straight out of the rifle. The crystal struck the dummy, which pierced about an inch deep into its torso.

"Perfect," Luke murmured to himself. In addition, what little recoil the compressed gas had seemed to be balanced by the top loaded weight of the crystals.

The Rangemaster took the rifle and pumped out a few rounds rapidly. No kick on the weapon meant even lightly trained personnel could rapidly switch targets between shots without much vertical adjustment.

Following this little practice session, Luke walked back to the main room as Lewis and Sabrina finished setting up the plan of attack on the facility.

"Well, the weapon design seems to work well. The people in the lab are just perfecting the design and making enough for our next mission. They should be finished by tomorrow morning," Luke stated as he approached the two strategists.

"Oh, great timing actually," Sabrina replied. "We just finished up plans here. Tonight, we will rest from the island troubles. Tomorrow morning Lewis will explain what our plan of attack is. Then we can all head to the range and test your weapons before we pack up and set out for the facility."

"Sounds good" Luke answered, now realizing just how exhausted he was from the recent events. He waved goodbye to Sabrina and Lewis, before making his way through the door John previously entered.

Down the hall, a cafeteria could be seen through a door to the right, while a door on the left led to another hallway. This hall looked almost like a hotel, except with names on the doors instead of numbers. Luke found the door with his name on it and spotted a fingerprint scanner near the doorknob. He placed his thumb on the scanner, which caused a magnetic lock within the door to release.

"Well, that's just cool," he stated to himself before entering his room.

The room was more like a hotel suite than anything else. To his right was the bathroom. A bath the size of a small hot tub took up one corner, with an ornate silver trimmed mirror that sat over a black marble countertop. A polished waterfall style faucet hung over the main sink, and a stand-up shower with a towel rack outside of it took up the far side of the room.

As Luke returned his gaze to the rest of the area, he spotted a king-sized bed across from a small TV seated on a heavy looking oak wardrobe. Beyond that, was a two-person sofa which faced a much larger TV. The sofa and second TV were through a large archway as if to separate the two spaces into faux rooms.

Luke strolled deeper into his living quarters and noticed that his clothes were all hung up or stored away in drawers; everything was prepared for him just like Lewis had stated upon Luke's first arrival at the facility.

Luke then proceeded to walk through another archway roughly the size of a door. Once he had entered this last area, he stood mouth agape as he looked around. To his left was a full-sized kitchen; cabinet doors left open and stocked with various snacks. He opened the fridge, which was lined with every form of beverage imaginable. From sodas to beers to wines and water, it seemed like a suite more befitted to someone much grander than himself.

As he turned to face to his right, a table with a bench came into view. The perfect spot to focus on his inventions; as the sofa would probably be more suitable for dining periods in front of the TV.

Towards the back of the room, the far wall contained a fully equipped bar. With various bottles of liquor and spirits ready for consumption. A small ice bin sat on the bar top alongside a cocktail shaker, with rows of different glasses hanging over the bar.

Luke strode back through the room and made his way to the bathroom. He was covered in smoke and grime from the trip to the island. Which meant he needed a deep cleaning before he even touched anything in this luxurious space.

Upon reaching the bathroom, Luke quickly threw his clothes to the ground and opened the shower. As he closed the door behind himself, he noticed a digital display with a few knobs secured into the wall. Luke pushed a button, which turned on the display to a temperature reading.

"Holy shit," he muttered to himself as he turned the dials to what he thought would be the ideal temperature. Following this, he pushed one more button to finalize his selections.

A quiet hum came from behind the wall as water poured out of the ceiling. Luke jumped towards the wall of the shower; surprised by the direction and flow. He peered up, and realized this shower imitated a heavy rainfall, rather than just spraying like the fancy hose set up he was more accustomed to on campus.

Luke stepped back into the controlled storm. The water was the perfect temperature and helped him unwind from the day's events. A small door was inlaid in the shower's wall, and once opened revealed various bottles of shampoo, body wash, and conditioner. Luke picked a few out and gave himself a deep cleaning. Once finished, he shut off the water and stepped out.

Luke strode across the bathroom to a shelf and pulled a towel down from a stack supplied on it. With the towel in hand, he wiped himself dry. Once he made for the exit of the bathroom, he threw the towel into a bin in the corner of the bathroom. A bin he had assumed was meant for dirty articles of clothing and the like.

Back in the kitchen, Luke grabbed a bottle of beer, which was labeled as a brown ale. He plopped down onto the bed and sighed. The mattress was surprisingly a thick, plush memory foam. As he settled in, Luke sipped the beer and turned the TV on to one of his favorite ghost hunting shows.

In light of recent events, the entire hunt seemed fake to him as memories of the island scrolled through his mind like a Wikipedia article.

This group on TV was hunting for the spirit of a child that died in the family home long before the age of vaccines and modern medicine, and he himself was hunting a demigod spirit hellbent on destroying the world. He chuckled to himself at the thought before he rolled onto his side and closed his eyes.

The thoughts of the day's events faded slowly into the depths of sleep.

Chapter 9: The Raid

Luke awoke to the intro of a random show playing on the TV. He reached for the remote and promptly shut it off, stretching his stiff muscles as he woke up. He was a little sore from the events prior, but nothing too extreme.

Luke then threw on some clothes, fitted his utility belt on, and looked in the mirror. In all honesty, the belt looked out of place with a basic pair of jeans and a T-shirt, and he made a mental note to change up his wardrobe once he had the opportunity to find more suitable attire for his new look. After all, he was no longer a college student, but rather a member of some elite secret organization that fought the real spirits of the world.

As he entered the cafeteria for some breakfast, Luke spotted John and Sabrina at a table already eating. A tray filled his hands as he grabbed some bacon and eggs, followed by a piece of toast which he buttered extensively. His meal was completed with a cup of coffee before he walked over to sit with his friends.

"Sleep well?" Sabrina stated with a smirk, noticing the grogginess still in Luke's eyes.

Once his tray touched down against the table, he lifted his hands to rub his eyes and took the seat next to her. "I did actually. Like a rock. What year is it anyway?" Luke replied, as he returned her smirk.

John seemed lost in thought, as he stared off into the distance while he chewed a sausage link. A moment later though, he cleared his throat and spoke up.

"Ya know... once we left that island, I discovered something about myself." This statement quickly changed the tone of the table from playful, to a more serious note.

"It seems my fear of ghosts came from the unknown. I had no idea what they were capable of, nor did I know what to do if I ever came across one. Now that I have answers to both of these questions, I've come to a conclusion."

Luke and Sabrina turned to face him as he spoke, with Luke being the first to reply. "Is that so? Well John, what is your conclusion?"

John took another bite of his food before he replied. "Well, I obviously froze up and was pretty useless on the island. However now that I've processed things, I think I am ready to fulfill my role. I spoke with Lewis this morning, and he has agreed with my decision to join the vanguard on our next mission. I don't have the calm observation skills of Sabrina, and I don't have the inventive mind of you." John stated as he nodded towards Luke.

A momentary pause followed as John took another bite of his food. "However, I do have some experience hunting. My dad was an avid hunter, and his favorite sort of game was the kind that could fight you back. From bears and mountain lions to more exotic creatures. And he took me on quite a few of his trips. I believe I can play the role of protector, as this just seems like another exotic hunt now. One with a much more dangerous sort of creature mind you, but a hunt nonetheless."

Sabrina smiled, "Well, I'm glad you've adjusted so well in your mindset. To be honest I was a bit worried you would be quick to drop out the moment we got back from the island. I think I can speak for both of us though, when I say we would be happy to have you guarding us!"

Luke nodded as he finished the rest of his food, agreeing with Sabrina's statement.

Sabrina finished her food as well, before she spoke up once more. "I believe it's time for us to get to work. The briefing is in a few minutes, followed by our range training as the convoy gets prepared for our journey out."

"We have lived in the shadows and taken on many small threats over our years as an organization." Lewis started to speak just as the three friends entered the room. He nodded towards them as they stood against a wall; looking over the room of men and women that were seated and listening intently.

"This, however, will be our first true test of our abilities. The Phantom Hawk's corruption was carried off the island by an unknowing agent of the military's secret paranormal division."

Pictures of the camera footage from the day before appeared behind Lewis as he continued.

"The carrier has fallen to this virus, and in turn the majority of their west coast base has been infected with her. Those that have been corrupted now wander the halls of the locked down facility, hunting for any that may still stand. If these creatures escape, then we will have a war on two fronts to fight, because the Phantom Hawk has taken Tokyo already. There is no telling how fast the spirits corruption will spread uncontained out east, but an escape near us could spread just as fast. Therefore, we will use this opportunity to learn if we have what it takes against this new threat."

Lewis paused for a moment, as he let all the personnel take in what this could mean before he nodded towards Luke. "One of our new members has devised a weapon with the capabilities to take down the creatures quicker and easier than old fashioned bullets. The weapon also has the means to contain and clean up the corruption in order to prevent its spread as well as give us the ability to study it more extensively. Following this briefing, you will all head to the range to gain familiarity with the firearm before loading onto a convoy towards the facility.

"Upon reaching the facility, you will be broken up into three squads. Alpha team will be the vanguard, entering from the front of the building and clearing the rooms one by one through the facility. Bravo's charge will be that of a flank position. You will enter from the rear of the building to help clear towards Alpha. Charlie will be our eyes for this mission and will be posted on a neighboring hill to ensure nothing escapes the warehouse unnoticed. Are there any questions?"

Lewis paused to take any questions. Once no one had anything to ask, he started to list members assigned to each team. Naturally, Luke and the other two were assigned to Alpha team. Since they not only already had firsthand experience with the creatures, but Luke was also the creator of the weapon they would all now wield.

Lewis dismissed the group, as the friends all followed the rest of the organization's members to the firing range.

Upon entering the room, Luke was quickly waved over by the Rangemaster from the day prior. "Since you have already created and tested the weapon, you will help me with training the others." he stated. The Rangemaster then promptly handed a fully refined version of the crystal rifle to Luke.

Following this, the officer turned to the rest of the members with Luke by his side. "This rifle was coined by Luke here as the Dawnbringer. It is fully loaded with what we now call duskshot, which are small crystals that embed into the targets and extract the corruption from within. They are only big enough to contain a single creature's corruption, so take care not to load spent rounds into the weapon. We have no idea what might occur if you were to fire a filled crystal into one of the monsters instead."

Whispers could be heard throughout the room at this statement, before the Rangemaster continued his speech. "They are top loaded round by round, so ensure that you are fully loaded prior to breaching the facility, as loading during the mission will be difficult. There are fifteen rounds including the one in the chamber. If you do manage to spend them all, then retreat to the back of your team to reload under cover."

With this introduction completed, the rifles were handed out and the Rangemaster took Bravo and Charlie teams with him. This left Luke in charge of the vanguard unit.

Alpha team received their weapons and followed Luke to the range itself, where he taught them how the weapon worked. "The target on these creatures is center mass. The crystal will function to extract the corruption regardless of where it is embedded. However, if you were to aim for the head and miss, the speed of the creatures would likely mean you won't get another shot off before it is upon you. And given the fact that even a small unnoticed scratch could turn you, this is a less than ideal situation."

Luke followed his statement with a patrol of the squad as they fired their weapons downrange. Luke stopped to observe Sabrina for a moment, as she fired a shot that flew straight over the left shoulder of her target.

"Ya know, I'm not exactly the best at this." She stated this to Luke with a shake of her head and a laugh. "You, however, seem to be a natural born leader. Given how well that little speech you said went over with everyone."

Luke blushed slightly at the compliment before he replied. "Thank you. By the way, you're missing because your stance is wrong. Lean into the weapon, not away from it. That way when you pull the trigger, your arms are more likely to stay stable instead of swinging to your side. Not that I have much experience myself... these are just some tricks the Rangemaster showed me earlier."

Luke helped Sabrina adjust into the position as he spoke it. "Ok, now exhale and fire on the exhale," he stated. To which Sabrina took a deep breath, exhaled, and shot.

The crystal now stuck embedded into the torso of her gel dummy. She jumped up in joy, as a smile quickly spread across her face.

Luke gave her a quick hug as he whispered in her ear. "Good job! But maybe don't jump with a loaded weapon in your hand."

Sabrina looked up at the rifle that was now pointed nearly backwards towards the rest of the personnel, and sheepishly returned its barrel downrange. "Whoops" she stated, before she returned to practicing her aim and technique.

Luke then continued past her to John. Once he reached his Viking built friend, however, he quickly froze in place. John was *not* kidding about his statement this morning. Luke watched as John rapidly pumped all 15 rounds into the dummy before him. As soon as the weapon had been emptied, his hands reached for more duskshot to reload. In the blink of an eye, all the open sockets on the top of the weapon were filled once more. John looked as if he had done this a thousand times. Which was of course not true, given that Luke had just designed the weapon. However, it seemed John's skills hunting easily carried over to this new weapon.

"Man, you should be the one teaching all these people instead of me," Luke stated with a laugh.

John shook his head as he set his weapon down. Unlike Sabrina moments before, John made sure to place his firearm down with the barrel turned towards the range. "I may be a good shot, but there's no way I could get in front of this group without freezing like a statue. Sabrina was right Luke; you are a natural leader. I'll take my place in the vanguard; you just make sure we get out alive."

Luke gave John a questioning look before he replied. "What do you mean get us out alive? I'm not in charge of the mission, I just made the gun."

"Oh? Are you sure about that?" John answered back as he nodded towards the back of the room, before returning to his rifle.

As Luke turned, he spotted Lewis and the Rangemaster in a private discussion with one another. Lewis noticed Luke's gaze and lifted his arm to beckon for Luke to join them.

"Yes sir?" Luke stated as he approached.

"I was just talking with Mike here," Lewis replied as he patted the Rangemaster on the shoulder. "It would seem that you are more than an inventive mind. You have the embodiment of a leader, and your quick adaptation of your crystal when assaulted by the plants tells me you can also think and adjust on your feet. So, with that in mind, congratulations. Alpha team is yours... you are now mission leader."

Luke stammered incoherently for a moment before he was able to finally stabilize himself for a real response. "Wait, but I have no experience leading. And why would these people even listen to me? I must be younger than at least half of them, and I am completely new to the organization."

To this, Lewis pointed towards the group Luke was assigned to help train. "They already listen to you. Your team focused so quickly after your direction, that they are ready to load up for the mission. And this is after you yourself learned to fire a weapon only recently. You are a natural born leader, as well as a good teacher Luke. Bravo and Charlie need a little more practice, but you should prepare Alpha to ship out."

Lewis winked to accent his statement before he returned his attention to the Rangemaster.

Luke inhaled deeply to calm himself with this new revelation. He was nervous given the sudden change of roles, but he was also excited. Everyone always told him that he had a sharp mind and was good at directing. But to be told this in such a vital mission, and to be handed the reins over all these people. The thought of the last part sank his stomach slightly though.

He was in charge of their safety now. If someone didn't make it out, it was on him.

Luke shook away these thoughts before he cleared his throat. "Ok everyone, we have clearance to load onto the convoy. Reload your rifles, grab an extra pouch of ammunition, and meet me topside."

John gave Luke a knowing wink as he loaded his weapon. Luke rolled his eyes in response, before his gaze fell upon Sabrina. Her lips formed into a proud smile as her face partially focused on the crystals in her hand, and also partially focused on Luke.

He blushed again at this, before he grabbed a fully loaded rifle himself, loaded a pouch of duskshot onto his belt, and turned to leave the room.

As Luke walked out of the hunting cabin topside the convoy came into view. Six black vans were lined down the road outside, with side doors ajar. Luke entered the back of the lead van as the rest of Alpha team slowly filed out into the open air and evenly filled the two front vans.

After he sat down, John and Sabrina joined Luke on a bench seat which faced backwards towards another seating area. Two more unknown agents that were part of Alpha team made their way into this open space and sat down.

Moments later, Lewis walked over to the open door and handed Luke a folder. "Inside, you will find the mission briefing, as well as our current information on the corrupted creatures. Be sure your team is well prepared for the enemy prior to arrival. There is also some additional information inside that may be of value to you."

As Lewis finished his statement, Bravo and Charlie teams subsequently filed into their respective vans. With a double tap on the front van, all the doors slid shut. The convoy then proceeded away from the hunting cabin and onward to Luke's first real mission as part of the team. Excitement and anxiety bubbled up inside his mind, so he turned his attention towards the folder in his hands to straighten his thoughts.

"Well, it seems we may have our work cut out for us," Luke stated as he started to read through the folder. Sabrina and John peered over his shoulders at the pages contained within. The two other agents also leaned in closer to be able to hear his next words.

"The facility housed roughly 250 personnel, with an unknown number having been corrupted. Unfortunately, we experienced an issue on the island related to this corruption. Although people were killed in the attack, there is a chance they can come back as puppets. It would seem that although living corrupted become the mindless creatures that now roamed the halls, the dead can come back with a more normal appearance; the corruption instead acting like a puppet master until they find a sufficient moment to strike. Therefore, we can't trust anyone that may still be alive within the facility. Any number of survivors could actually be corrupted creatures in disguise."

One of the two operatives proceeded to speak up following this. "But sir, what even *are* these creatures?"

Luke had forgotten that almost everyone in the prior expedition was now lost. So, none of these people had any experience with this kind of threat that they were now heading towards.

"Well..." Luke started, before he cleared his throat and continued. "When the corruption infects a living person or thing, it acts as sort of a spiritual virus. Instead of infecting the body, it infects the energies of the target. This leads the victim to then adapt its physical form to the corruption's demands, essentially killing what is left of the living and using it as sort of conduit to its own will."

He paused once more as he recalled the first creature that charged the camp. "The monsters we will face have semi-translucent skin. In addition, their gums grow down over their teeth into sharp, needle-like weapons. The bones in their arms also seem to reform into dagger like talons. They have yet to be seen carrying weapons and the like, so their intelligence is probably no higher than a savage beast. However, they move far faster than the humans they once were. This makes their teeth and claws just as effective as the rifles we carry."

With one final pause, Luke decided to attach a warning to his explanation of the monsters; to reiterate the importance of acting fast to this threat.

"Do not hesitate to fire at anything moving our way, as the duskshot is deadly to the creatures, but should cause only minor injuries to any living."

The man's grip on his rifle tightened as he nodded in reply. His hand was shaking slightly, and it was clear he was nervous about this mission. Actually... this may have been his first mission in general, as the woman that sat next to him seemed to calmly take in the information while she nodded along.

She gave him a pat on the back before speaking. "It'll be ok. We just go in, clear these assholes out, and come back in time for a nice hot meal and a few drinks."

The man nodded along to her words, which seemed to calm him down a bit.

The group was mostly silent following this as the vans carried along on their journey. Eventually, the driver called back to let the team know that the city was now in sight.

Upon entering the city, the vans split down different exits from the highway. Luke assumed that this was to prevent any curiosity as a convoy of black tinted vans may draw much more attention from civilians than one van on its own. Only the vans for Charlie team continued forward down the highway. This was probably to set up their lookout positions in case any random people decide to walk past the warehouse during the breach and assault.

As time went on, the distance to the warehouse shortened steadily, until their van finally came to a stop as it pulled up alongside three other vans in the nearby parking lot.

Luke looked up at the warehouse. It was massive for sure, but from the outside it looked like nothing special. Just a large plain rectangular building you could spot in any other warehouse district of any other major city. That was probably the point though, as the military would not have wanted random people poking their noses around in so confidential of an area.

The vans emptied as Luke pulled a radio out from the van's wall. He turned it on as Alpha and Bravo both separated into their respective groups, still within earshot of him.

"Alpha One to Charlie One, what's your position." Luke felt so proud for a moment, for he always wanted to say something like that. He felt like a badass, as if he was playing a video game in real life. Unfortunately, in real life you don't get any second chances if you died.

"Alpha One this is Charlie One, we have eyes on you and the perimeter is secured. Approach when ready."

With this, Luke bladed his hand before he pointed it towards the building's corner. The motion signaled Bravo team to unshoulder their rifles and proceed to the backdoor of the building.

As they moved around the building, Luke's gaze moved to Sabrina. A hint of worry could be seen behind her eyes, but for the most part she hid it well. Luke then peered over at John, who was definitely much calmer than he was on the island. Not even his hands shook as he held his rifle across his chest, ready to sway it out once a target was in sight. Finally, Luke's gaze crossed over the other seven men and women of his team. These members were in different stages of readiness, but that was to be expected given the circumstances.

After this final check, Luke led the way to the facility's front door.

As Luke approached the door, John and the other three members of the vanguard ran to the front, with two leaning against the wall on each side of the door. Once Luke gave the signal to Charlie team, the doors security protocols would be disabled. The vanguards for both Alpha and Bravo would then breach the doors on opposite sides of the building, and the sweep would begin.

Luke looked to the hillside where a spotter and sniper pair from Charlie were stationed and waiting. A moment later, the spotter's arm swung up. This signal meant that Bravo had finished getting into position themselves.

Luke clutched the barrel of his Dawnbringer rifle with his left hand, as he raised his right hand in a similar motion. He then took a deep breath and splayed his right hand wide open to signal Charlie to disable the locks.

As his hand quickly returned down to the trigger of his weapon, a click could be heard as a magnetic lock was disabled. Following this, the vanguard turned the door handle and pushed the door open.

As it swung, a creature that was kneeling in the hallway turned to the group, let out a high-pitched scream, and charged.

Chapter 10: Security Breach

A crystal buried into the creature's chest, which was fired reactively from John. It clawed at the duskshot for a moment before its talons retracted back into its arms. The flesh hardened teeth returned to their normal human shape, and the semi-translucent skin turned to a tanned shade. The body then dropped to the ground; the only sign that it was corrupted being its hollowed charred eye sockets where living shadows danced a moment ago.

The Alpha team strode into the hallway and breached a door to their right. Shots fired as two more creatures collapsed to the ground, returned to the bodies of their previous life. The bodies of people that once walked these halls, conducting research and making discoveries. Now, cursed to wander as mere husks of themselves. Hellbent on killing anything they could feast their eyes on.

Luke directed the vanguard to guard the hall as the remaining members of the team moved into a nearby room. Both to prevent the group from being flanked, as well as to prevent any creatures from possibly slipping past them and out into the open. With the location temporarily secured, he then took the chance to explore the space.

This seemed to be the lab where they intended to test the blood sample taken from Liz. Luke walked with Sabrina through the room, looking for any information the researchers may have gained from their analysis.

"Hey Luke, I just had a random thought that may be important to our mission." Sabrina stated this as she froze in front of one of the lab desks. "Do you remember what had happened to that blood sample?"

Luke listened to this before he absentmindedly replied while sifting through some folders on the desk. "Yea, it fell off the desk, and into the... Shit!" he yelled. The change of dynamic in the room now caused every head in the room to turn to face Luke.

"We need to get out now!" Luke barked to the rest of the members of Alpha team. In a cruel twist of irony however, the vanguard backstepped into the doorway as a cacophony of screams could be heard down the hall.

"What's the problem?" John inquired as he backed towards Luke's side. A veritable army of creatures now rushed towards the doorway. Crystals embedded one after the other as body after body dropped. This merely slowed the onslaught down however, as the monsters began to climb over the corpses like ants over a twig.

Some of them got lucky and were able to make their way to the group's defensive position. Suddenly, two men from the vanguard yelped as they each took a claw to the chest. Ribbons of blood flew out as they fell aside and clutched their chests in pain, the acidic burn from the corruption already spreading quickly.

Luke reacted instantly and shot a crystal into each of the men's wounds, which caused the pain to subside in their chests. Or at least, the pain from the corruption.

"Get these two men bandaged and prepare to escape now!" Luke commanded, before he turned to John and replied to his question. "The blood sample fell into the HVAC system, *that* is how all these people got infected. So that means, if the air conditioning kicks on..." Luke trailed off as John's eyes got wide.

His reply stammered out at the sudden realization. "We would all become infected as well..."

Luke swiped his radio from a holster on his belt and quickly keyed the microphone. "Bravo team you need to get out asap! Charlie, cover our retreat. Abort the breach! I repeat, abort the breach!"

"This is Charlie, we have both doors in sight. You are clear to exit."

Luke confirmed Charlie's statement with a quick "copy that," which was followed by only silence. For whatever reason, Bravo team was not replying.

"Bravo come in; do you copy?" Luke tried again.

A broken transmission came through after a moment, as screams and shots could be heard over the radio. "This... Bravo... pinned down ...can't exit."

"Damn, we have to try to get to them," Luke stated as Sabrina quickly replied with a short "how?" He took a moment to think as the last few creatures fell in the doorway. The team was finally able to start making progress in clearing the opening of corpses while collecting the filled crystals to be studied back at the base. It seemed there was only one course of action available to them now.

"Reload your rifles. We lock down this side of the building again, then wrap around and aid Bravo team. We need to get everyone out of here before-" Luke was interrupted by a low hum from within the walls as the air conditioning started up.

"Everyone out. Now!" Luke barked. Realization struck as the entire team bolted for the door. "Cover your mouths and noses! Hold your breath until outside!"

Alpha team rushed outside of the door; rifles held low. It had seemed that the twenty or so creatures that attacked them earlier were the only ones down this hall. Which would explain why Bravo was pinned down. Most of the fiends probably congregated on the other side of the building and easily flanked them.

Alpha team made it out of the building quickly. Once the last operative exited the doorway into fresh air, Luke held his arm up and made a fist. A series of clicks could be heard as the magnetic locks once more secured into their place within the door. What the team did not realize in their hurried escape, however, was the wisps of corruption that came through the ventilation.

The wisps of corruption which had slowly filled every duskshot loaded into their rifles. Every crystal in the Dawnbringer rifles was filled to the brim with corrupted energies.

Luke turned to the group to make sure everyone was still alive. The two wounded were quickly dropped off at the waiting vans, as the remaining eight members of Alpha team rushed to Bravo's point of entry. Yelling and screams could be heard from just inside the door. It did not seem like Bravo had made it far into the building before they were assaulted. More importantly though, they did not sound like they were corrupted yet.

Luke opened the door and Bravo team could be seen in the middle of the hallway; no more than thirty feet from the entrance. However, the situation Bravo was in looked bleak. Flanked on all sides, creatures constantly filled the hallway from doors that led from the surrounding rooms.

"Clear them a way out! Drop anything between them and us!" Luke directed. He was then the first to act, as he fired a shot into the back of the nearest creature. A crystal that was unknowingly filled with corruption during their retreat.

The duskshot struck true and embedded between the monster's shoulders. But for some reason, the creature seemed unfazed. Luke faltered for a moment. Which quickly turned to surprise as Sabrina shoved his barrel down to the ground.

"Luke, we can't help them..." Sabrina stated with a somber tone. as he turned to her.

"And why not?"

In reply to Luke's question, she pulled a crystal from his gun and held it up at eye level. While gazing upon the crystal, he noticed that it already glowed the eerie shade of red that signified it was filled.

Luke's shoulders dropped in defeat as he realized the open top design of the rifle left the crystals exposed to airborne sources of corruption. Corruption for instance, like the kind that spewed from the ventilation. They were never in any danger of being infected, as the crystals served as a barrier. Unfortunately, this also meant that *all* their ammo was now spent.

Luke pulled his radio out and keyed the microphone. "Bravo team, our ammo is tainted. Focus the majority of your gunfire on the creatures in front of you. Try and make your way to the exit." His instructions were pointless however, as seconds later a hum could be heard from within the walls. The air conditioning was about to start blowing on this side of the building.

It seemed to work in stages, not that the specific design mattered at this point. Alpha team watched helplessly as Bravo's ammo slowly filled with the corruption in the air. Ammo which they then fired repeatedly into one of the creatures that was blocking their escape. A creature that for reasons unknown to them would not drop.

Bravo team managed to fire six or seven shots into the creature before they were overrun. Screams filled the air as talons ripped and tore through them. A pool of blood had begun to expand from underneath the dogpile of carnage as the screams slowly quieted. A fog of despair started to cloud the minds of Alpha team as they witnessed Bravo's sudden mutilation.

Within this moment of silence, one of the crystals fired into the foremost creature shattered. A reddish-black cloud escaped from the destroyed prison and started to seep into the monster's body. Within moments, a flash of what looked like red lightning shot through the creature's muscles.

One by one, crystal after crystal shattered and filled the creature with an increasing amount of corruption. It let out a screech, which slowly turned into a roar as its spine reformed into a long row of spikes. Muscles bulged and grew as the creature turned more gorilla-like instead of human. That is, if gorillas could also grow to be ten feet tall crouched down. With massive biceps the size of tree trunks ending in forearms that could be used as battering rams.

The monstrous abomination turned slowly towards the open door that Alpha team currently stood on the other side of. As a loud snapping sound echoed down the corridor, its once humanoid skull split in half and reformed into a pair of forward-facing horns. The living shadows in its eye sockets shifted from the solid black flames to a hellish combination of red and black.

Once this abomination's transformation was complete, it roared again and started to stomp towards the door. Walls were shoved outward from its massive size; snapping support beams and framework as it made its way closer to its prey.

Shaking the horrors of what he had just witnessed from his mind, Luke slammed the door shut. As Alpha team began to backpedal away. He then signaled Charlie to lock it once more. The magnetic locks clicked into place just as a massive dent appeared in the door.

This creature would not be contained so easily.

"Alpha team this is Charlie. You need to get out now. We have just intercepted military communications indicating that they have discovered what has happened in the facility. An airstrike is en route to destroy any evidence of the events that have happened here."

Luke looked down at the radio before he gave the door a sideways glance. An entire squad was lost because of a simple fault in his weapons design.

Another massive dent appeared in the door, as the creature pounded against the barrier which kept it from its meal. In the distance, the unmistakable drone of military jets could be heard closing in on their location. The pounding on the door continued as the metal was reshaped under the monster's fists. As if it was a massive god-like blacksmith hammering away in its forge.

"Get to Charlie team! Go go go!" Luke commanded.

Alpha team replied by switching to a full sprint up the hill. As they reached the top of the hill, the military jets had finally come into sight. With one final dive to the ground for safety, the first set of missiles struck the building. Luke covered his head as explosion after explosion popped off into the structure. The moment the abomination managed to finally smash through the doorway, a missile struck behind it. Every creature in the hallway instantly exploded and their corpses were engulfed in the flames.

A heat wave washed over the remaining members of the mission as Luke looked around to make sure John and Sabrina were safe. Sabrina clutched the ground below her tightly as if at any moment a blast would send her flying in the air. John was turned to face the facility, which was now an inferno. Smoke and fire shot up high into the sky as the last missiles struck true. The jets had already turned to return to base.

Leaving only the smoldering ashes of the dead in their wake.

Chapter 11: Captive 187

"Bomb them," the Director stated calmly as he watched the unknown group of people enter the fallen facility. He continued, "I want an airstrike on that location ASAP! Nothing is to get out of containment, do you hear me?"

"Yes sir," an agent behind the Director replied before he exited the room; with a phone in his hand as he punched in the number for the nearby Air Force base.

Director Johnson sat back in his chair; his eyes glued to the satellite feed of the facility. He watched as the two teams from this unknown organization entered the building from opposite doors. In their hands they wielded a strange looking futuristic weapon with sharp pinkish objects thrust within them. Less than ten minutes from when they breached the recon facility, one of the teams exited and ran to the opposite side of the building, only to lock the door before they ever entered. He leaned in close as he watched the group bolt the moment the air strike commenced. It had seemed that this group lucked out, even though their partners within the facility were not as fortunate.

Once the facility lit up from the airstrike, the Director turned off his monitor and turned to a man in a lab coat nearby. "How is your progress on the control harness?"

The head of research and development dropped his head to focus on the clipboard in his hand. "The harness has just been finished and is currently awaiting your permission to test."

"Good," the Director replied. "I want to see this test myself."

Director Johnson led the way down a brightly lit hallway, the walls of which were a very sterile and very blinding shade of white. Door after door passed him, with the head researcher following closely behind. Two agents in black suits took up the rear of the entourage.

The group stopped in front of a metal door with a biometric security pad. The Director placed his thumb onto the pad as he keyed in a passcode. Then, a light flicked green as the door slid open for the party to enter.

A long spindly leg was the first thing to come into view, which was separated from the observation room by a sheet of one-way glass. One by one, seven more of the massive legs could be spotted as the Director walked fully into the viewing area.

Each of the limbs had to be at least ten feet long, all of them ending against a black shadow-laden body. Melding with these shadows, the entire creature was also draped in a sickly green aura. When it turned, its eight eyes seemed to match; small orbs of green flames seated above two large black fangs. The massive spider was alert and ready to pounce, as it sat partially crouched within its room.

A man in the room stood up and handed the head researcher a small tablet, which was then subsequently handed to the Director.

"To activate control once the harness is attached, push this," he stated as he pointed to a rectangular green button on the screen of the tablet. "We have tested the harness on some of our Class B specimens with a perfect success rate. However, this is our first test on a Class A subject. If all goes well, we will begin production on a second harness to be used on the Phantom Hawk."

"Good," returned the Director. "Harness the Broodmother."

At his command, a small door opened in the room on the other side of the glass. Four men armed with assault rifles entered the room and began firing as they formed a perimeter around the Broodmother. This got the spirit's attention immediately, as it lunged for one of the soldiers. His screams could be heard through the glass as the specter's fangs pierced deep for a moment, only for it to back off.

Another soldier tripped on what could've been assumed to be just a thick strand of spiderweb, if not for the screams that followed as he fell into a web. The material was extremely corrosive to any victims that were caught unaware, and the man slowly fell silent as he slipped straight through the openings between the strands into a pile of chunks below.

A fifth man quickly entered the room as the events unfolded. In his hands was a large metal box, with LED lights flickering over the surface. Four straps jutted out from the sides of it, making the whole device look like some kind of technological backpack.

The man tossed it into the air towards the Broodmother just as it turned and impaled the third soldier with one of its legs. The moment the device landed on the spirit's back, the straps wrapped around and locked into place as blue LEDs started to rapidly flash over the surface of the pack. The man that carried the harness in quickly sprinted out the door, with it shutting behind him at the same time as the spider sunk its fangs into the final soldier. The Director pushed the green button on the screen of the tablet in his hands just as the spider withdrew its teeth.

An eerie hollow screech escaped from the Broodmother as it stood in place shaking. The harness lights sped through their cycle rapidly across the machine's surface before they finally stopped. The pack now glowed with sporadic solid lights across it, and the spirit had stopped moving.

The Director looked down at the screen, which now had a variety of commands strewn across it. There was a button for attack, patrol, and recall. A box on the other side of the screen was empty for inputting specific coordinates to move the subject, and in the middle were simple basic command arrows. The Director pushed a button labeled *turn left*, and the Broodmother immediately spun in place to now directly face the glass barrier.

"Excellent work," the Director stated with a grin. "We will need to field test this of course, but this should give us a weapon to weaken the Phantom Hawk. Begin construction of a second harness, as well as a method of launching it. I highly doubt we can get as close to it as we did the Broodmother considering the Phantom Hawk's tendency to corrupt every living thing nearby."

With a nod, the man in the lab coat left the room to begin this next project. The Director then turned to the glass again.

Medical personnel were on their way down to aid the two bitten soldiers, but it was too late.

The first to be bit started to clutch at his chest, a look of terror on his face as he moved to scream. However only a slight rasp managed to escape his lips. His flesh then liquified and reformed into an almost cocoon-like shape. Just as soon as this fleshy cocoon had formed, it exploded.

The explosion flung the dead bodies in the room through the air as the second man that was bit cocooned as well. The force of the detonation was strong enough to crack the reinforced glass that separated the rooms.

From where the cocoon used to sit was now a spider about four feet tall. Its own legs and body were completely unlike the Broodmother's however, as they looked to be made of remolded flesh and muscle tissue rather than the shadows of their matron. The second cocoon exploded, which further damaged the glass as a second spider joined the first. The two stood still, facing the Broodmother and waiting calmly.

"What's going on here?," The Director asked, as a nearby seated man typed away at the computer in front of him and replied.

"During our testing, we discovered that the Broodmother has two primary abilities. The first of which is a highly corrosive web it uses less to trap prey, but moreso to create traps for possible aggressors. The second, is that people and animals bitten by the Broodmother seem to undergo a complete biological change. A portion of the victim's matter forms into a cocoon, as the rest liquifies inside to be reformed into the spiders you see now. In addition, as the body reforms, the cocoon starts to produce a volatile chemical. When the spiderling inside pierces the cocoons wall with its leg, a reaction takes place. This reaction then leads to the explosion we witnessed as the spider hatched."

The researcher then pulled up the file on the Broodmother as the Director strode over to read through it. As his eyes met the screen, the man continued to explain the creature.

"The cocoons don't always hatch immediately, however. The first set of cocoons we saw hatched the moment they were formed. Within seconds of hatching, the spiderlings then began to try to attack the walls of the room. The fact that these ones don't seems to confirm our theory that the smaller ones share a hivemind, with the Broodmother at its core.

The next cocoons that had formed in one of our tests laid dormant for two weeks. We sent a man in to take a sample of one; thinking that they were failed transformations. However, as he approached the cocoon it exploded and killed him. The Broodmother seems capable of commanding them to hatch, and if not commanded they instead act as landmines. There is... one other thing though," the man trailed off.

"Yes? What is it?" The Director asked impatiently. The man then turned to face the Director as if to emphasize his last statement.

"The control levels both the Phantom Hawk as well as the Broodmother have shown over their creations shows an extremely high level of intelligence. To be able to function while separately coordinating a few, or in the Phantom Hawks case hundreds of its own creations is something that would drive a human insane from all the incoming information. While Class B and some Class C captives have shown signs of intelligence, Class A seems to be smarter than any human. Our theory is that the only reason we have been able to capture them is because they don't understand our world yet. If one of the creatures was able to return to its own world, there is a chance that we lose control of the portal, and a war would break loose."

The Director pondered this for a moment before he replied. "Well, then you better make sure we don't have another escape like the Phantom Hawk. Prepare the containment cell for a field test." With this he exited the room; the metal door sliding shut behind him as he strode down the hallway with the tablet still in hand. He then called the head researcher to meet him at the helipad for a bird's eye view of the field test.

Winding hall after winding hall the Director walked, before a final portal led him outside to a waiting helicopter. He climbed inside as the researcher caught up and jumped in as well. Shortly after, the helicopter lifted off from its pad. It climbed about a hundred feet into the air before it started to fly in circles centered around the facility.

"Prepare the containment bay of 187 for release", the researcher relayed into a radio. The ground next to the facility split open shortly after, as the structure which contained the Broodmother lifted above the surface. A solid metal box covered in a crystalline shell now sat in contrast to the unassuming military base's nearby walls.

Director Johnson checked the tablet to make sure the harness still had control over the Broodmother. Following this, he nodded to the researcher seated next to him. "Drop containment protocols on 187."

Following the head researcher's command, the wall opposite the bay's personnel door slowly dropped open. Darkness flooded the opening as wisps of green were the only thing easily spotted on the spirit in the nighttime air.

The Director punched in coordinates for a clearing in the desert roughly 100 yards away, and pressed *move*. The giant spider took no time to respond and skittered quickly into the moonlit desert terrain. It moved much faster than could be expected for something that colossal in size. The helicopter lit a spotlight focused on the creature to follow its path as it moved to the coordinates. The Broodmother then sat still at this new location, awaiting its next orders.

The Director moved it to various locations around the desert in the test before a cow was released roughly 200 yards from the creature's current location. The Director then pushed the *attack* button, which caused a new screen to pop up. It had various options such as attacking anything on site or attack immediate threats, as well as a radar display with a single red dot at the cow's location.

The Director pushed the red dot, and the words *target locked* appeared on the screen. He then looked up as the spirit turned to face the direction of the cow. Within moments, the Broodmother lunged at the cow, piercing it with two of its legs. It then pulled the impaling legs apart, ripping the cow in two. Both halves of the animal flew in opposite directions far across the desert from the force of the attack.

"Perfect," the Director stated. A devilish smile slowly spread across his face as the Broodmother was returned to containment.

On a nearby hill that overlooked the facility, a man with binoculars and a radio transmitter laid in the dirt. "Headquarters is going to want to hear about this," he stated to himself. After which he switched the frequency on the transmitter and pulled a microphone out from its side.

Chapter 12: Emotions

"It's all my fault" Luke stated to himself, seated at the mini bar in the back of his room. He took another sip of the beer in his hand before he hung his head once more.

How could he have been so stupid? Leaving the crystals exposed to the open air like that was just begging for something to go wrong. Ten members of the team he led, all of Bravo team. They were all lost because of his mistake. Why was he even put in command to begin with? How could Lewis of thought he would be capable of handling the responsibility?

Luke and the remainder of the mission's members arrived back at the underground headquarters a few hours ago. The sun had just started to set, just like Luke's mood. Upon arrival, he had somberly briefed Lewis on the details of what happened during the mission. As Lewis dismissed him and set about to direct the weapons lab to make design changes recommended by Luke, Luke himself retired to his room to be alone with his thoughts. He just couldn't shake it out of his mind that those lives were lost because of him.

A knock rapped against Luke's door from the other end of his condo-like room. He sighed hunched over before quickly draining the remnants of beer from its bottle. A hollow thud echoed as he sat the bottle onto the bar top, getting up in the process to answer the continued knocking upon his door.

Luke slowly swung the entrance open to reveal John and Sabrina on the other side, drinks in John's hands and a tote bag in Sabrina's.

"We thought you could use some company," Sabrina stated with a soft smile as the pair entered Luke's room before he could reply. They made their way back to the kitchen area and Sabrina sat the tote bag she was carrying on the table.

"Oh, it looks like you started without us," John observed as he sat the drinks he was carrying on the bar top next to the empty beer bottle Luke had previously abandoned. He turned around and winked at Luke as if to emphasize the joking nature of his comment.

Luke allowed a sad smile to cross his face as he shut the door and shuffled towards the bar again. "Thanks guys, but I'm not really in the mood for a party today."

Sabrina rolled her eyes before she replied. "It's not a party. We just thought you could use some distractions." To accent her statement, she pulled a game system out of the tote bag. This was followed by various board games, trivia games, and a net with paddles that could be used to turn the dining table into instant table tennis.

John opened three bottles of beer and passed them out as Sabrina attached the net to the table. She then slid the table out with the opposite end facing Luke. Next, she pulled a small ball out of the bag and threw it into the air. Luke followed it with his gaze as it bounced against the table, got slapped by a paddle, and smacked him right in the center of his forehead.

Sabrina keeled over laughing as John stifled a chuckle.

"Oh. I see how it is," Luke stated as he smiled and shook his head, before he bounced the ball against the table and slapped it back with the second paddle.

Sabrina was clearly more ready than Luke however and shot it right back over the net. It went back and forth like this for a few rounds before Luke spiked the ball down and out it went.

"Point for me," he stated with a grin on his face. The events of the day slowly faded from his mind as he got lost in the game.

Back and forth the rounds and points went, with both players jumping every which way to fight for victory over the other. Eventually though, Sabrina won with a score of 11 to 8. She tucked her hands behind her back and gave a playful bow as Luke returned the motion. The two of them smiling as Luke moved aside for John's turn against the champion.

Luke watched as the two started the battle dance that he and Sabrina were doing moments earlier. John was definitely more clunky with this game, as Luke watched Sabrina bounce back and forth scoring repeatedly on him. Her dark brown hair flowed and waved with each maneuver she made, fluttering through the air like an ocean wave.

Sabrina gave another bow to John as she won again, this time with a score of 11 to 3.

"Wow, I suck at this" John stated as Luke slapped him on the shoulder and took his place across from the champion once again. This time, Luke was more prepared.

The two went at it until Luke finally won. This game dragged out quite a bit longer as Sabrina kept the points close until he finally pulled ahead at 15 to 13. This time, Luke gave the mock bow first and winked at her as Sabrina rolled her eyes and returned the gesture. She then handed her paddle off to John who proceeded to lose to Luke at 11 to 5. Doing better this time, but clearly unable to keep up against his more agile friends.

They played a few more rounds of table tennis as the first round of bottles emptied. This was their sign that it was time to switch games. The friends moved onto a trivia game, which Luke subsequently won hands down. John then quickly pushed aside the cards and dropped a board game in the middle of the table instead.

"I feel like this is a little fairer," he grumbled.

All three of them then burst out laughing and grabbed another round of drinks. Roughly an hour passed as they played, with John ultimately winning his first event of the night. He quickly stood up and let out a triumphant "Yea!" knocking the board game straight off the table.

Everyone grew silent for a moment as the pieces scattered across the floor before laughter again filled the room. Luke tried to stand up and tripped over his chair in the middle of the laughing fit, which had only caused both his and his friend's laughter to double in volume. He wiped tears from his eyes as they next turned to video games. The mood now far lighter in the room, with Luke fully distracted by the company of his friends.

The console was plugged into the larger TV across from the sofa as all three of them sat shoulder to shoulder on the two-seater couch. Luke sat in the middle, with Sabrina on his right and John to his left. Once everyone was comfortable, they loaded a perfect transition game onto the screen.

A digital game board lay strewn in front of their characters as they made their way around it. Mini games divided the rounds up as each person fought each other for rewards... or stole others rewards if their digital dice rolls were lucky enough. The game ended with Sabrina fist pumping her victory as she adjusted to lay on the couch, her legs strewn across Luke's lap.

John got up to grab some more drinks for the group as Luke picked their next game. As John stumbled back from the bar area Luke locked in a free-for-all fighting game and gave John a wink. John looked at the screen before he rolled his eyes and picked up a controller after he handed out the drinks.

This game was one of Luke's favorites, and John fully expected him to dominate the competition. As the three of them locked in their characters however, it was clear there was some collaboration going on. Once Luke was the first to be knocked out, something was definitely amiss. He glanced at his friends on both sides and let out a humored sigh.

"You two are ganging up on me, aren't you?" he inquired.

Sabrina slyly looked in the other direction as she replied, "I have no idea what you're talking about."

Her and John laughed then as Luke retorted, "Fine then, have it your way."

On the next round, Luke waited for the other two to lock in a character before he held his head up high and locked in his own.

"Oh great," John stated. Afterwards waving his hand in Luke's direction as he continued. "He locked in his favorite character, looks like the fun is over."

Luke smiled as Sabrina gave the two of them a questioning face followed by a simple "oh?" She then promptly learned what he meant as their two on one strategy fell apart, and Luke took them both on.

He gave a half bow in both directions and smiled as Sabrina and John agreed not to team up anymore if Luke agreed not to play that character. An accord was made, and round by round the three of them took turns earning victories over the others. All laughing as they cycled their way through more drinks.

"Whelp," John started. Slightly slurring his words as he stood up with a stretch and a yawn. He continued, "I theenk itsh about time I went to bed."

Luke and Sabrina stood up as well, and Luke followed his bulky, stumbling friend to the door.

"Get home safely," Luke stated jokingly with a glazed wink and a clap on John's shoulder.

John slowly mimicked the motion as he rolled his eyes. Luke then closed the door behind his friend, before walking back over to the front of his bed.

Sabrina had already shut off the console, so Luke turned on his ghost hunter show and sat at the edge of his bed. Sabrina sat down next to him and stared at the screen for a moment before she gathered the energy to make a statement.

"Do these shows feel the same anymore to you? I feel like with everything that has happened that the enchantment would be gone."

Luke thought for a second about his reply before he answered. "Well, the enchantment is gone with everything I've seen now. However, watching something like this gives me... Well, idk. It gives me stability in everything that's happened. They may look more fake now, but these shows are something I'm used to."

Sabrina nodded in understanding as Luke tried to adjust his position, then drunkenly stumbled, and fell backwards onto his bed. Sabrina laughed at him as he let out a defeated sigh, then decided to follow suit and lay down next to him. Her head rested in the curve of his shoulder as he looked over with a smile on his face and wrapped his arm around her.

The two of them laid like this as the hunters on the show entered an abandoned insane asylum. Conversation sprouted from the screen about how this was a hotspot for malevolent creatures as Luke rolled his eyes. "I'll show you a malevolent spirit," he muttered. Which had managed to force out a giggle from Sabrina.

A few more moments passed before Sabrina decided to speak. "You know, what happened wasn't your fault," she stated. Although her eyes were still semi-focused on the TV, her attention was now on Luke. "I know you're probably still going to beat yourself up over it, but there was no way of knowing that our ammo would've been corrupted the way it was. That was a field test. A field test with grim results, but a test nonetheless."

Sabrina paused for a moment before she continued to attempt to reason with Luke's mind. "Plus, look at it this way. Had you not called us out to rescue Bravo team, then we would *all* be dead now. It didn't look like that airstrike cared if it hit any of us, and we would've been deep inside the building otherwise. So, in a way you saved ten more people than someone else might have."

Luke tightened his grip on her for a moment to symbolize a hug as he rested his head on top of hers.

"I know. It's just, I feel like I could've done more. In the end, those men and women depended on me... and I let them down.

Even if the alternative was worse, maybe there was a way I could've saved them all."

Sabrina looked up at Luke as he stated this. He then gazed down into her hazel eyes as she replied once more.

"Well, there's no use worrying about that now. It has already happened, so now all we can do is plan for what comes next time. We still have a long way to go before we can stop the Phantom Hawk, and we will need you to get us through it." Sabrina accented her statement with a smile, as Luke subsequently smiled back.

Maybe because of the alcohol, or maybe just because of the moment, Luke had a fleeting urge. After a moment passed, he finally gave in to it as he leaned down and softly kissed Sabrinas lips. She quietly returned the gesture, before she cuddled deeper into his shoulder.

Luke then closed his eyes; a smile now on his face, as the two of them drifted off to sleep with the TV playing quietly on the other side of the bed.

Chapter 13: Breakthrough

Luke woke up with a yawn the next morning. As he blinked the sleep from his eyes and tried to stretch, he felt a weight on his right arm. He looked over and remembered Sabrina was there, her hair now a jostled mess from sleep. He slowly moved his arm out from under her so as to not wake her and walked to the bathroom.

Luke shut the door and turned on the rainfall style shower. Once the water flowed at his ideal temperature, he stepped in and let the warm water flow down every inch of his body. While he washed the smell of alcohol away, he noticed a throbbing in his head. Not enough to be painful, but more of a mere annoyance.

The slight hangover was a fine price to pay, however, for the previous night. Luke smiled to himself as he proceeded to wash his hair. He then shut off the shower and grabbed a towel, drying himself off as he threw his pants back on from the day before and left the bathroom.

As he entered the room again, Sabrina was already awake. She wiped her eyes and yawned as she sat on the edge of the bed.

"Good morning sleepy," Luke stated with a smirk.

She rolled her eyes before pulling the towel from his hands and walking off to the bathroom. "My turn" she stated, as she groggily shut the door behind her.

The shower could be heard turning on as Luke made his way to the kitchen. He grabbed a couple of bottles of water and sat down at the table. The first bottle was promptly opened by Luke, as he downed about half of it. The cold water felt like it was sealing away the dry walls of his throat as it washed down. He then got up and changed into some fresh clothes before walking back to the table and finishing the bottle off. By that point, the shower could be heard turning off in the bathroom as Sabrina finished.

The bathroom door opened, and Sabrina walked out. Her hair was up in a towel as another towel was draped around her torso. The towel formed into the shape of her hips, and Luke thought to himself how much more attractive the towel looked on her than it did on him.

She moved to the table, took a sip of water from the second bottle Luke had pulled out, and grabbed a handful of clothes that were in the tote bag still. Luke realized at this point that she had always intended on staying the night, as she returned to the bathroom to get dressed.

The door slowly shut behind them as the two made their way to the dining hall. Once they entered, they spotted John seated at a table with his head in his hands. He waved them over before he returned to this position. Clearly his hangover from the night's events was affecting him more than the other two. Although Luke did have some spotty memories of John grabbing quite a few more drinks between the rounds he brought the rest of the group.

"Good morning, John," Luke stated as he sat down with a tray of breakfast.

"Mhhmh" John replied, as he tenderly lifted a cup of coffee to his lips.

Luke chuckled at this and slid over to make room for Sabrina as she returned with a tray of her own.

"John might have a few more regrets than we do," Luke stated as he motioned his head towards the man currently resting in his own hands. John promptly raised a finger in Luke's direction, which caused a laugh to escape from both Luke's and Sabrina's lips as the three of them dug into their food.

Following this, the three of them strolled into the main room. Standing by the command table was Lewis, in conversation with a man none of them recognized.

Lewis beckoned the three of them over as the man looked their direction. His short military style haircut stood atop a worn-out face with sunken shadow engulfed eyes. This man seemed to have been through just as much as they had in recent days, although Luke didn't recognize him from their mission. When the group finally reached these two, Lewis directed their attention at the man next to him.

"I would like you all to meet Adam Smith. He was on the military's expedition to the island you visited. He is also the sole known survivor of the facility you were at yesterday."

Adam held out his hand to shake hands with each member of the friend group, before he moved it once more behind his back.

"We found Adam during a final sweep of the area that Charlie team had made to ensure nothing escaped the facility. It would seem that he is untouched by the corruption, and upon learning that his division was responsible for the Phantom Hawk's escape, he has agreed to help us capture it.

"To that end, a clearance code he took on the way out may just be the breakthrough we could use. Luke, I think you specifically would be highly interested in this." As Lewis finished his statement, he nodded to Adam as encouragement to take over from this point on.

Luke peered at Adam curiously, as Adam directed Luke's attention towards the digital display above the command table.

"It would seem that the researchers at Area 51 have devised a means of controlling the spirits", Adam started. Plans popped on the displays one after the other, showing a strange backpack-like device.

"Unbelievable," Luke muttered, as he dissected the plans in front of him. "Whereas my crystal traps the spirit by using angles designed to reflect its energy to keep it contained within, this backpack seems to use electrical energy as sort of a mental takeover."

Luke continued as his fingers floated in front of his face near the digital display, pointing out bits and pieces of information in the holographic view as he spoke. "Instead of containing the creature's energy, it sends pulses of electricity out in the same way a brain's synapses do when sending instructions through our bodies. Initial pulses are sent to calm the creature down and make it passive, which then makes it possible to use additional pulses to command its movements."

All eyes were now on Luke as the wheels started turning in his brain. He pulled out a notebook and began to scribble notes and equations across its pages.

"We thought this might be of interest to you," Lewis started. Pausing only to make sure he had Luke's attention before he continued. "Do you think it would be possible to mimic this design? If we can control some lesser creatures, we may be able to use them to our advantage in our fight against the Phantom Hawk."

Luke grinned at this, as he glanced sideways at Lewis and replied. "Mimic it? Nah. This device is far too bulky to be brought with into the field. And you would need a separate man controlling each creature. The tradeoff would mean less people aware of their surroundings, and subsequently more deaths. A single man would have to toss the pack onto a creature, wait for it to fall into a passive state, and then focus on controlling it. The rifles would be more efficient against the numbers of corrupted the Phantom Hawk is creating. I do, however, have a different idea."

To accent his point, Luke held up his notebook to show a sketch of a new crystal design. Still small enough to fit into someone's hand, but not nearly small enough to fit into one of the rifles. A small metal box was attached to one side of it, with metal tubes jutting out of the box to wrap around the crystal's exterior.

"This is a modified crystal using some of the technology in the backpack, albeit on a smaller scale. You would activate this crystal by pushing a button located on the attached box. This would then prime it to capture the next thing it hits when thrown. The crystal will next use similar pulses to the ones that the military backpack uses to pacify the spirit. Except this crystal offers a more permanent solution, as it instead will bind the spirits will to the owner of the crystal. Although this process will take longer to finalize its control than their backpack."

Luke paused for a moment as he pointed to a small sharp object in his sketch. "Each crystal would have a single use needle that will prick a drop of blood from the holder. The box will then use the DNA blueprint pulled from the blood to train the spirit within as to who to listen to. That way it can't be used against us in the field, or by an unsuspecting wielder if the crystal were to somehow get lost."

"Wait, so what you're saying is we could literally capture spirits within, to then summon back on our side instead?" Sabrina asked with her mouth slightly agape.

Luke nodded, "The only downside is with the device being much smaller, it would take longer to turn the spirit. This isn't something that can be used immediately after, and my assumption is that the more powerful the spirit is, the longer it would take to convert. In addition, I assume something like the Phantom Hawk would need to be severely weakened before capture could even be a possibility. At full strength it may just destroy the device and pop out more pissed than it was before."

"Interesting idea," Lewis started deep in thought. "What would you need exactly to create this device?"

Luke joined him deep in thought as he replied. "Well, for starters I would need a toolkit capable of working with extremely small materials. Soldering alone would need nearly a microscopic soldering gun with solder small enough to not overflow between wires. Small batteries like those found in a watch could do for a source of power, as the pulses won't need much energy to work. The crystal would help the cables with containing the pulse to amplify its effectiveness."

He continued, "It would also need materials to form a controller microchip; to both read the DNA as well as send out the pacifying signals. And it would also need to be small enough to insert into the box alongside the battery. Stuff that you probably wouldn't be able to find at the nearest electronics store."

Lewis winked at this last statement, "Lucky for you, we have suppliers perfect for this. Flesh out your plans and bring me a list of what's needed, and I'll have them ready for a prototype."

Luke nodded, before he excitedly strut to his room. He pushed his door open and strode across the area, letting the door close itself as he took the table tennis net off his table and fixed its position.

In a flash, he had a pen in hand and a full-sized notebook open in front of him as he jotted down more extensive notes and equations. The page was littered with variables and labels as he fleshed out his ideas. Within an hour, he had every small detail finalized on the control mechanism for the crystal.

Luke transferred over design notes for the crystal itself next, using his original model as a baseline, but with small adjustments to suit the nature of this new device. The resulting crystal looked almost like a 20-sided die, which would both help increase surface area affected by the pulses as well as become easier to handle than his sharper, elongated design. Luke gave the entire new blueprint one final look over, before he ripped a page out of the notebook. He then scribbled a list of supplies in required lengths and sizes needed to craft his creation.

Luke returned to the main room a couple hours after leaving and found Lewis leaning over the command table. "Here's what I need to do the prototype" Luke stated, as he handed the torn-out page to Lewis.

Lewis took the page and nodded as he called someone over from a nearby desk. Luke listened as the man was told to retrieve the items ASAP. The man then quickly set to work sending calls out from his desk.

As it was around lunchtime now, Luke decided to head down to the cafeteria to grab a bite to eat.

He made his way towards the line and grabbed a tray; filling it with a bowl of what looked like clam chowder, some fries, and a thick, juicy burger. Luke then sat down at a table John was currently seated at and popped a fry into his mouth. His stomach grumbled in approval as he realized he was perhaps a little hungrier than he had thought.

"How has your day been?" Luke asked John, as he took a spoonful of what indeed was clam chowder into his mouth. Followed by another and another as the ache in his stomach slowly subsided with the weight of the food now building in his belly.

John raised an eyebrow at Luke and chuckled his reply. "Less distracted than your morning it would seem. I took a nap to nurse the rest of my hangover away and then decided to come have a bite to eat. Were you able to figure out your sci-fi mumbo jumbo?"

Luke nodded in reply as he finished scooping the last remnants of his chowder into his mouth. He then took a long drink of the soda he grabbed with his tray and swallowed.

"I gave Lewis the materials I will need just moments ago. From what he said, I should have everything needed to work on my device by this afternoon. The rifles design has apparently also been adjusted to better protect the crystalline ammunition the next time we are out in the field. I haven't seen the changes yet though because I've been so distracted with my work."

John nodded as he looked upwards in thought. "Ya know, I discovered a gym further down this hall earlier. I realized last night during our table tennis matches that I could really work on my cardio. Plus, with how much running around we will probably be doing in the coming days, I think it would be a good idea if you got some exercise in as well. You know, while we have the time to do so. Care to join me after we finish eating?"

Luke hadn't thought about it before, but John did have a good point. Although he was fairly athletic already, Luke's recent days in class were so focused on his crystal finally coming to fruition that he completely forgot about his health. He hadn't gone for a run in at least a month. And although the rifles and crystals weren't that heavy, a more extended mission would probably take its toll on his energy levels.

"That's a good idea John. Yea let me finish eating and grab something else to wear and Ill join you."

A silent nod of confirmation was John's reply, as the two friends finished their meals with discussions of the life they left behind at school. A lifestyle that was now long abandoned.

Once finished eating, Luke placed his tray in a stack of other dirty dishes as he walked out the dining area and back to his room. He quickly threw off his current clothes and slid on a pair of athletic shorts and a moisture wicking shirt. Following this, he exited his room again and returned to the main housing hallway. He then walked past the cafeteria, and further down the hall to a door labelled *Training*.

"How have I not seen this door before?" Luke muttered to himself. Although that would make sense that he missed it; seeing as the one time he didn't have an immediate task at hand in this headquarters, he was heavily distracted by the losses on their most recent mission.

Beyond the door was a room far larger than expected. It looked pretty much like a full-sized public gym. A row of treadmills and exercise bikes started the room on the left, with various weightlifting machines coming into view as Luke's eyes panned right. The room's right wall was lined with dumbbells and bar weights of all sizes.

Towards the far back of the room, a hallway on the back wall led to what he had assumed was showers and bathrooms. A door in the back right corner sat next to the end of the free weights, with big bold letters splayed across it labeling it as the swimming pool.

"Pretty magnificent, isn't it?" John stated from behind Luke as he tossed him a towel and a bottle of some sort of blue sports drink. "You'd have to pay a pretty penny for all this, and we have unlimited access for free."

Luke gazed into the room for a moment longer as he admired the amount of effort these people went into for their personnel. "You've got that right," Luke replied as he began to walk towards the exercise bikes.

Luke was never much for a treadmill. His stride when running was elongated, and as such using a treadmill usually ended up with an awkward jog as he tried to adjust to keep his balance. This stride often led to stepping off the moving part of the device, with a trip up always following. If he ran, he ran outside and off road. Years of cross country trained his balance and pace, so he felt much more comfortable in that environment. Thankfully though the gym also had bikes, so he could get his cardio in with a bit of leg training at the same time. He did want to check out that pool later if they had time as well.

John took up the last treadmill, which stood next to the first exercise bike. Luke sat down next to his friend and turned the bike on. He chose a pre-set course setting on the bike and began peddling as his friend started up the treadmill and began a relaxed jog.

"It really is weird to go from classes every day to supernatural zombie fighting," John stated. His breathing slowly adjusted to the pace of his workout as he spoke. "A few weeks ago, I was worried about how to pass my tests. Or even what homework needed to be done on any given night. Now, I'm using guns loaded with hippie crystals to shoot the undead."

Luke rolled his eyes and smiled at this statement. "I'm not sure that hippie crystals would exactly work in the same manner as mine do," he replied. Making sure that John saw the air quotes he put around the phrase *hippie crystals.*

"Yea, well classes certainly seem a lot easier now. Calculus seems like nothing compared to the fact that there is a demigod currently hellbent on causing an apocalypse. Oh, and we are the ones that are somehow supposed to stop it."

John was right. Although Luke was more focused on his little side project than his classes most of the time, this was a massive change. Every time he messed up one of his crystals in the past, all it meant was going back and checking his work again. At most, he would have to buy a new crystal to reshape. But now... now if he messed up then lives could be lost. Not to mention that they didn't even know if the Phantom Hawk could be contained. All this work in the end could mean nothing. For all they knew, humanity was going to come to an end regardless.

All because the military became enthralled by the thought of a new secret weapon.

Luke shook his head as he pedaled to clear these thoughts. "Well look at it this way. You are getting an all-expense paid internship in special operations. Put this on your resume and I'm sure any job would be glad to hire you."

Luke stated this last part jokingly, as both friends knew that they would probably never be allowed to speak of this place. Not that anyone would believe them anyway. Going around telling people you worked for a secret organization that hunted real life ghosts would probably get you thrown in a nuthouse before anything else. But still, joking about it helped Luke to lighten his mood from his previous thoughts.

John and Luke continued bantering back and forth throughout their workouts. The conversation slowed to a snail's pace over time as John focused on breathing and Luke became lost in thought. He went through the steps of mentally checking his work on the recent invention he thought up. Just to make sure everything involved in the object would have the best odds of working as intended... once he got the materials and was able to get started on it that is.

Luke's course hit the cooldown phase just as John shut off his treadmill.

"I think that's it for me. I'm gonna go to my room and shower." John stated to Luke as he wiped the sweat off his forehead with a hand towel, his breathing heavily labored from the workout he just endured.

"Sounds good. After this cooldown cycle, I think I'm gonna check out the pool. I have a bit more energy left so might do some laps and cool off in the water."

John looked at Luke like he was an exotic animal yet to be discovered. "I don't know how you still have energy, but you do you."

The two friends waved goodbye to each other as John walked off. Luke's bike had just finished the cooldown portion of the course, so he shut it off and stood up.

Luke wobbled for a moment as he realized how tired his legs had gotten. Maybe he wouldn't spend too much time in the pool after all. He wiped off the bike as well as the sweat on his forehead. Then, he began the short walk across the room to the door which supposedly led to a pool.

Luke was overjoyed when he walked through the tinted glass door and spotted the swimming pool. Easily an Olympic sized body of water sat in the middle of a tiled room. Most of the natatorium must have been at least 16 feet deep, however there was a shallow strip to one side for wading in: Probably to rest between workouts.

On the opposite side of the room was another tinted glass door, although this one was labeled *Sauna and Steam Rooms*. He wasn't currently in the mood for a sweltering experience, but he would

114

have to check those out in the near future. For now, Luke dropped his hand towel into a bin and slowly lowered himself into the shallow portion of the water.

The pool was warmed to a lukewarm temperature; probably since it was indoors and underground. Luke submerged himself fully under the water for a moment. He let his muscles relax as the water washed over him, easing the tightness out of his muscles from his bike session. He then re-emerged and brushed his hair back from his face with his hands.

His eyes opened towards the far side of the pool, as if to laser in on a target. With a lift of his legs and a kickoff from the wall behind him, he was off swimming across the contained body of water.

Luke's legs kicked as he sliced through the water with his arms, turning and kicking off the far wall once he reached the end. Luke lost track of time as he burned off his remaining energy swimming laps. As much as he enjoyed a good workout on a solid surface, nothing could beat the feel of water splashing around him as he darted through it. Even though it was a workout still, it almost felt therapeutic to be in the calm pool alone.

Finally exhausted, Luke sat in the shallow end of the pool with his eyes closed. In this moment of relaxation, his mind wandered to recent events again. This time though, he was a lot more accepting of the failures.

Sabrina was right, things couldn't be changed now. All they could do was look forward to the future and improve. His mind then started to replay the events of the previous night. As his mind drifted off, he could hear his name being called close by.

"Hey, Luke!" Sabrina shouted.

He opened his eyes and swiveled his head to her, spotting the smile across her face.

"Enjoying yourself there?" she continued teasingly.

Luke looked down and realized he relaxed enough to be laying on the water's surface. He sat up before he could drift off out of the shallow end and replied to her. "Oh, for sure. Nothing beats the water for relaxation." He stated this while he returned her smile.

"Well, Lewis wants to see us now," Sabrina responded. "Your supplies have come in, and assuming all goes well with the device he wants to brief us on a mission to test it."

Chapter 14: Capture Tech

Luke entered the main room with John and Sabrina at his sides. The group walked up to Lewis as he peered over the command table, a familiar image showing on the 3D display.

"Ah good, you're all here," Lewis stated as he looked up. He then motioned to a box on a table nearby before speaking once more. "Here are the materials for your test Luke. Before you take them and get started, however, I want to talk about your next mission.

Trying to comb his damp hair with his hands, Luke replied to Lewis. "I assume the mission is somehow related to my new device?" Luke recalled Sabrina's statement a bit ago about how the mission depended on if the device worked. So, Luke assumed it had to be something to do with capturing spirits.

"That is correct. If your device appears to work as intended, then you will leave on a covert op mission to test it. We have decided on the perfect spirit to test it on as well. One that is also partially from our world. In addition, this achieves the goal of cleaning up a mess we left behind earlier."

Luke thought for a moment about what this could mean. Realization hit him when he looked down at the command table and finally processed what was being displayed.

"You want us to return to the island and capture the banshee that was created when the corruption infected the ghost I caught, don't you?"

Lewis nodded, "That is correct. We will be sending a small group this time to the island. You three as well as Adam will be going, since he also knows the general layout of the area. Two guards will be sent to accompany you all, making sure you have sufficient protection in case something goes wrong. The mission objective is to simply field test the device. Attempt to capture the banshee with it. If the invention somehow fails, then the new objective would be to evacuate the island. No need to lose anyone trying to kill the banshee after that, as it's contained to the island anyway."

"Understood," Luke replied. Hopefully, they would be able to sneak in and capture this spirit with no hiccups. After all they could use a break. Mainly because almost every mission so far had gone wrong in some way.

Lewis gestured once again to the box of materials. "Go ahead and take your supplies then and let me know if there is anything else you should need. We will plan the start time and date of the mission based upon when you finalize the device."

Luke grabbed the box and walked off to get to work. Sabrina and John stayed with Lewis, as they had a few questions for him about specifics on the mission.

Back in his room, Luke sat the box on the table next to his plans and began to unpack various wires and tools for the task at hand. He quickly retrieved his utility belt and pulled the portable grinder out, as well as a fairly large crystal from the box.

Following his new crystal design, Luke began to grind down the rough edges of the piece of quartz. Bit by bit the crystal slowly began to take the shape shown in his sketch. He started by grinding it down into roughly a cube shape. Next, he grinded the corners down, evening these new surfaces with the existing ones. This process was repeated a few more times on new corners that popped up as he continued grinding. Eventually, the crystal reached the 20-sided design he had sketched out earlier. With this done, he set aside the crystal and pulled the new tools in front of himself.

Inside the box was a magnifying glass and a small microscope to magnify his working area. There was also an extremely fine tipped soldering iron, with a roll of nearly microscopic solder. Luke set these items out in front of him; surrounded by the various electrical components needed to build the metal box that would give the crystal its controlling capabilities.

First thing to do was program the controller chip to emit the electrical pulses needed to pacify whatever gets captured inside. Luke used a laptop provided to write the programming required.

Programming wasn't his strongest subject, but he took enough classes to figure out how to create a simple artificial intelligence-based program. The program would read the DNA of the owner, then use that to teach the spirit inside whose commands to follow. The AI based design was a fail-safe that Luke planned as a way to adapt the control methods to the spirit captured: If a certain array and pattern of electrical pulses failed to make progress with the entity, then the artificially intelligent software would adjust until it found a pattern that would work best.

Hours passed as Luke typed away the code for his new program. Although it was simple in the vast world of programming, it still required pretty in-depth syntax (and more than a few compiling errors) before it ran properly when compiled.

Once finalized, Luke began the process of transferring the code to the controller chip. He sat back as the code began to upload and realized the time was almost 7 PM. He had been working nearly five hours on the program. Once his stomach began to growl while waiting, he realized that maybe it was time to take a break for some dinner.

While the upload time wouldn't take as long as eating, this was probably the best moment to take a break. Luke shut his room's door behind him and made his way to the cafeteria. Since he had a poor habit of waiting to eat until he was absolutely famished, the various smells within the room made his mouth water almost instantaneously.

He grabbed the juiciest looking steak he could find; medium-rare of course. Following this, the rest of his plate was filled with some steamed asparagus and a heaping spoonful of some chunky mashed potatoes. With a ladle of peppered gravy spooned over the top of his potatoes, he grabbed a cola and went to sit at an empty table.

Not that it was hard to find one as the dinner rush had already come and gone. In fact, Luke looked around to notice there was almost nobody in the room period. He didn't think seven was *that* late of a time to eat.

Luke started to quickly devour his food, as he was eager to return to the work needed to complete his prototype of the invention. This benefited him in a different way however, as about halfway through his meal Sabrina burst through the cafeteria door.

"Ah there you are Luke! Come quickly, there's an update on Japan, as well as a problem we may have related to the military."

Luke sensed her urgency and stood up quickly to follow Sabrina out of the room, leaving his half-finished tray on the table as the pair left.

He realized why the dining room was so empty once he entered the main room of the underground base. The room was packed; with personnel standing or seated throughout it. Everyone was looking up at the monitors splayed across the walls of the room as the news showed across their screens. Scenes of what could only be described as an army of corrupt creatures came into camera shot of the helicopter's birds-eye viewpoint, while the reporter continued their updates.

Tragedy has fully struck Japan as the quarantine on Tokyo has been broken. Reports have been coming in of outbreaks all across the island now as the Japanese military is losing more ground against these creatures.

The reporter paused for a moment to let their words settle with viewers before they continued. The images of the horrific events in the island nation continued to cycle across the screens during this time.

It would seem that any dead or wounded turn into these demonic abominations. Furthermore, experts have no idea as of yet on how to stop the onslaught. Strikes made against the giant bird-like creature flying above Tokyo have been futile, as they have been unable to harm the monster. To make things worse, any aircraft that have attempted an assault have undergone a transformation simply for being near the threat.

Recovered wreckage has shown the fighter jets reshaped into discs of razors and spikes, the very metal of the craft somehow turning into a bone-like plating. The pilots have also become fused with the very technology they were flying, turning into hulking abominations of man and twisted machine. With these abominations reinforcing the smaller monsters on the ground, it's only a matter of time before the whole of Japan falls.

The camera footage changed to the news anchor's grim visage as the last part was stated. Once the news changed to discussing expert's opinions on the matter, all heads in the room turned towards Lewis.

Lewis, however, turned his head to Luke. Speaking calmly, his tone was even more serious than usual. "It would seem that we are shorter on time than anticipated. How is your progress coming along?"

Luke replied quickly to the question. "The crystal has already been prepared and I wrote the program to run the conversion technology within it. The software was transferring as I grabbed some food, but I should have the prototype finished before the night is over."

"Good," stated Lewis as he turned to look at the command table. "We will go ahead and slate the mission for around noon tomorrow then. While it is less than ideal to attempt a covert mission in the middle of the day, I'm afraid that we don't have much time on our hands. Not only because of the Phantom Hawk, but also because of a discovery we made on the military's side of things."

Luke tilted his head in confusion. Did the military discover their location and somehow decide they knew too much?

Lewis began typing at the edge of the command table and as a new image showed, Luke got his answer. A 3D display of a spider now rotated above the table. A file was then pulled up on a digital display next to it titled *Broodmother*. The creature would have looked like any other spider, if it weren't for the strange green shadows coming off it like an aura. Its eight green, shadowy eyes peered listlessly off in the distance.

"We have discovered the reason for the controlling backpack design. The facility has begun successfully testing its use on another spirit named the Broodmother. They intend to begin further field testing of the creature soon. Upon successful results, they intend on using it as a weapon in an attempt to regain control of the Phantom Hawk."

"There lie a few issues with their plan, however. The first of which is that upon seeing how the Phantom Hawk corrupted the fighter jets, we have reason to believe it would do the same to this control module they attached to the Broodmother. Whether this would destroy its function or give control over to the Phantom Hawk matters not, as either outcome leads to a second spirit being unleashed and out of control."

Lewis paused for a moment to let everyone process this new information, as he detoured the subject slightly.

"Furthermore, we have discovered a classification system the military is using for the spirits. According to them, both the Phantom Hawk as well as the Broodmother have been labelled as Class A entities. A characteristic of a Class A spirit includes signs of immense power. In the Phantom Hawk's case, this would be its ability to corrupt matter in an aura around itself. For the

Broodmother, it would seem it has the ability to weave corrosive webs to kill prey.”

Lewis continued, “In addition, it has the capability of turning living beings into mine-like cocoons that explode when near a target, leaving behind a smaller spider that is then directly controlled by the Broodmother. The mental link is much like a hive mind, with the Broodmother at its core.”

Sabrina interjected now as she had a sudden realization.

“Hold on, the Broodmother directs the spiderlings? Wouldn’t this require some level of higher thinking?”

Lewis nodded, “That would be the other characteristic of Class A spirits. The current theory the researchers at the military’s facility came up with is that these spirits are highly intelligent. And by highly intelligent, they mean an intelligence level above humans. These spirits are practically demigods in their own world.”

This time it was Luke’s turn to speak. “So, by the military’s classification, what would that put our banshee at? It doesn’t seem to have any level of thinking above instinct, as it blindly attacked the corrupted creatures on the island before it tried to hunt us.”

Lewis turned away from the command table to face Luke. “If we go by their classifications, then that would put the banshee at around Class C. Class B shows signs of intelligence similar to humans, with the ability to also lead other lesser creatures. Class C is the highest classification of instinct, while retaining some stronger powers. An example would be that Class C spirits are kind of like the top of the food chain for animals in the wild here on Earth. Strong enough to rule their biome, and that’s about it.”

Lewis paused for a moment to think before he continued. “It should still be useful for us to capture it though. As it would seem that the spirits themselves can only be harmed in two ways. Either by capturing their essence in your crystals, or through the actions of another spirit. With you controlling it, the banshee would be similar in strength to a Class B spirit. This would be at a disadvantage against the Phantom Hawk still, but maybe it would give us the ability to at least weaken it for a subsequent capture.

"To that end, I urge you to finish your meal and return to the device. We will need it sooner rather than later."

Luke nodded to Lewis and waved goodbye to his friends as he returned to the cafeteria. As he sat back down to finish his meal, his mind raced with the information he was just given.

Things were looking more dire every day, as now they had two major threats to contend with. Especially if the Broodmother broke free from the military's control as well. Knowing the banshee would be useful was a boon to Luke, however that also meant that the entire fate of the world practically rested on him. If he wasn't up to the task with the help of his own spirit, then all would be lost.

His stomach turned at this thought, but he forced his way through the rest of his food regardless. He would need his energy for the mission tomorrow, as well as to complete his project on time. Although he had a lot of weight on his shoulders, taking it one step at a time seemed like the only viable course of action now.

Luke finished his food and set the tray in the dirty stack. As he left the cafeteria, people that were previously watching the updates about Japan had now begun to file into the cafeteria; all eager to start their own meals. They talked amongst themselves about the news as they entered, and they were all clearly a degree less stressed than Luke now was.

The door to his room shut behind him as Luke moved to the table and sat back down. The software had now finished transferring to the controller chip, so it was time to build the box itself.

He slid the magnifying equipment in front of himself and slowly got to work soldering the miniscule wires into place on a chipboard. The controller chip was seated mostly in the center, as a spiderweb of wire led to resistors, capacitors, and the like around it. A socket was placed onto the board for a small battery, as Luke continued to fervently work on the prototype.

An hour must have passed before he finally finished soldering. Luke sat back and stretched, his head growing lighter as the blood rushed back through his stiff limbs.

He took this moment to stand up and grab a drink from the fridge, chugging half of it before he sat back down to continue. With the entire controller finished, he seated the technology into the back half of the small box meant to protect and hold the parts together. Luke then inserted the back end of a small hollow needle into an opening he created earlier on the board, before securing it in place. This would be used to extract the blood used to link the crystal owner's DNA to the spirit. The needle was also programmed to retract after confirming a successful blood draw. This would ensure to the holder that their device was primed and ready.

Once this final component was seated in place, Luke got to work attaching the box to the shaped crystal. He drilled small holes into the crystal, which aligned with small metal spikes protruding out of the back of the box. This would give the box a more efficient method of reading changes in the crystal to relay back to the controller.

He then filled the holes with a strong adhesive and aligned the box to be secured in place. Following this, Luke began wiring the flexible metal arms into the sides of the box.

Each of the arms had a set of metal spikes that jutted out from the back as well; although these ones were for efficiently delivering the pulses of energy to tame whatever was inside. A quick session of drilling followed as Luke pathed his way across the crystals surface, creating lines of holes that wrapped around its surface in the manner he wanted the tendrils of the box to sit. These cavities were then filled with the same adhesive as earlier, and he went to work aligning and seating the pulse cables against the crystal.

Luke finished the design by placing the metal box's cover on. Once the cover was snapped into place, its creator leaned back in his seat.

He picked up the finished crystal and admired his work. It was small enough to be thrown like a softball, and the tendrils that curled around it could be used as a sort of grip. Luke then took a deep breath as he placed his thumb on the tip of the needle that jutted out from the box... and pushed down slightly.

The minor pain of a prick came expectantly, as the needle then slid slowly into the box's casing. The box and cables next sent out a flowing series of blue LED's that eventually solidified into a glowing light. Blue now scattered across the surface of the instrument, fading out before fully lighting up again repeatedly. Almost as if the crystal was breathing and alive.

Luke grinned to himself and set the prototype back down on the table. His design worked, and it was ready to be tested tomorrow.

A quick glance at the digital clock on the wall told Luke that it was nearing midnight now. A yawn escaped his lips as he stretched one final time, before standing up and walking towards his bed.

After he shed his clothes from the day in a trail leading to the edge, Luke plopped down on his bed face down into the pillow. This was the moment of truth. Tomorrow they would know for sure if they had a weapon against the Phantom Hawk. And if it worked, then this spreading disaster could finally be halted and averted.

Luke's breathing steadied and calmed, as he slowly drifted off to sleep.

Chapter 15: The Banshee

Luke awoke early the following morning; his thoughts were already racing about the mission.

He grabbed a new set of clothing from the wardrobe and threw it on quickly before he left his room for some breakfast. Almost forgetting the new device, he turned back in and pocketed it before making for the cafeteria once more.

"Ready for the big day?" John asked Luke as both of them set their trays down at the table. An assortment of breakfast meats, eggs, and breads lay between the two of them.

"Well, ready as I'll ever be. The prototype is done... and it's already been primed for me to use. The ultimate test of course will be once we reach the island and encounter the banshee though."

Luke paused for a moment as he made a realization. "Speaking of which, I think we need to figure out some names for the things we encounter. What do you think?"

"How about we just call it the Banshee?" Sabrina chimed in as she sat down with her own food. "It's pretty suitable of a name, and it's not like anyone is going to confuse it with a different creature or anything."

Luke shrugged "Yea, that makes sense. But what about the corrupted things? It just feels... I don't know. Weird? To just call them corrupted. Especially since we may need to differentiate between different kinds in the field one day. We don't want to confuse the small ones with something like that hulking abomination we saw in the warehouse."

John's eyes shot wide open as he quickly swallowed his food. "There ya go! The big one can be an abomination!"

Sabrina nodded to John's statement before she turned to face Luke. "Well, we both named one. Looks like you get to name the last one."

Luke stroked his chin for a moment to mime being deep in thought. "Well, I don't think I'm going to take the easy way out like you two did." He followed this statement with a side-eyed smirk towards the other two.

Sabrina rolled her eyes, "I don't see a reason to spend a lot of time on naming the very things we're trying to get rid of." She ended her statement with a grin to show Luke she wasn't that serious though.

Luke grinned back devilishly, "Ok, then regular ones are corrupted. There, I win the battle of laziness, and that was all pointless." Luke ended his statement with a laugh.

"Yea yea Luke, you win. We should probably finish up here though and get to the briefing room."

John stated this with a flat tone to his voice. It seemed he was a bit nervous about going back to the island. Not that Luke could really blame anyone for feeling nervous. Hell, he was nervous as well. They were going to actively chase after something that was able to kill a small army of the corrupted.

The three of them agreed though: Focus had to be on the mission entirely if they were to get everyone out of here alive.

The friends finished their breakfasts in thoughtful silence; running various scenarios through their minds of what could possibly happen. A few minutes later, Luke was the first to stand up and leave the cafeteria. He strolled down the hall to his room and grabbed his utility belt. The belt was then strapped around his waist, setting the prototype crystal into a holster on it as he left his room.

Luke entered the main room, joining both Sabrina and John by the command table as Lewis cleared his throat to speak.

"Today's mission as some of you already know will be covert ops. The five of you will first take a helicopter to the coast. Upon arrival, a boat will be waiting to take you back to the island. We have reconnaissance set up off the coast of the island to ensure your landing will be at a safe distance from any of the corruption or the banshee. Upon landing, a vanguard will be formed between Emily, Adam, and John."

Luke looked over and noticed this was the same Adam from the military facility they attempted to clear. He looked much more rested and less haggard now as he stood and listened to the rest of the briefing.

"You are responsible for ensuring Luke can get to the Banshee safely. Even if it managed to kill all the creatures, the plant life might still pose a threat. Assumptions, however, are that there are still a few creatures scattered across the island. Which is why you three will be outfitted with our updated version of the Dawnbringer rifle."

Lewis pulled out the rifle, which now had a transparent bubble over the crystalline ammunition. He pushed a button towards the back of the weapon and the bubble popped open.

"Simply push here to open the ammo shell, insert new duskshot, and shut it again. The shell is made with powdered quartz mixed into the plastic. So, while it may not work to trap any spiritual energies, it should do well enough to repel airborne corruption away from the crystals inside."

He set the gun down on the edge of the command table before continuing the briefing. "Sabrina is on observation duty for this one. Her keen eye should work well to spot any ambushes, and maybe collect more extensive field notes that we may use for our assault on the Phantom Hawk. We are going to need every advantage we can get when the time comes, and the entire environment is going to be unrecognizable in Japan. The island may be able to give us the little insider knowledge we need to not stumble into a trap."

"Speaking of advantages though, this all depends on your success in capturing the Banshee. Are you prepared Luke?"

Luke nodded in reply, holding up the prototype to show Lewis that it was primed and ready.

Everyone went their own ways to prepare for the mission. John, Emily, and Adam went down to the weapons lab to practice using the updated Dawnbringer, as Sabrina left to gather some tools for her newly assigned position.

This left Luke, who promptly went to his room again. He flopped down onto his bed, eyes shut in contemplation. This would be the ultimate test. If it worked, then they had the weapon they needed to take on the Phantom Hawk.

Luke's mind wandered through every scenario past and future about these spirits. His mind somehow settled on his utility belt in the process, which gave him an idea.

He promptly jumped up from his bed and went to the table where he had previously crafted the prototype. A brush of his arm cleared the center of the table, as he produced a pen and notepad. Luke spent the remainder of his morning sketching and scribbling notes for his new idea. This time, it was something for his personal use.

Noon came around, and the party loaded into the helicopter that was waiting outside. Nerves filled Luke as he took his seat, going over in his head what they've already witnessed of the Banshee before.

It seemed to have two major strengths. The first was its scream. The group had brought noise cancelling headsets linked to their radios to prevent incapacitation if they were to get caught. Since even at a distance the scream was painful, they could only imagine how it would be up close. With their headsets though, they would be protected from this threat.

The second strength was how it actively assaulted the corrupted. With the way the creatures exploded when it flew through them, it must have had a way of attacking from the inside. The corruption that tainted the spirit might have given it a way to interact with biology in a similar manner to the corruption's virus-like effects. Except instead of morphing its targets, it aimed solely to destroy them.

Otherwise, the creature might have just physically ripped them apart once it flew inside. The only thing that was for certain was that if it reached you, you were dead.

As Adam and Emily had not yet seen the Banshee, Luke spent the remainder of the flight briefing them on how it acted.

"So, you're telling me this spirit is capable of both a debilitating scream, as well as simply blowing us up by touching us? Where did it even come from?" Emily asked. Her blue eyes seemingly pierced Luke as she gazed in his direction. Her thin, sharp jaw was lined with her straight blonde hair, which she brushed back with her hand as she waited for her answer.

Luke dropped his head slightly as the piercing stare made him uncomfortable, and he rubbed his neck while replying. "Well, it was originally just a ghost. I was testing an older crystal design at a haunted house near our university and ended up catching it successfully. I then discovered that we could capture the corruption in my crystal because the corrupted energies were pulled from a plant that attacked me on the island.

"The corrupted then ended up attacking our camp, and in our escape the crystal was shot. In the process, the corruption inside morphed the regular passive ghost into something far more destructive. This new specter ended up killing everything in its sight. Except us, of course. We were already on the boat and escaping the island by the time it tried to catch us. It gave up chasing fairly quickly though. Which might be because it's part ghost. It's probably now bound to the island where it was transformed into its new form; unable to leave in its current state."

"Hold on go back," Emily stated with surprise in her voice. "What do you mean a plant attacked you?"

In all the excitement, Luke had forgotten that she had never actually been to the island.

"Well, the corruption the Phantom Hawk emanates and used to transform the people on the island? Turns out it doesn't only affect humans. Plant and animal lives are corrupted in a similar way. A flower shot a spike at me and attempted to pin me, but the spike grazed me and ended up grappling onto my crystal instead. That's how we discovered that the crystal could purify the corruption."

Sabrina chimed in now, to further explain to Emily. As well as to Adam, since he probably knew as much about the corruption itself as most people.

"The corruption acts kind of like a spiritual virus. Instead of attacking your body, it attacks your energies. Your corrupted energies in turn then attempt to reform your physical self into their new identity. And although the crystals can in a way cure the corruption, they can't save the organism once the corruption has fully taken hold. This is because in the process it ends up destroying the balanced biology of what made you, you. Without the corruption holding everything together anymore, your physical form perishes immediately."

"Wait," Adam started. "But if the corruption attacks your spiritual energies, why did the fighter jets that attacked the Phantom Hawk change as well? There isn't a living part to them."

Sabrina looked towards the ceiling, leaning back as she crossed her arms in contemplation. "It's possible that since the pilot was strapped into the jet when hit with the full-strength aura, that their energies assumed the jet was merely an extension of their body."

She continued, "Since it's not biological, it wouldn't know that our skin is the outermost barrier. Which would explain why the metal of the ship was replaced with more of a bone style plating. That was probably the corruption trying to graft the bone and tissue of the pilot around what it thought was the whole body."

"Well, that's not terrifying or anything," John stated with a shudder as the group sat in silence for the rest of the trip. One could only imagine how painful that would be. To have your body stretched over a vehicle. Would you even feel it? There had to be a point where you were no longer yourself. A point where the corruption took over and you felt nothing.

Not that anyone in the group knew for sure, or even wanted to find out for that matter.

Eventually, the helicopter made its way to a landing pad near the beach. The party of five disembarked and walked across a strip of sand to a dock with a speedboat at the end of it. It seemed that this time, they were ready for a speedy getaway if needed. They then made their way down the dock and loaded into the boat one by one.

As the boat left the shore and started to speed off in the direction of the island, Luke began to go over the plan in his head again. With John, Adam, and Emily as a vanguard, they were to sneak a path through the island to wherever the Banshee may be. He then had one chance to catch the spirit... and they wouldn't be able to help him. For if the rifles captured it they had no way to safely transfer it over to the controller crystal. Not that their mission was exactly safe in the first place.

This also didn't include the fact that he was sure there were still corrupted on the island they would have to quietly remove or avoid during their search.

The boat bounced along the waves, the only sound being that of the hull crashing against the water as a salty spray was kicked up a few times over the occupants. The island now slowly came into view; its silhouette jutting up in the distance against the horizon. Once the island was close enough for more detail to be seen, the boats Helmsman pulled out the radio built into the craft.

"This is Skipper One to Scout One, do you read me?" A short pause came through before the return call was heard on the radio.

"Scout One here we read you loud and clear. The beach looks to be currently clear of any hostiles. You may proceed with caution."

"Copy that," he replied, as he returned the radio's microphone to its place and proceeded closer to the island.

As they neared the shoreline, remnants of their previous camp could be seen now. Tattered walls of tents clung to debris scattered across the red stained sand. Like a field of flags, marking the destroyed structures as well as the graveyard that sat upon the area's surface. Luke noticed though that there wasn't a single body left anywhere in sight. At least, not a whole one.

"Wait a minute, where did everyone go?" He questioned.

Sabrina replied "Well, I think there are two outcomes. Either the dead came back as corrupted later on, or the Banshee put a quick end to their resurrections."

John then chimed in, "Either way, that is a lot of blood... and we were so close to joining them."

Luke noticed something just then. Whereas before, John would have probably been shaking and scared out of his mind, he actually stated this as more of a cold observation. It seemed he had finally gotten his bearings together; really fitting into his new role on the vanguard. Especially considering all the pressure he was probably under to keep Luke and Sabrina safe. If Luke fell, there was no one else that would be able to capture the Banshee, since the crystal was bound to him.

If Luke fell, they would all be dead before anyone could get back to the boat.

The speedboat came close to a makeshift dock that was built on their prior expedition, and the skipper tied the boat off. He then helped the group one by one off the rocking vessel and onto land.

Although the land was more solid, the boat definitely felt safer to be on. Luke walked to where the platform met with the sand of the beach and handed out everyone's headsets and radios.

Once everyone made sure the earcups tightly covered their ears, they took turns completing radio checks. One by one the checks went to make sure that everyone could be heard through the equipment. The last thing they needed was for someone to spot a threat on the island, only to be rendered mute when they attempted to warn the rest of the party.

When everyone was finally geared up and prepared, Luke threw forward a hand to signal the beginning of their mission.

John took to the front of the group and led the way with Adam. Behind them, Luke and Sabrina filled out the middle as Emily took to the rear in case of an assault from behind.

They followed the beach along the shore in order to cover one of their flanks, as the vanguard clutched their Dawnbringer rifles in both hands. Ready to shoot at anything that may charge at the small party.

Luke himself kept one hand close to the holster for his crystal, ready to throw it at a moment's notice if the assailant so happened to be the Banshee itself.

As they cleared the beach, Luke and Sabrina surveyed what remained after the last battle. John was right, there was a ton of blood. Almost every visible inch of sand from their previous camp was dyed a reddish brown. And while there wasn't a single body in sight, appendages could be seen strewn sporadically across the ground.

Hands, arms, legs. Parts that couldn't function without the whole were left abandoned. Luke turned away as he spotted a decapitated head, mouth frozen open mid scream. The skin of the person's face was now stretched and dried across their skull; their eyes already rotted away into blackened empty sockets. As Luke refocused on other aspects of the scenery, he spotted Sabrina out of the corner of his eye taking notes of everything they came across.

The group finally made their way slowly to where the forest joined with the beach. As they reached this junction, Luke signaled the party towards the trail they had previously partially explored. The group then left the safety of the shoreline to move deeper into the island.

Something stood out to him, however. The plants on the edge of the forest seemed to be dead now. The corruption perhaps finally ran its course, and the plants with nothing to feed on, must have withered away into blackened stems and leaves.

He tapped Sabrina's shoulder and pointed towards this, as she replied with a nod and took notes on his observation. The group quietly continued their journey to the trailhead. Once they reached their next checkpoint though, a scream split the silence.

John swiveled towards the forest and fired off a crystal, which promptly embedded into a corrupted that had leapt from the entrance of the trail to the party.

The group split down the middle as the creature crashed down, already returned to a body Luke recognized as one of the other personnel from their camp. Someone that had previously been dead on the ground when they left the island prior in fact. This confirmed one of Sabrina's theories; some of the dead did resurrect once the Banshee was gone.

Everyone regrouped and stood in silence, their heads on a swivel as they looked around for any more creatures ready to answer their ally's call. A few minutes passed however, and nothing seemed to be close enough to join the attack. Luke then signaled forward, and the group started to make their way down the trail once more.

As they looked around, one thing became abundantly clear: The forest was no longer a threat.

The bushes and flowers that once lined their path with spines and thorns were now blackened and wilted. It was as if the corruption fed upon its own form when it was unable to find a suitable source of nourishment. Trees that once stood as hardened barriers were now cracked and bowed down in various directions. A few more weeks, and this island might be completely devoid of any sign of plant life.

The group passed by areas with more natural looking dead flora, as Luke recognized this to be the areas which he cleansed with his crystal on their last visit. The group then ventured deeper down the trail past these areas, into a portion of the trail that they had yet to explore.

The journey continued quietly down the trail, as a light could be seen ahead of them. Everyone took to the left side of the trail now that the plants were no longer a threat, giving them some feeling of protection as they reached the end of the forest and stepped back out into sunlight.

Ahead, the trail could be seen pathing down into what used to be a tribal village. Huts lined the clearing; abandoned long ago by the people that once lived here.

In the middle of the village though... a battle currently ensued.

The Banshee let out a scream, as the cry was returned by at least two dozen of the corrupted. The group moved ahead towards a vantage point in the clearing as the first of the corrupted leapt at the Banshee.

The spirit quickly flew to the side as it lashed out with long black claws, instantly severing the creature's head from its body. Its corpse had barely landed on the ground as the rest of the corrupted joined the fray.

Group after group of them jumped at the Banshee, dagger like claws ready to tear the spirit apart. The specter was too fast however, as it dodged the next attack and promptly flew into one of the assailants. Within moments the corrupted exploded in a spray of viscera, the ghast now unveiled again like a surprise toy in a chocolate egg.

As it swooped down and entered another corrupted, Sabrina started to scribble down some notes. Luke looked onward and noticed that as it was about to enter a creature, it momentarily converted into a shadowy form. It wasn't attacking the chemistry of the creatures, it was simply shedding its physical body and then reforming inside of them. Pushing everything out of the way around it in a split second.

As the battle continued, Luke pulled his prototype out of its holster and signaled for them to move closer; there was no way he would be able to accurately throw it at this distance. Everyone crouched as they moved closer to the action... taking extra care to avoid stepping on anything that might alert the hostiles to their location.

The Banshee continued to fly around, using its agility to take out the corrupted one by one. As the group reached the edge of the village, Luke took a deep breath to prepare for his throw. Just as he pulled his arm back though, a corrupted pulled everyone's attention when it scrambled up from the tall grass nearby.

The monster let out a scream as it spread its claws and crouched to leap at the party. The vanguard quickly filled it with a series of duskshot however, and everyone turned back to the village proper.

The Banshee had finished with its battle and was now staring directly at the group... Its red glowing eyes pierced Luke's brown ones as it seemed to gaze into his very soul. It leaned back to let out another one of its piercing shrieks, then flew straight for the group.

Luke pulled his arm back again, quickly threw the crystal forward at the flying spirit, and... missed.

The Banshee swerved out of the way of the crystal as it bounced harmlessly against the ground in the middle of the village.

"Shit," Luke muttered, as everyone dove out of the way of the spirits first attack. Luke quickly scrambled to his feet and sprinted towards the crystal. Everyone depended on his ability to capture the Banshee. Everything from their lives, to averting the entire apocalypse that now loomed over the world.

Adam aimed his rifle and shot at the Banshee. However, it was able to dodge the crystal and lashed out at him. He was able to roll out of the way, but Adam lost his weapon in the process as it flew from his grip.

The entire group was now scattered as everyone attempted to build distance between themselves and the raging spirit. During his sprint for the crystal, Luke looked over his shoulder and witnessed Sabrina trip over a rock and fall.

Unfortunately... the Banshee noticed as well. The specter now had a lock on its new target, and angrily flew in her direction.

Sabrina turned to face the spirit as she tried to crawl away; with it quickly closing the distance between them.

The crystal now close, Luke dove towards it. Once he felt the invention within his grip, he quickly turned and used the momentum to chuck the crystal in Sabrina's direction. The Banshee continued its charge, as it raised one clawed hand into the air. Sabrina covered her face and closed her eyes as the spirit brought down its hand towards her, fully expecting her life to end in that moment.

With its claw inches from Sabrina's body, the Banshee froze in midair.

The crystal had struck true this time, as the lights spanning its surface began to flash at various intervals. The specter then burst into its shadow form; the wisps of black smoke being drawn completely into the crystal.

Silence filled the air as the prototype landed with a thud at Sabrina's feet.

Luke panted as he laid on the ground, his upper body propped up by one of his elbows. He then fell over onto his back with his limbs splayed out and laughed.

Sabrina breathed a sigh of relief as she joined his laughter, and the rest of the group solely following suit as John let out a "Hell Yeah!" followed by a fist pump into the air.

They had done it. They had caught the Banshee.

Chapter 16: The Spider's Web

"Sir! We can't do this!", A researcher exclaimed to Director Johnson.

The Director simply ignored the man as he used the tablet to command the Broodmother to load into a shipping container. Once the container was sealed, the Director began walking towards a nearby helicopter.

"Do you really intend to unleash this thing on our own people? What kinds of lines are we crossing just for this test?" The researcher continued as he kept pace with his determined leader.

The Director replied, still making his way to the helicopter.

"It's a small town in the middle of nowhere. We need to test the Broodmother before we take her to Japan, and if a few hundred people must die to achieve our goal then so be it. Billions will be saved, but more importantly the world will know we hold all the cards now. So, you can either shut up and return to your post, or you can join the townsfolk. Your call."

With this the researcher stopped. He motioned as if he was going to argue, but quickly fell silent and returned to the facility behind them.

The Director climbed into the helicopter and directed it to take off. It lifted above the shipping container as men on the ground secured cables between the two. Once the container was secured, the vehicle began to ascend further into the sky.

The Broodmother needed to be tested against something more akin to the corrupted creatures the Phantom Hawk can create. And what better way to do this than to test it against actual corrupted?

A small town was chosen in Montana for this initial test, and as they began their flight the Director pulled out his phone and punched in a number. "We are on our way, release the catalyst," he stated coldly before hanging up.

After their coastal facility was lost and before the airstrike was initiated, a few agents had managed to sneak into the warehouse and recover a sample of the corruption. This sample was smuggled into the towns water treatment facility earlier in the day, and at the Directors command was now being administered into their water supply.

By the time the helicopter arrived, the entire town should be filled with nothing but corrupted. Roadblocks and a perimeter were also set up to ensure nothing could leave the town before the Broodmother arrived to clean up the mess.

Their timing seemed to be impeccable, for once the helicopter arrived the streets could already be seen filled with creatures. They wandered aimlessly, yet the moment a survivor attempted to make a break for it the creatures were ready to redirect and lunge. No one survived the carnage as pained screams from the last remaining locals matched the hunting shrieks of their corrupted neighbors.

Eventually though, silence once again filled the air. This was the moment to test.

The helicopter hovered close to the ground and unlatched the container from its cables. With the push of a button, small explosives popped the door off safely to unveil the darkness within.

The Director input a command, and the Broodmother walked slowly from within and into the daylight of the afternoon sun. As this test was to see how the Broodmother would work uninhibited in combat, the Director input a broad command. The spirit was to clear all life from a zone drawn on the tablet around the town, then wait for further instruction.

A button was pressed, and the command was relayed to the harness.

The Broodmother stood still for a moment as it surveyed its target area. It then skittered forward and began weaving a web across the road that entered the town. The web glistened in the sunlight as the monstrous spirit finished its work.

It then let out a shriek, which drew the attention of a group of the creatures nearest to the edge of the town. As they spotted the massive spider, their bloodlust led them to break into a sprint across the road and straight into the web trap.

The first few moved seamlessly through the web... and landed as a pile of eviscerated flesh and bone on the other side. More and more assaulted the web though until it eventually wore out, with four of the corrupted being able to climb over the pile of slaughtered brethren and make a beeline for the Broodmother.

As they got close, however, it quickly swung one of its legs out to sweep three of them away. While they tumbled across the ground a short distance, the Broodmother bit into the remaining creature. A shriek escaped its mouth as it underwent a new transformation; the mutilated human form now slowly reshaped into a fleshy cocoon.

The three thrown creatures recovered quickly, this time setting their sights on the nearby cocoon. As they got close, however, the cocoon exploded.

Shortly after the eruption occurred, a smaller spider leapt out of the spray. It quickly bit down on another of the corrupted, which then promptly began to form a cocoon of its own.

The Director grinned as he saw this. Apparently the Broodmother wasn't the only one capable of spreading her spiderlings. This would be good to quickly take out the creatures on their path to the Phantom Hawk once they invaded Japan. Especially since here there were a few hundred, but the island nation was filled with millions of these beasts.

The two remaining corrupted were transformed into cocoons, then spiderlings, as the Broodmother set its sights on the town itself.

Long black legs skittered down the main street as spiderlings began smashing through the windows and doors of various houses.

Battles could be heard throughout the village as the two different types of thralls met.

It appeared as if the corrupted were an even match for the spiders though. This observation was confirmed as a few corrupted sliced through some of the spiders in one of the houses and made their way into the street.

They weren't a match for the Broodmother however, who quickly impaled some of the corrupted onto its giant legs. One by one it lifted its assailants to its mouth to gift them an infectious bite, and one by one corrupted turned into pulsating fleshy cocoons.

These cocoons waited until more corrupted came close before they then detonated and sent limbs flying through the air in every direction. The Director watched as explosions slowly spread throughout the city; spiderlings clearing a path through the wreckage to hunt as houses began to collapse. Their structural integrity was destroyed by the onslaught of explosions targeted at the spider's enemies.

Out of nowhere, a pack of the corrupted leapt from hiding near the Broodmother. As it began the process anew of impaling and infecting these targets, one of them had managed to get underneath the spirit's body. With a quick lash of its claws, it missed the spirit entirely... but managed to slice a long gash across the backpack portion of the harness.

The Director quickly shot his gaze down to the tablet in his hand, as an error read across the screen.

Battery compromised, estimated time until failure: one hour.

The Director gritted his teeth and quickly input a command for the Broodmother to abort and return to its container. As he relayed this command, it quickly skittered out of the town and back into its temporary home.

The helicopter secured the container once more into place as it lifted off back to their facility. The battle was mostly over now anyway, as various cocoons laid spread across the city. Some of the recently fallen locals had yet to be resurrected as corrupted, however they couldn't risk losing the Broodmother within their own country now. A perimeter would have to be set up to monitor the situation and contain the creatures until a further course of action could be taken.

The helicopter began its journey back to base as the Director watched the time with clenched teeth. They had only about ten minutes to spare once they arrive to resecure the Broodmother in its cage, before all hell would break loose.

He made a hurried call to the facility to have everything prepared for locking down the Broodmother the moment they arrived back and waited. Every minute that passed seemed like a bomb ticking down; with the error message consistently counting down towards power failure. The base was getting steadily closer, and with eight minutes to go they arrived at the landing pad.

The container was quickly dropped as the Director input a command. Within moments, the Broodmother's housing was lifted to the surface and the wall slid open. The spirit itself skittered calmly across the open desert terrain and into its housing. The wall then slid back into place and the prison slowly receded back underground.

He breathed a sigh of relief as the helicopter landed. With tablet in hand, he jumped out of the vehicle and made his way back into the facility.

Corridor after corridor the Director strode through with purpose as he made his way back into the observation room that linked with the Broodmother's cell. He looked down at the tablet in his hand as the countdown reached zero and a large *connection lost* displayed across the screen.

When the Director looked back up, the Broodmother let out a crazed shriek. It then proceeded to rip the harness off and tear it into a pile of scrap metal before tossing it through the air, with enough force to cause it to shatter into a spray of parts upon connecting with a wall.

Moments later the Directors cell phone rang. "What is it," he stated, frustrated at the turn of events.

"Sir, we are in position and the perimeter has been set. It looks like there aren't any new corrupted yet, however the spiders in the town have begun to move again. It looks like they're searching for something."

The Director gritted his teeth again as he muttered "dammit" before hanging up the call. With the loss of control over the Broodmother, that meant the spiderlings were back under its will as well. They were probably being commanded to find the spirit now. However, it would take them a while since the Broodmother was faced towards the back wall of the container. It would have had no idea as to the distance it was carried before it regained control over its own actions.

The Director turned to the head researcher, who had now entered the room upon hearing that the test was complete. "We need another harness for the Broodmother, and make sure to reinforce it. One of the corrupted was able to damage the previous one and we nearly lost control during the test."

"Yes sir," the man stated, as he directed someone to relay the instructions back down to their lab. The researcher then turned back to the Director. "We are currently processing video recording of the field test and should have a finalized summary soon. From the looks of it so far though, it would seem the Broodmother test was a success. It should give us the edge we need to take down and capture the Phantom Hawk again. This time, with full control over its actions."

"Perfect," stated the Director, his demeanor now returned to his normal calm and collected poise. "Once our harness design has been improved and reimplemented onto the Broodmother, we will prepare for our frontal assault on the Phantom Hawk's corrupted army. Soon, the spirit will be ours again."

A few days had passed, and the Director entered his office one morning to look over the details of their planned assault. A call came through moments later though on his desk phone's intercom. With the push of a button, the Director answered, "What is it now?" The voice on the other end seemed to be from their surveillance team.

"Sir, we may have a problem."

The voice stated this hesitantly, before finishing its report.

"It seems that a group is now entering the testing site where we have the perimeter set up. And what's more, is that they have some sort of spirit under their control."

Chapter 17: A New Look

Luke peered down at the crystal in his hand, relief washing through his veins as they sat in the helicopter.

The invention had still not finalized control over the Banshee; with a flashing array of red lights crossing over the metal arms that wrapped around the piece of shaped quartz. But that was fine. The hard part was done, and the spirit was captured. Even more importantly, they were able to do so without a single loss of life this time.

Hope began to swell in everyone as they realized how close they were to averting the apocalypse once and for all. Not that the Phantom Hawk would be easy to take down, but they were getting more and more tools under their belt in preparation for the final battle.

Once the helicopter reached its usual landing outside of the small hunting cabin, the group of five hopped out. Luke led the way as they made it back into the secret base below the unassuming structure. When the party made it down into the underground room, Lewis could be seen standing by the command table once more.

Luke held up the crystal in his hand, as applause could be heard reverberating throughout the room. Everyone was overcome with excitement as they saw that the mission had been a success. Lewis himself even grinned, before he beckoned the party to his side.

"I see that you made it through the island, and without a single casualty, nonetheless. Well done." Lewis accented his statement with a nod before he continued.

"Seeing as we won't be able to field test your control over the spirit until the prototype has finalized the process, you can all enjoy some well-earned relaxation. Our weapons lab is already hard at work producing more copies of your controller crystal now that it's been tested in the field. The final mission in stopping the Phantom

Hawk will soon be upon us though, and you will all need every ounce of energy you can muster for it.”

John, Emily, and Adam all left for their respective rooms to finish their day off with some showers and food, while Luke and Sabrina stayed behind.

“Actually sir, I had an idea before we left for our mission. An idea that has to do with our trip to Japan. Do you happen to have any access to a tailor?” Luke questioned, as Lewis’ eyebrow raised in curiosity.

“We have a few specializing mostly in combat related gear. What was your idea?”

Luke motioned for Lewis to hold on a second as he walked to his room at a quickened pace. Sabrina decided to take this moment to pass on her gathered information on the island’s current inhabitants as she pulled her notebook out and held it in front of herself and Lewis.

As soon as Luke reached his room, he hurried across to the table in the back. He then grabbed the notebook he had hastily sketched a design into before they left for the island. Without wasting a moment, Luke spun on his heels and exited the room, once more making his way back to the command table.

Sabrina had just finished informing Lewis about what they discovered regarding the corruption’s life span when Luke once more reached the pair. All eyes turned to his notebook as he laid it open on the edge of the command table.

A rough sketch could be seen of pants, a long-sleeved shirt, and a long coat on one page. With some details and information scribbled on the page after.

“Before we had left for the mission, I had an idea for an outfit that would better match my new belt. Furthermore, the design notes I have here detail an array of powdered crystals throughout the outfit that should be able to reflect airborne corruption as well as the Phantom Hawks aura."

Luke pointed to his design notes as he stated this last part, followed by him quickly clearing his throat to continue.

"The pants and shirt designs offer full protection from the corruption for anyone that joins us on the mission. The coat is an add-on I designed for myself that could protect the controller crystals on my belt from being corrupted prior to use. It would also add a further layer of protection against impact force in case things get a little rough in the field."

"Ooo," Sabrina stated as she leaned in closer to the notebook to look at his design. Lewis stroked his now stubble covered chin as he listened to Luke's explanation and nodded.

"We do have the network to get these materials made, and this solves our problem of how to get you all close enough to the Phantom Hawk to capture it. Good job, you made our job even easier. In fact, I think we could probably have a design ready to be used in the field test for your Banshee."

"Do you mind if I sketch up my own outfit for use?" Sabrina asked Lewis as she ran her fingers across the sketch Luke had drawn earlier.

"Not at all," Lewis replied. "We will have someone send these notes out to one of our connections to get Luke's coat as well as the general designs for the broader use outfit started. Just bring me your design when its ready and we will have it made shortly after."

Sabrina smiled widely at this as she quickly ran off to start working on her own outfit.

"We can easily follow these design notes to create a matching pair of boots for further protection. However, wouldn't your designs head exposure still allow an opening for the aura to corrupt our field operatives?" Lewis asked this as Luke gazed into the corner of the room deep in thought.

"For the Phantom Hawk mission, something akin to a riot helmet with a facemask should be able to easily accommodate the crystalline barrier. The crystals are small enough that they shouldn't inhibit vision while also giving protection from the aura. I don't believe we will need the helmets for the field test though, as airborne corruption seems to only exist when blood from a corrupted person enters a strong concentrated force of wind. Such as the kind you could find in an industrial ventilation system. It doesn't seem light enough to carry itself through the air in any other way."

Lewis nodded as he called a messenger over to pass the design notes as well as information on the mask and boots off to their tailors. With this done, Luke excused himself from the conversation to start his period of relaxation. Now calmed since the most recent of his innovations was now in the works to be crafted.

As he reentered his room, Luke quickly stripped off his clothes, set his belt and the prototype crystal onto his table, and walked towards the bathroom. A quick shower then cleaned away the grime and sweat from the day's mission.

Following this, he pulled on a pair of shorts and a plain T-shirt. His stomach then grumbled; clearly wanting sustenance from earlier exertions. This grumbling continued until Luke left his room once more and made his way down to the cafeteria.

One filled tray later, and Luke walked over to a table where Adam, Emily, and John were currently midway through their dinner. John scooted over to make room for Luke as Emily continued talking.

"When I joined this organization, our day-to-day tasks mostly involved research. On occasion we would do some fieldwork if there was enough evidence of a cryptid in an area or if a spirit seemed especially malicious in sightings, but we mostly just documented events. Never once did I think our purpose would become necessary to humanities survival."

Adam finished his bite of food before he now took up the mantle of conversation.

"Tell me about it. When I joined the paranormal wing of the military, I thought of it as mostly a joke. We had a few missions to gather intel on supernatural occurrences in the world, but I mostly felt like a glorified ghost hunter. Objects falling, reading EMF in abandoned buildings. It all seemed like bullshit to me. On occasion we had someone get attacked by a spirit, but it was mostly just scratches and the occasional bite mark... but then we were assigned the island expedition."

Adam took an extra-long pause to gather his thoughts before he continued.

"Nothing could have prepared me for what we witnessed. I was lucky to be assigned a lookout position. That was probably the only reason I was even able to escape. Almost everyone else was slaughtered when they went to scout out the village. The same village that we came across today. Even my lookout partner died, as we didn't know her wound was infected with the corruption at the time. The same infection that would be what ultimately led to my facilities demise."

"At least you two were already involved in the field," John started. "Imagine my surprise when I am getting ready to go home from our university for a visit, only to be interrupted by some men in black looking folks that told me ghosts are real and I was needed to fight them.

John continued, "I was terrified of ghosts. The only reason I could see them wanting me was because I was friends with Luke. Ya know, the one responsible for literally every tool we've used to fight our way through so far." With this last part John gave Luke a pat on the back.

Luke... who was currently face deep in a bowl of soup and passively listening to the conversation. As John patted his back, Luke looked up from his food like a deer in headlights. This surprised expression proceeded to get a laugh out of everyone around the table at his expense.

He swallowed his mouthful and wiped his lips with the back of his hand to contribute to the discussion. "Yea well, when I was designing my crystal trap, I didn't exactly expect it to be used in this manner. I was looking for a method to both prove the existence of ghosts as well as capture them. It seems like the proving the existence part was kind of unnecessary though, given that the Phantom Hawk is doing that one for me."

Emily smiled at Luke, "Well it's a good thing you were able to succeed. Who knows where we would be now without all the things you've designed for us."

John then looked around before returning his eyes to Luke. "Speaking of where people are, where is Sabrina? Did she decide to just call it an early night?"

Luke grinned as he replied. "Oh, far from it. I gave Lewis some designs for clothing to protect us from the Phantom Hawks corruption. I think you all will be pretty pleased with the design, but Sabrina ran off to adapt it a little more to her own tastes."

Emily perked up at this last part. "Wait, I'm not going on our next missions wearing the same unflattering gear as the rest of you. I need to have some input on this."

The rest of the table laughed as she quickly got up and deposited her tray, before running off in the direction of everyone's rooms. Certainly, to meet up with Sabrina and get her own design ideas done.

"So, how exactly is this gear supposed to help us?" Adam asked, now curious as to Luke's ideas.

Luke gave him his full attention for a moment as he went on to explain his thought process. "Well, before we went on our mission, I had an idea. The angles on the crystals are what allow them to contain the spirit's energies. Or in the case of the prototype, the angles also allow it to function as a taming mechanism."

Luke continued, "I decided to use a similar concept, but with powdered quartz instead as an inlay for clothing. If the powder is weaved in at the correct angles, it should function similarly to the walls of the solid crystals. Acting as sort of a mirror and reflecting any corruption away from our bodies. Without it, we probably wouldn't be able to get anywhere near the Phantom Hawk without instantly turning."

Adam nodded to this as everyone returned to their food. He was then the next to get up, passing along his goodbyes as he left to get an early night of sleep in. It had seemed that he wasn't fully recovered from his warehouse escape yet, and the recent mission drained him entirely.

Luke took this moment to move to the opposite side of the table from John to have a better conversational angle.

"So, John, how do you feel after our last mission? It seems like you have gotten over your ghost fears entirely. Are you ready for field testing the Banshee?"

"I feel," John started, as he calmly wiped his mouth off with a napkin. "That you need to work on your aim. I mean c'mon, you couldn't hit the Banshee when it was coming straight at us?"

John accented this statement with a devilish grin, as Luke rolled his eyes.

"You know damn well it dodged the throw. I think the only reason I was able to hit it the second time was because it wasn't looking at me. Besides, you have to admit, my fadeaway throw was badass."

This time it was Johns turn to roll his eyes. "Yea yea. In all honesty though, good job. And to answer your previous question, yea I think I've pretty much adapted now. I think most of my fears surrounding spirits were related to the fact that I knew nothing about

154

them. Even though things we are seeing now are far worse than I could've imagined, at least we have knowledge as to what they're capable of. And even better, we have ways of fighting back. I doubt I would be this calm if we didn't have the Dawnbringer rifles or your capture crystals."

Luke nodded as Emily and Sabrina strolled to the table in conversation and sat down. Sabrina next to Luke, and Emily next to John.

"So, did you two figure out what you wanted to wear to the dance?" Luke jokingly stated to Sabrina.

"Oh definitely, I think you will like the designs we came up with," Sabrina replied with a wink to Luke.

This caused John to choke on his food as he took a drink to clear his throat. "Well, just make sure you don't distract him too much. Otherwise, he may miss another throw."

"Oh my god," Luke replied. Making sure to draw out the last word as everyone at the table laughed. Spirits were at an all-time high with the recent success of their mission.

Talk slowly steered away from the mission and clothing to the table tennis and games that were still littered across the back of Luke's room. Everyone waited for Sabrina to grab a bite to eat as they made plans for how they were going to spend the rest of the night. Once her food was gone, the four of them made their way out of the cafeteria to Luke's room.

John groaned as the first game decided was table tennis, since he knew he would surely lose again. He wasn't wrong, as even Emily was far more agile than him, and he was subsequently knocked out repeatedly. He had improved though, and at one point almost beat Luke. Although Luke was able to turn things around and pull ahead by a few points towards the end of their game.

Drinks were drained and laughs were shared as the friends and their newest member enjoyed the distraction from their upcoming contest with a demigod.

They then decided to return to the fighting game Luke was so proficient at.

As the group walked over to the couch, Luke whispered something in Emily's ear. As he finished his statement, she replied with a devilish grin and a nod.

Everyone sat down on Luke's couch; with Sabrina sitting in his lap to make room for Emily. Luke then wrapped his arms around her waist so that he could grip his controller, and they turned the game on.

The first game they played was a free-for-all. At least, that was the game mode they had selected. It became clear what Luke whispered to Emily as they tag teamed Sabrina, followed by John. Knocking each of them out before finishing the match in a one versus one.

Luke of course, using his favorite character and coming out as the ultimate victor.

"Oh ok, I see how it is. A little payback now?" Sabrina stated to Luke as she grinned. "Fine, let's just change this to teams then. But Luke and Emily must be separated, as she clearly has played this game almost as much as he has."

Emily gave her a cheeky grin as she replied. "This may be one of my favorite games."

Luke then chimed in, "That's fair. Sabrina is on my team though since I'm going to need to keep my eye on her." He followed this with a wink as the teams were set, and the next match began.

This time, the match was far closer. Luke had decided to switch characters, but Emily decided to keep what everyone now discovered was her own main fighter. In the end, John threw a fist pump into the air and Emily cheered as the two of them defeated Luke and Sabrina.

"Ok ok, I feel like we just need to avoid our favorite characters if we are to make things a little fairer here," Luke stated as he laughed and shook his head. The terms were agreed upon, and round after round was played with both teams collecting their fair share of wins.

The night went on like this for a while, with the newly expanded friend group slowly drinking their way through Luke's supply of beers. Eventually though, exhaustion from the day slowly crept into everyone. As tiredness mixed with the warm buzz of the alcohol, the party decided it was about time to call it a night.

Luke held his door open as the other three left to go to their respective rooms. He then walked back inside and sat on the edge of his bed. With a tired sigh, he turned on one of the typical ghost hunter shows he so enjoyed. It was a rerun episode, but that didn't really matter since he was just going to use it as background noise to fall asleep to.

Once sounds began to flow from the bed's TV, Luke threw off his shorts and shirt he put on previously and began to walk through his room cleaning up a bit.

There was a trash can in the kitchen area that he tossed the various emptied bottles into. Following this, he shut off the couch's TV and the game system they were playing just moments ago.

Luke paused to stretch, before he fixed the position of his table and moved the table tennis net to the side. The prototype crystal was then returned to its rightful place on the tabletop since it was moved aside to the counter for their games earlier in the evening.

Once he had finished cleaning up for the night, Luke started to return to his bed. He froze however, as he did a double take of the controller crystal.

It no longer was covered with the array of red lights, and instead the entire thing shone with a soft breathing green light.

The Banshee was now tamed and ready for testing.

Chapter 18: Ghost Town

As Luke entered the main room the following morning, everyone was scrambling about chaotically.

"What's going on?" he inquired to Lewis, who waved him over.

"We just obtained information that the military has tested the Broodmother in a small town in Montana. And by tested, I mean they intentionally corrupted the entire town to give the spirit some targets to take out."

Luke's jaw dropped as he processed this statement. The military actually killed off an entire town, just so they can see how their demigod worked. Where was the morality in this act?

Lewis pointed towards a display of the town on the command table and continued to speak. "We have a new emergency mission being prepared. You will take a contingent of operatives into the town to clear any signs of corruption, as well as the spiders that were left behind."

Luke raised his eyebrow as he faced Lewis. "Wait, what do you mean left behind?"

Lewis answered as he pointed to various giant cocoon shapes and spiders scattered throughout the streets. "During their testing of the Broodmother, it appeared that their harness was damaged by one of the corrupted. They were able to contain the Broodmother long enough to return it to their facility. However, it would seem the harness fully malfunctioned shortly after. Since the Broodmother controls the spiders it creates, this caused the ones spawned during the test to fall back under the Broodmother's direction."

Lewis continued, "We believe they are currently searching for the spirits location to free their creator. It would seem that they don't know how far the spirit was taken though, which works to our advantage. Since they don't have the capabilities to assault the Area 51 facility without that knowledge. However, if they fully sweep through the town and find nothing, they might decide to expand their search. Who knows what kind of destruction could be caused if they encounter a large city in the process. The spiders could spread like a plague if that were to happen, and quickly become uncontainable."

Following this, Lewis gestured in the direction of a stack of boxes Luke previously had not noticed. "While I'm afraid we can't wait for you to gain control over the Banshee for this mission, we did receive the clothing you requested. We need you all to get changed and prepared to fly out to Montana. You will be provided with ten operatives in addition to the five of you that went to the island yesterday."

"About that," Luke started, as he revealed the glowing prototype controller crystal that finalized its taming the night before. "The prototype is actually ready, so we can use this mission as a field test for the Banshee's capabilities in addition to how well the taming worked."

Lewis took the crystal into his hand and inspected the green lights as he handed it back to Luke. "Well, we can possibly consider this situation a blessing then. Although the military's actions are unforgiveable, we now have a location to test the spirit against an actual foe. One directly related to the Phantom Hawk, nonetheless. In addition, we have received word that with the harness destroyed, the military has been set behind. Their Broodmother assault on the Phantom Hawk is now delayed massively, which gives us a chance to field test the Banshee before they attempt to use the Broodmother again and fully lose control."

Luke grabbed his outfit which was folded on top of the contents of one of the boxes and nodded to Lewis. He then returned to his room to prepare for the mission.

As he stripped down out of his more casual clothes, Luke pulled on his new black pants and matching long sleeved shirt. The clothing was made from a lightweight moisture wicking material it seemed, which would do well to keep them cooler. Even with the total coverage the clothing provided for protection.

As Luke pulled on the black combat boots, he noted that they did not spare any expense in the craft of this gear. They could have simply made the cheapest basic design, but they opted for comfort instead.

A pair of sleek black gloves were the next items he pulled on. They went roughly halfway up his forearms and were lined on the inside with the same soft, moisture wicking material used on the rest of the clothing. It was a good thing the designers decided to create these, as Luke somehow forgot to think up protection for their hands. Probably the most important area as well; since their hands were the most likely to get scratched up and become susceptible to corruption.

As Luke pulled on his utility belt and holstered the Banshee's crystal in place, he grabbed the elongated coat specially made for his outfit. Before putting this piece on, he decided to walk to the nearby mirror to see how the new outfit looked.

With a wide arced swing, he pulled the coat behind himself and slid his arms in. The lengthy outerwear fluttered into place from the motion, ending up more than halfway down his legs.

With the coat thrown on, Luke's new look was complete. He then took a moment to admire the overall appearance of his design come to life.

The powdered crystals inlaid between the layers of fabric gave the entire outfit a semi-gloss sheen when in light. Not blinding and shiny, but it gave the entire set the appearance of a wax-like coating. With the flowing black design and his utility belt for carrying various tools and crystals, Luke looked like an apocalypse survivor. Which was probably not far from the truth if they failed at stopping the Phantom Hawks rampage.

After one final sweep of his room, Luke made sure that he had not forgotten any portion of the outfit. The protection probably would not be needed for the current mission, but a field test with the whole set would be better than missing pieces. Plus, he looked badass, and looked forward to flaunting it when testing the Banshee.

Nothing was missing during this last sweep, so he promptly exited his room and returned to Lewis.

As Luke entered the main chamber, his jaw dropped once more. This time, the reaction was caused less by a town's destruction at the hands of the Broodmother, but rather Sabrina and Emily's outfits.

Their boots were both longer and slenderer than Luke's own, ending just below their knees. Instead of the black pants, the two of them each had vibrantly colored leggings. Sabrina's were a velvety red, while Emily's were pure white. The lower half of each outfit was finalized with a black skirt, which probably promoted movement just as well as Luke's pants. If not better, all things considered.

Their shirts were closer to the standard design, albeit they were short sleeved. In addition, the black cloth was fitted more tightly around the waist. The cut around the collar was also deeper, without being too revealing or exposed. To make up for the short sleeves, their gloves went halfway up their biceps rather than stopping along the forearm.

Sabrina's outfit was completed with a coat relatively similar to Luke's own. Although hers was a shade of red that matched her leggings and covered more of her legs. A clip kept a field journal clasped to the outside of her coat, which fully cemented her as more of the observational type.

Emily's outfit was completed with a white shawl. Which just like Sabrina, matched her leggings.

"Do you like them?," Sabrina asked as she posed.

"Honestly? You're beautiful" Luke stated, which caused Sabrina to blush. It was true though, as she looked like a much better dressed version of himself.

"Your outfit is attractively badass by the way. You kind of look like a well-dressed assassin." Luke stated in Emily's direction. Which was absolutely true, and Sabrina nodded in agreement. Something about the shawl gave Emily a very mysterious look.

John and Adam were also with the group, however their outfits blended more with the other operatives Lewis had assigned to the mission. Their gloves were shorter than even Luke's, and the remainder of their outfits only consisted of the boots, pants, and shirts. Luke definitely stood out as the leader with his unique look, while Emily and Sabrina easily could be made out as specialists.

Once the remaining operatives that had not yet arrived filed in, Lewis began the briefing.

"As this is a larger group than the previous mission, you will be taking the vans rather than the helicopter. The helicopter would be faster, however not all of you would fit. Time is of the essence but having more numbers for safety matters above all else. You will unload and prepare outside of town along this road." Lewis stated this as he began pointing at the town's display, starting with a street that ran through the center of the town.

"John will lead the Alpha team vanguard while Adam will lead the Bravo team. Your objectives will be to split onto both sides of the road and clear houses of any hostiles found within. From what intelligence we gathered from the military's reports, there won't be any survivors in town. This, coupled with the fact that our ammunition is non-lethal to humans, means we are taking a shoot first approach to anything we come across."

With the majority of the personnel having their assignments, Lewis then directed his attention to Luke, Emily, and Sabrina.

"You three will be taking to the center road of the town. As the vanguard clears both sides, Luke will be in position to give out orders to either side depending on whatever obstacles he observes. He will also be testing a new weapon in the field; dubbed the Banshee. Vanguards must ensure not to shoot this spirit, as we will be using it on our assault against the Phantom Hawk. Losing it to stray fire here would surely spell doom for us all."

Next Lewis motioned to Sabrina.

"Sabrina will be tasked with observing and noting anything we may not know about either the spiders or the corrupted, as well as acting as an extra set of eyes for passing necessary information to the two vanguards. We must make sure they don't get flanked and overrun while they are clearing the structures."

The only person left to be assigned a task was Emily. As Luke pondered what could be left, his thoughts were quickly answered by Lewis' next statement.

"Emily will be taking on the role of guardian from this point forward. Her task is to ensure Luke and Sabrina's safety at all costs, since the two of them are vital to the success of our Phantom Hawk mission and beyond."

Emily nodded to this, as Luke realized even more why she looked like an assassin. She had one of his Dawnbringer rifles strapped across her back, but strapped to her boot was a weapon that must have been designed by the weapons lab for her.

A quartz crystal about the length of her forearm was carved into the rough shape of a blade. Luke recognized a milder version of his capture crystals angles along the edges, and realized the blade probably had a way to absorb corruption and then bleed it off over time. An interesting design that could safely fight the creatures in close quarters without risk of becoming full of corruption and rendered useless.

The end of this specially designed crystal was seated in a black grip, which completed the appearance of an assassin's blade.

Lewis wrapped up the briefing and waved his hand towards the stairs, signaling that it was time to leave.

Luke then took to leading everyone out, while his friends followed close behind. "Everyone ready? It seems like we are about to walk into a full-on battle." Luke stated this as he remembered how their warehouse breach went. The mission failed completely, and he lost an entire team of operatives. In fact, other than the Banshee capture, it seemed as though most of their missions had been failures with a massive cost of lives.

Luke would test the Banshee here, but his primary objective was to make sure he would get everyone out if possible.

A series of nods were the only reply from his friends as they all made their way upstairs, outside, and into the three vans that waited for them. With all of them being in leadership or specialist roles, all five of the island mission's members were in the lead van. The remaining ten personnel filed into the second and third vans, as all three shut their doors. Engines turned on, and one by one the vans began the long trek towards the fallen town in Montana.

"By the way Emily, nice dagger," Luke stated with a grin as he gestured towards her boot.

Emily bent down and gripped the handle as she lifted it out and handed it over to Luke. "You like it? After our close encounters with some of the corrupted on the island I figured I might need something easier to use than a rifle if the creatures got too close. The people down at the weapons lab mimicked some of your crystal designs to be able to pull corruption spirit energies out with the blade. However, they altered the design enough that hopefully it will release those energies from the crystal over time rather than keep it trapped. Ya know, the blade would be kind of useless if it filled up after a handful of slashes."

Luke nodded, as this was what he surmised earlier based off his observations. He held the blade between both hands as he ran his fingers gently across the crystal. It was definitely sharper than he had expected, and it seemed the weapons lab did an immaculate job on the angles: They were able to use the necessary designs perfectly in conjunction with the angles needed to create the sharp edge.

He then gripped the weapon in his right hand and noted that the balance was perfect. It almost felt like an extension of his arm when he gave it a few waves through the air, slicing at imaginary foes.

"Maybe I should get one of those as well, they did an amazing job on it," Luke stated to Emily as he returned the blade to her.

Her face beamed with pride as she re-holstered the weapon and replied. "Thank you! I was actually the one that drew up the design for it. The lab just adjusted some of the angles since they had the notes you gave them with your math."

Luke was highly impressed by this, and she seemed extremely capable in her role now. An eye for weapon design and the fighting skills to match would be a perfect asset when they finally left to fight the Phantom Hawk.

"So, how long is this drive again?" John asked this to Sabrina as he stretched his arms wide above his head. They hadn't been on the road long, but it seemed he was a bit antsy to get out and do some moving.

She replied, "Our total trip is supposed to be about six hours to the town. So, I would say we have a little over five hours left. Prepare to die of boredom."

John groaned at this reply as he leaned back and closed his eyes.

Adam was seated next to John, with his arms crossed over his knees and casually hunched forward. He looked over to John as the large man groaned and shook his head with a smile. Adam was clearly more accustomed to these long road trips in windowless vehicles than the rest of them.

Well, everyone besides Emily. Who had her legs crossed one over the other as she kicked her foot to an unknown rhythm inside her head.

The journey continued in mostly silence as everyone tried to keep themselves entertained. Adam sat in his bent position and mostly just stared at the floor waiting, while Emily continued to listen to her mental radio. She occasionally quietly hummed the song she was thinking of, but it was too quiet for anyone else to make out what song it was over the sounds of their journey.

John apparently decided to use this time to take a quick nap. After his earlier groan, his eyes had not opened again, and his breathing was now calm and steady.

Sabrina took this free time to look over her previous notes, as well as scribble down some questions she asked of herself to observe from the corrupted and spiders they would find.

Luke simply read through the briefing folder in his hands, trying to plan for any hiccups that may arise as he read through the information obtained from the military's field-testing reports.

Eventually, the small convoy of vans came to a stop as they reached their destination. Luke slid open the van door and stepped out into the sunlight. As his eyes adjusted to the glare after being in the back of a dark van for so long, he looked over to see the other ten operatives for the vanguard exiting their own vans and stretching as they looked around. Luke then walked around the vehicles to take in the sight of the fallen town.

It was small for sure; maybe only a few hundred people once lived here. The main street they would go down was pretty much the only major road within city limits. Honestly, it looked more like a village than anything else. Rows of houses lined both sides of the road, followed by a few gas stations and small stores for various goods the locals would need in day-to-day life.

Back when the town was alive, he could have easily walked from entrance to exit in less than an hour with a casual stroll. Now though, it was a stark foreshadowing as to what the world would look like if the Phantom Hawk was not stopped.

The structures were mostly dilapidated; probably due to the Broodmother related test more than anything else. Walls of some of the houses were splintered and roofs were bowed down as if some kind of explosion pummeled the exteriors. Glass was also shattered out of occasional windows, although some still held up with a few scratches and dirt covering their surface.

The street was lined with various cars, some of which were still parked neatly in front of the houses. Others were not so lucky; now crushed, flipped, or pummeled and pushed aside. Luke could not tell if this was because of the Broodmother test, or the prior corrupting of the townsfolk. The corrupted had probably done whatever it took to hunt what little survivors that were left. After all, the creatures' strength was still fairly unknown. The only variant of the monsters to show its strength to Luke so far had been an abomination: The abomination that almost smashed its way through a solid steel door trying to escape from the warehouse facility, shortly before the air strike had turned everything in the area to ash.

One thing stood out to Luke though, and that was that there was no sign of *human* dead. Sure, mutilated spider corpses and the bodies of fallen corrupted littered the street and yards, but not a normal human was in sight.

This meant that any who died late to the party were already risen; probably hidden somewhere in the maze of walls and debris.

Luke sighed at this thought as he unholstered his new controller crystal and looked down at it. John and Adam had walked over to the operatives in order to organize the Alpha and Bravo vanguard teams, but Sabrina and Emily were now side by side behind Luke as he peered down at the glowing combination of crystal and technology now in his hand.

"Let's hope this worked," he muttered as he tossed the crystal up into the air.

In a burst of shadows and smoke, the Banshee materialized floating a short distance in front of him.

A few members of the vanguard quickly reached for their Dawnbringer rifles, but it soon became apparent that this was an unnecessary reaction.

The Banshee was at the very least pacified, since it simply floated in the air with its gaze locked on Luke. This caused him to shiver, as only days ago it had wanted to rip everyone apart. He remembered how it seemed to peer into his very soul. And although it still felt like it was gazing deep within his body, it seemed more like it was waiting now. As if it needed Luke's permission to do anything.

John and Adam joined the other three with their teams organized behind them. Everyone looked onward in awe at the Banshee, for almost none of them had seen an actual spirit this close before. Let alone one that was directly tied to the corruption that now plagued their world.

Luke pondered for a moment how much of the human spirit was left and how much was simply the corrupted energies controlling it like a puppet. He turned back to face the human portion of their group and spoke.

"Everyone's roles should be clear from the mission briefing earlier. John will lead Alpha team through the left side of the town, as Adam will lead Bravo through the right. Your job is to cleanse any corrupted and or spiderlings left behind from the military's field test in order to prevent their future escape into surrounding areas. We will keep to the main road to provide support and direction from a clearer viewpoint, as well as take out any hostiles that escape into the open."

Adam and John nodded as their operatives gave a salute and gripped their rifles. The two teams then moved to the front, cautiously walking around the Banshee in the process. Everyone assumed it would turn on them at any moment and thus decided to play it safe. It had made no move in any direction however, and simply stayed with its eyes locked on Luke.

Luke then cleared his throat as he met the spirit's gaze. "You will stay by my side and look for any of the corrupted creatures or spiders we may come across. If any come into vision outside of the houses, kill them."

Luke had hoped the spirit understood what he meant by corrupted and spiders. Maybe it was able to share in his own knowledge since it was now linked to him biologically as well as spiritually? Either way, they would find out soon enough. After all, that was the purpose of this field test.

The Banshee seemed to understand the first part at least, because it slowly floated to Luke's side and faced the same direction as him. Sabrina and Emily took a cautious step back, which was understandable given that it just recently had tried to kill them both.

With everyone in position, Luke gave the order to proceed, and the group slowly entered the town. They made their way across city limits as the two vanguards then proceeded into yards on their respective sides.

Although the mood was fairly calm when they entered, it did not stay that way for long. Soon, screams could be heard from the two closest houses.

A small group of corrupted sprinted out from the buildings on each side; some taking the open doorways while others smashed through what remained of a few windows. The vanguards were prepared however, and quickly dropped the creatures before they could close any meaningful distance.

This was the call to action needed to set everyone in the right mindset, and both Alpha and Bravo team promptly jogged towards the openings and began their breaching.

Shrieking could be heard from within the buildings as the teams locked in combat with corrupted hidden throughout the rooms. Luke quickly noticed a few spiderlings skitter across the roof tops; alerted to the sounds of conflict within the houses below. They looked about waist high in height, and the tapping noises from their legs sent a chill through the spines of the three grouped on the street outside.

What was more chilling than that, however, was that you could see where human flesh had been melted down and reformed to create these horrors. Reshaped flesh and muscle covered every inch of their forms; the only humanoid aspect left to these monstrosities. Finalizing their look was a set of eight glowing green eyes peering forward. A small aura of green wreathed itself around their bodies as well, mimicking the same aura the Broodmother had in the 3D display back at headquarters.

The fleshy arachnids leapt down from the houses, ready to hunt the now flanked teams inside.

Luke's Banshee took to its commands well though, as it shot off to the left house where the action had started. While it flew, it extended a clawed hand and promptly tore apart a spiderling mid leap. Without pause, it then dove down and flew through the body of another; bursting back out in an explosion of flesh from what was once the spiderlings mutated form.

One by one the spirit flew around and eviscerated the new creatures, before finally returning calmly to Luke's side.

"I think she likes you," Sabrina stated jokingly.

When Luke looked back to roll his eyes, he spotted the smile that was spread across her face. The field test seemed to be going well, and people involved had gained hope for the future.

The various teams made their way slowly through the town. The vanguards breached house after house, and the Banshee easily clearing any corrupted and spiderlings that targeted the group in the street. Things were going smoothly, until a yell could be heard from the house Bravo team was in the process of clearing.

A corrupted fell backwards out of the house with a duskshot buried in its chest, as one of the Bravo operatives shortly followed. He fervently clutched at a gaping wound on his arm, while blood flowed freely over his grip.

"Use a crystal!" Luke shouted, hoping to stop the man from a painful reawakening. Through the burning pain however, it seemed that his judgement was flawed. The operative quickly snatched the crystal from the chest of the fallen corrupted and pressed it against his wound."

"No!" Luke yelled, but it was too late. Rather than purifying the man's wound, the sated crystal instead emptied its stored corruption into the already infected operative.

His yell turned into a full-on scream as his joints all seemed to lock up in agony. The excess corruption formed a small cloud of shadows around him as the outline of his body could be seen changing. Muscle and tissue exploded outward from his entire body as they reformed into larger masses throughout.

The screams were now matched with the sounds of ripping and snapping as bone followed down the path of change; reshaping into a larger brutish form as it resolidified. As the man laid on the ground locked in torment, his screams slowly fell away. In their place, a deep roar slowly erupted from the mutated form. He stood back up in the now towering hulking shape of an abomination and turned to the group on the street.

The abomination charged as Emily swung her rifle around and fired a quick burst of crystalline shots at the creature. It was surprisingly quick given its size though, and managed to swat away the barrage before they could hit their mark.

Sabrina jumped back to give Emily a clearer sight of the creature as she tried again. Somehow this thing knew what she was trying to do though. With a deep guttural growl, the abomination lifted a large chunk of debris to shield itself in its rampage towards the exposed party.

Luke had to think fast, since for some reason the Banshee had no reaction to the assault. He realized why moments later, as they all dove out of the way of the massive arm that smashed down into the road at their location, leaving a small crater in its place.

Even though it was the same corruption that had infected the other people, they had given this one a different identity. The Banshee didn't think of it as a corrupted or a spiderling, the spirit viewed it as an abomination. Something entirely different.

Being entirely focused on avoiding getting smashed, Luke couldn't think of a way to explain this thing as a target now though. Instead, he yelled out "Protect us!" which was enough to get the Banshee's attention.

The three of them clutched their ears as the Banshee drew the abominations attention with a high-pitched scream. It was more controlled than some of the screams they had heard further away, but it still served its purpose.

With the abomination now charging the larger threat of the spirit, the Banshee made a laser focused flight directly at the beast.

The debris the abomination was using as a shield meant nothing to the specter, because it converted into its shadowy form and flew straight through the obstacle. The abomination dropped its shield as the Banshee continued onward... straight into the monster's hulking form.

A roar filled the air as Bravo team rushed out to reinforce the street and watched as the beast grabbed at its own chest.

A set of claws pierced outward from its right shoulder, before they quickly sliced along through the creature's chest and down to its abdomen. This motion repeated at various angles, as viscera flew from the abomination in every direction. It was almost as if it swallowed a massive blender. The deep guttural roars it spewed were slowly being choked out by the destruction being wrought within its form.

A set of claws then pierced straight up through the creature's head, and promptly swung straight down the center of its torso. Moments later, the beast collapsed in a pile of flesh, with the Banshee calmly floating where it once stood. The spirit pulled its clawed hands back down to its sides and hovered back over to Luke.

"What the actual fuck," Adam managed to get out through his shock, as everyone stared at either the pile of meat or the now calm Banshee. Luke, Sabrina, and Emily just kneeled on the ground breathing heavily from the workout of dodging the abomination's onslaught a moment earlier.

Luke was the first to stand up as he finally replied to Sabrina's earlier joke. "Yep, I think she does like me."

He then helped her up to her feet as she rolled her eyes at him, still catching her own breath.

Emily quickly hopped up as well, and the three of them reformed their position on the street. Luke looked toward Bravo team and thought this would be a good moment to pass on some information that was previously overlooked.

"So, in case it wasn't clear to anyone before. If you get wounded and need to stop the corruption from turning you, use a *fresh* crystal on your wound to purify it. Otherwise, you're just going to turn into one of those."

Luke accented his statement by pointing at the oozing pile of viscera that now laid on the ground. Nods were promptly returned from the semi-frozen Bravo team as they finally processed what had happened. Adam then directed them onto the next house, and they began the task of catching back up to Alpha team's progress.

The rest of the town's cleansing proceeded much smoother and more efficiently now. Corrupted and spiderlings were cleared from the houses by the vanguards as the Banshee continued cleaning the street of any outliers. Both teams had a few more injuries in the process, but no new abominations were created. John probably instructed his team already on how to purify any corrupted wounds; since he was present for both Luke's discovery of how it worked on the island, as well as the creation of the abomination in the warehouse.

With Bravo now informed on corrupted first aid as well, they managed to avoid any more hiccups along the way. By the time everyone had reached the far side of the town though, Luke counted three Alpha operatives and two Bravo that were left uninjured.

John managed to make it out unscathed, but Adam wasn't as lucky. A deep gash clear across his chest now bled profusely down the man's torso. The wound was obviously purified given that he had not turned, but he had to be quickly bandaged up before he lost too much blood.

"Ok, mission completed. Both teams aid your wounded and let's get back to the vans. Our field test was mostly a success, and the town will no longer be a threat to anyone." As Luke finished his statement, everyone joined him on the main road. The group then proceeded to make their way back to the direction they came from.

What they were not aware of however, was that about halfway through their path through the town, they had managed to walk into an exposed area. In the distance outside of town, the military's perimeter had watched their every move. A man prone on the ground now had a clear shot of any given party member.

The sniper on the outskirts had just been given a command relayed from the Director: These people were a threat, and the one controlling the Banshee was to be taken out when the opportunity arose. As he looked through his scope, the sniper adjusted his rifle until the crosshairs overlapped Luke's chest.

With a calm pull of the trigger, a shot fired off towards the group leader's heart.

Everyone's heads swiveled in the direction of the gunshot, as it was clearly not one of their Dawnbringer rifles. In the blink of an eye, the Banshee adjusted its position, and a bullet quickly hit its physical form. The shot then pierced through its body, before landing harmlessly on the ground behind it.

No sooner than the hole from the bullet closed, had the Banshee now let out a shriek. With the command "protect us" still floating around in its mind, the specter shot off in the direction of the assailant. The sniper saw its piercing gaze lock onto him, and his hands began to shake as the man turned from hunter to hunted.

Everyone in the party was now both confused as well as on edge due to the recently attempted assassination. Luke grabbed a pair of binoculars from one of the operatives so that he could follow the spirit's path with his eyes.

In the distance, he spotted the sniper at his post alongside a few more men. The militaristic group was well blended into the nearby foliage due to their camouflage.

"Oh shit, I think the military knows about us now," Luke stated as the sniper fired another round at the Banshee. The spirit completely ignored this, and a scream could be heard over the town as the Banshee entered the sniper and reformed.

Blood and flesh exploded in every direction, covering the remaining members of the perimeter control. Luke dropped the binoculars away from his eyes as chorus of screams followed. He knew that the Banshee would take out every single person in the group, and as it returned to the middle of the street calmly, everyone knew that the spirits objective was now complete.

With wounded being escorted back by the healthy operatives, the field test group managed the rest of their way through the town and back to where they had entered.

Luke picked up the crystal he had forgotten about earlier and held it up to the Banshee. "Uhh, get back in?" he stated, and it seemed like this simple command was enough. The Banshee returned to its shadowy form and promptly re-entered its controller crystal. Luke holstered it back onto his belt before he and John helped Adam back into the first van.

Once everyone was seated and the doors were shut, the convoy began to move. Back to headquarters they travelled with this new information and test results.

But more importantly, they were almost ready to take on the Phantom Hawk.

Chapter 19: The Landing

When the party entered the secret underground base upon their return, the wounded were promptly taken to the infirmary to get their injuries checked in a more sterile environment. John left as well to assist and check on his team members; making sure that they would be ok.

In the meantime, Luke, Sabrina, and Emily made their way to the command table where Lewis stood facing them.

"Welcome back, I assume all went well?" Lewis inquired; his eyes locked on Luke.

"Well, as well as it could have been I supposed. We did have one casualty due to an oversight into how the operatives were to treat a corrupted injury. After the resulting abomination was taken care of and the remaining members informed though, clearing the rest of the town proceeded smoothly. We had a large number of wounded, but it looks like they will hopefully all survive."

Luke paused for a moment to pull out the controller crystal on his waist before he continued. "The Banshee also performed better than expected. And while we don't know how it will do when faced with the Phantom Hawk, it fought its way through the creatures with ease. There was, however, an issue that arose upon leaving."

Lewis tilted his head as he listened. "Oh? What was the issue?"

Luke took a moment to organize his thoughts before he replied. "Well, the military had left a perimeter behind to keep an eye on the town it would seem. Furthermore, once we cleared the town, a sniper attempted to take us out. The Banshee did not take to this threat too kindly and killed them all, but I think it is safe to say that they are now aware of our existence. At the very least, they know we have the ability to control spirits better than they can."

This news caused Lewis to lean against the command table as he processed it, stroking the newly grown stubble across his chin as he opened his mouth to reply. "This is troubling news indeed. If they learn of our location, everything we have worked for could be lost. I'm afraid this means we will have to push the assault on the Phantom Hawk ahead of schedule. Luckily, we have finished making preparations for everyone, and we will be ready to brief later tonight."

Lewis then handed Luke an object he recognized as another controller crystal. "Our lab finished mass producing your design, let me know what you think."

Luke observed every small detail on the crystal as he rolled it around in his hand. The shape was correct, and although he couldn't check if the software was done right, it was an easy assumption. After all, he gave them his code. So, all they had to do was download it onto the device.

"Yea, this looks like a perfect replica of my prototype. How many have they made?"

Lewis replied, "They have finished at least fifty of them, with more to come. You and the specialists will be given six each. You three will have the better view in the battle, and the extras are in case you miss the first throw. We can't make it this far only to lose because our single weapon was lost. Now that they're approved though, we can finalize preparations for the mission. I suggest you go get some food and rest, as we will start the briefing at midnight. Shortly after, you will all head out for Japan."

With a nod Luke walked away to get some food, leaving Sabrina and Emily behind to pass along additional information as well as Sabrina's observations from the mission.

As he sat down in the cafeteria with his food, he realized just how exhausted he was. His arms felt like they were filled with lead as he lifted the fork to his mouth bite after bite. The room was mostly empty since most of the personnel were preparing for the trip to Japan. Which was convenient for Luke, as he had to focus entirely on eating to get his fork to his mouth accurately.

With the mission of eating now a success, Luke dropped his tray off with the other dirties and made his way back to his room.

Luke set aside his field outfit to get cleaned as his door shut, and walked to the back of the living area where the kitchen and dining portions were set up. The Banshee's controller crystal was then set back down, and he pulled the new, empty crystal out and pressed his thumb against the needle. Within moments this controller crystal was primed as well. Luke then set it on the table next to the Banshee's one.

With his preparations made, Luke flopped down onto the bed and quickly drifted off. Giving his body the nap, it craved.

A few hours later, Luke sat up in bed as he stretched and yawned. The nap was much needed, and he could easily sleep for longer. However, the briefing was in twenty minutes, and he had to get dressed. Seeing as the journey was all the way to Japan this time, it would be easy finish sleeping on the journey.

Luke had a weird dream regardless, and he could have sworn that someone stood over his bed earlier in the night. But when he looked around the room, everything seemed to still be in place, and nothing was there to threaten him. It must have been the cleaners bringing back his outfit for the mission.

With his long coat now draped around his form and utility belt in place, Luke grabbed the crystals he left on his table and once more seated them next to each other in the holsters along his waist. One last check across his room told him that he had gathered everything needed, and the door was opened and shut as Luke made his way down the hall to the command room.

John and Adam were already inside and stood slightly behind Lewis, the three of them facing a room full of chairs with the desks pushed aside to make room.

As Luke approached them, he noted that this was going to be more of a full-on battle than a small mission. Looking around the room, there had to be at least 50 seats in the center.

Personnel were still slowly filing in, talking amongst themselves. The more serious people at the briefing were discussing the upcoming mission and the possibilities it involved, as well as the risks. While the less seasoned members of the organization mostly talked about their plans upon return; mostly involving an excessive amount of drinking.

Lewis motioned for Luke to stand by his side, and he quickly took this new position in front of the room.

Once more, Luke peered around the room, and he spotted Sabrina and Emily mixed in with the regulars. Although with their individual specialist outfits they did not blend in well, and broke free from the entourage to flank Luke and Lewis; with Sabrina joining Luke's side and Emily standing off by Lewis. Eventually, the line of people thinned out before ultimately disappearing, and everyone had taken their seats and focused on Lewis as he began to speak.

"Here we finally are, with mission after mission behind us gathering intel and testing our new weaponry. The time has come for us to begin our assault on the Phantom Hawk. As our most recent intelligence indicates, it is currently still taking up residence above the city of Tokyo. The vehicle of choice for making the journey there is a C-130, which we have obtained access to for the purpose of this mission. It has the capacity to easily hold everyone and their gear for the mission."

Hushed whispers could be heard throughout the room, as clearly this was new for the organization as a whole to be taking such a massive strike force. Luke himself was excited at the prospect of flying in the aircraft of choice, as he never once thought of joining the military. Because of this, he did not expect to ever get the opportunity to experience the kind of vehicle he would now be in.

The whispers died back down slowly as Lewis continued the briefing.

"We will be using Haneda Airport in Tokyo for our landing zone since it gives us the shortest journey to reach the Phantom Hawk. Because of its proximity to ground zero, however, prepare to be assaulted the moment you touch down by the corrupted in the surrounding areas. Your objective will first be to secure the site and set up a forward camp for this operation.

"The Phantom Hawk will not be an easy objective, and this entire mission may take longer than expected. As such, special crates of food will be provided that are lined with a crystal barrier to prevent contamination in such a corruption heavy zone. Prior to disembarking from the aircraft, also ensure your helmets are in place. With such a close proximity to the Phantom Hawks aura, even momentary exposure could easily turn you into one of its thralls."

Luke followed Lewis' gesture as he motioned at a few open crates. It would seem the helmets were prepared just in time for this final mission.

While they matched the colors of Luke's outfit and the general semi-gloss look, they definitely did not match the design. His clothing fit more into the wasteland theme of their mission, and the helmets very much resembled what you would see riot teams wearing. It did, however, match the more simplified outfit the main force of operatives would be wearing.

Luke noted all of this to himself before Lewis folded his arm back in and continued.

"The commanding officer in the field as well as the man in charge of spearheading the mission here is Luke. He has proven himself a competent leader in every mission he has gone on since joining the organization. He is also the mind behind virtually every tool we now have against the Phantom Hawk. The Banshee under his control has also recently been tested in the field and will prove a valuable asset in your assault."

Lewis then waved his arm in Sabrina's direction. "Sabrina is the next in command. Her experience in observation and quick thinking under pressure has earned her the position in charge of navigation and communications. She will be keeping in touch and reporting back to those of us who remain here. Just in case plans change or reinforcements are required."

Luke had wondered what Sabrina's role would be now that they were no longer gathering information for the assault. His assumption had been that she would be more of a field tutor to the small army, but this new role would suit her just as well.

She had also been the only person Luke knew that had been to Japan anyway. He himself never travelled far since he was mostly a shut in and focused heavily on his ghost hunting hobby. That, and the crystal invention which led him down this path into a secret war for the survival of humanity.

Lewis cleared his throat and gestured next to Emily. "Emily here will function primarily as Luke's personal guard because he is the sole person able to control the Banshee and thus his survival is the most vital. He also has the most experience with the controller crystals; considering he has both created them as well as actively tested their usage in the field."

Lewis detoured as he continued to describe Emily's role. "When scouting and covert ops are required however, Emily will be the strike force leader. Not only does she have expansive experience in the organization, but she is our most skilled member in terms of subterfuge and assassination. If covert ops are necessary, she will hand pick a team from you to craft a strike force with. For more typical battle situations, John will be your commanding officer."

Lewis followed this statement with a hand wave in John's direction, who nodded to the room in response.

"John is also new to the organization but has proven his skill with the Dawnbringer rifle you will all be carrying. He has also shown aptitude with leading vanguards during prior missions. His efficiency in combat will help us to minimize casualties, as well as give us the tactical edge we will need against the army of corrupted."

Once more Lewis paused, and Luke noticed that Adam was missing from the room. Given the size of his wound, it would make sense if he was not on this mission. However, Luke had come to appreciate the calm aura Adam gave to the missions he had been on with the party.

"Adam was to join John in dual command on the battlefield, however he was injured in our last mission. As such, he will be receiving treatment at our outpost in South Korea with a helicopter on standby. During his time in the military's paranormal division, he had received extensive flight training. With these skills, he will oversee object recovery. Once the Phantom Hawk has been captured, Adam will ferry the crystal containing it back here, while the assault force waits for a larger craft to retrieve them."

Luke wondered as to why the controller crystal would be taken first. Would the corrupted somehow still be a threat once the Phantom Hawk was removed? What could possibly threaten the loss of the crystal? He mentally slapped himself however, as Lewis' next statement reminded him that the Phantom Hawk was not the only factor involved in all of this.

"Prior to the briefing, we have received word that the military has finished their design of a new harness for the Broodmother. As such, they will be attempting to stage their own mission in the coming days to use it against the Phantom Hawk and regain control of both spirits. The crystal with the Phantom Hawk will be removed from location in case they show up after the mission is completed and attempt to take it from us."

A display of the Broodmother now showed above the command table as Lewis continued to speak. "There is also the possibility that they will once more lose control of the Broodmother, in which case we will need to safely extract the crystal to ensure it does not get destroyed. The Broodmother does not have the same infectious reach as the Phantom Hawk, which makes it a lot easier to contain on the island than its flying brethren."

Lewis then paused for a momentary thought before he finished his briefing with a personal note.

"Understand that not all of you will make it back from this. We are facing an immensely powerful threat in territory where it ultimately has the advantage. A threat we have never in the history of our species had to face before. But know that your sacrifice if you fall, will be rewarded with the survival of humanity. You will not only be saving your brothers and sisters in arms, but also everyone worldwide. I thank you for this... and pray for your safe return."

An operative walked down the stairs and quickly whispered into Lewis' ear. With a nod Lewis dismissed the man, and then turned back to the room full of waiting personnel.

"The vans are outside and ready to take you to the airstrip to board. Everyone is dismissed, and we will be waiting back here for your success."

Following this, Lewis pulled Luke aside as everyone else began grabbing helmets and exiting upstairs to where the vans would be. He placed a hand on Luke's shoulder and looked him in the eyes with a grave expression as he began to speak in a hushed tone.

"Just to let you know Luke, there has been a slight hiccup in our plans. It seems that a fatal flaw has been discovered in the quartz we used to produce the supply of controller crystals. The one I handed you was produced from one of your own crystals on a separate shipment, and as such is the only working one we currently have. Protect it well and make absolutely sure you hit your mark with it. There might not be a second chance."

With this Lewis walked off, leaving Luke even more stressed with the stakes at hand. The Phantom Hawk would probably have to be weakened first, and as such would be less likely to avoid the crystal when he threw it. Regardless though, this did not make things any easier.

Luke grabbed his own helmet and strode up the staircase to the hunting cabin above as he tried to keep a calm composure.

Outside, the only lights seen were the headlights of the full convoy of vans that stretched down the road. That and the moonlight given off amidst the clear skies above.

Luke looked up as he walked towards the front van, gazing at the full moon, and wondering if it was a sign of luck or a curse for their mission. Did nature want them to win? Or was the world sick of humanity and this was its way to remove such a widespread pest?

Luke's thoughts continued as he hopped into the van, the door closing behind him, and engines starting as the convoy began its journey to the airstrip.

"Are you excited?" Emily asked, clearly less affected by the importance and stress of the mission than everyone else. She had been involved in many field missions already though, so this could have probably been expected. For someone used to this life, an assault of this proportion must have felt empowering more than anything else.

Luke, however, was nervous. So were John and Sabrina, judging by the looks they wore upon their faces.

"I'm ready, although I wouldn't say I'm excited." Luke stated, with matching nods coming from the other members of the command group.

John laid his Dawnbringer rifle across his lap and leaned back in his chair. "On one hand, we have faced creatures no one could have ever believed existed before and come out on top. On the other though, this is the Phantom Hawk itself we are talking about.

Everything we have fought before was simply its creation--barring the spiderlings."

Sabrina joined in on John's observation, further hypothesizing the possible issues involved with this demigod.

"More importantly, the creatures weren't even created through active influence by the Phantom Hawk. It was simply its aura that corrupted the living around it. Who knows exactly what kind of power it has when confronted and forced into a battle itself. Whether the aura was intentional or not, we can expect more destructive actions from it when we threaten the spirit inside its newly owned territory. Some hawks in our world are known to be fiercely territorial, and judging by previous actions the Phantom Hawk may follow that ideology."

Emily leaned back with her arms folded behind her head as she spoke now.

"Well think about it this way. We should enter this assuming we will succeed. If we win, then the world is saved, and we have experienced things most people couldn't even imagine. If we lose, then there is nothing we can do anyway. The world will end, and the problem will go away with our extinction."

Luke nodded as he processed this. While that was a pretty bleak way to view failure, she was right. It wasn't as if they would come back home to an onslaught of hatred from the general public. No one knew about their mission, or even the organization's existence for that matter.

Except for maybe the military, but that would only pose a problem now if they succeeded. Somehow Emily's comments gave Luke a twisted sense of calm, and his nerves relaxed slightly at this new viewpoint.

Their journey was fairly short as there was no traffic at this time of night. Most of the trip was through backcountry anyway, but even the towns they drove through were quiet. The people filling the population of the areas were calmly asleep, unaware of the events unfolding that would decide their fates in the coming days.

There was a shift in the terrain below their van, which Luke assumed was the airstrip, judging by the sudden drop in speed of the vehicle. A few moments later, the van came to a stop, and Emily hopped up to slide the van door open and jump out.

Luke followed suit and was quickly awestruck as the aircraft they would be taking came into view. It was massive; a rounded nose leading into probably a hundred feet of mankind's ingenuity.

As they walked under one of the giant wings jutting from the side of the craft, Luke couldn't help but tilt his head back and let his eyes wander across the machination again. Excitement welled up inside him, as this experience was new and ultimately a thrilling one. While the plane itself was probably much smaller than the commercial ones used daily at this airport, he had not actually stood near them like this before. The gate that led to the door of the planes he had been on was elevated, and mostly obstructed the external view of the vehicles.

The rear of the plane opened as they approached, and Luke staggered for a moment to get one last look at the outside of the C-130 before he climbed the metal ramp into the transport bay.

Once inside, Luke's boots clattered against the metal floor as he made his walk up into the body of the plane. Once at the deepest point of the craft, he sat in a seat to his left and strapped the harness-like seatbelt into place with a series of clicks.

Sabrina took up the seat next to him, as John and Emily sat across the way on the right side of the plane. Everyone followed suit and buckled up as the remaining personnel filed in from the rest of the vans and into their own respective seats. This mission was a massive undertaking, and the number of people coming along was unreal.

Once everyone was seated, supply crates were then filled into the plane. All designed with the same crystalline barrier in their walls to protect the contents from the Phantom Hawk's aura. A final check was made that everything was on board, and the back door of the craft was secured.

"This is Flightdeck One to Invasion One, we are cleared for takeoff at your command."

The voice came from Luke's radio he had forgotten about at his side. With a quick look around the room to make sure everyone was secured and ready, he keyed his microphone to reply. "This is Invasion One, we are all clear and ready for takeoff."

"Copy that," the voice spoke over the radio.

Seconds later, Luke could hear the engines on the wings begin winding up. The mild humming of the idle engines slowly grew into a muted roar that could be easily heard through the metal walls. A slight jerking motion followed, and the plane moved to take its place at the end of one of the nearby runways.

A few minutes passed as the plane waited to be cleared by the air traffic controller. As soon as the wheels began moving again, everyone knew that it was finally time to take off.

The engines picked up in sound as the craft shook with the motion. Their speed increased rapidly as they sped along the runway before a sudden drop in Luke's stomach had told him that the plane had finally left the ground. The aircraft climbed into the sky steadily, and eventually a change in motion told Luke that they had reached the desired altitude.

Luke sat back and closed his eyes as the flight continued onward. The motion of the plane in the slight turbulence rocked him into a calm state as the excitement of the start of the adventure slowly faded away. His tiredness now caught up with him as he processed the flight in his head.

They would arrive probably close to midday in Tokyo, with a refueling midflight. Luke knew that some variants of the C-130 could do in-flight refueling, and judging by their flight distance he assumed this was one of those variants. However, the thoughts racing through his mind slowly faded out as sleep took over.

An unknown number of hours later, Luke awoke to a small thud against the plane. He realized that they were probably in the refueling stage somewhere over the Pacific Ocean.

As the various sounds came in from the plane being refueled and then freed to continue its journey, Luke began to drift back off into his sleep. The exhaustion from the constant stress and excitement of his last couple of weeks finally took its toll.

The last thought to cross his mind was that he would probably sleep through the entire flight as he once again drifted off.

"We're hit! We're Hit! Brace for impact!"

The words came over an intercom system just as Luke awoke to a massive jerk in the aircrafts motion. He scrambled to grab his radio as he keyed the microphone. "Copy that! What's going on?", he asked as he looked around the room to make sure everyone was aware of the situation.

Emily wore a serious face, as she mentally prepared for the change in plans, while Sabrina and John looked worried and in disbelief. Who would attack them? Was it the Phantom Hawk?

Luke's radio sparked life as they received the troubling news.

"We are being assaulted by American fighter jets! Prepare for a crash landing!"

"Shit," Luke stated as realization struck him. The perimeter at the village must have relayed enough information for the military to track this mission. They were going to try to blow this mission out of the air so that they could take on the Phantom Hawk and capture it themselves.

Another explosion struck as it blew away a massive hole towards the back of the plane. A handful of operatives seated in the area were quickly sucked out from the hole where their seats were once secured. Most were dead on impact, but screams could be heard from the living as they were pulled out to their inevitable deaths below.

The roar of the engines could be heard more clearly now, however the sound slowly faded away as they started failing.

"We are going down! Everyone brace for impact!" Came over the intercom once more.

"Where are we?!" Luke spoke into his radio; since being stranded in the middle of the ocean was an easy way to fail the mission before it could truly begin.

"We are approaching the coast of Japan! We will try to make a landing on the water!"

Not the worst place to have a crash Luke guessed, but this was a problem, nonetheless. "Everyone get your helmets on!" Luke shouted over the noise of the wind, as he quickly strapped his own helmet into place upon his head. It may not do much in the crash, but if they landed within the Phantom Hawk's aura the last thing they needed was for any survivors to be killed by corrupted operatives.

Everyone quickly followed his command as another explosion rocked the aircraft. More chunks of wall exploded off the side of the vehicle as additional personnel were sent flying below to their doom.

Moments after, the nose of the plane dipped as the engines fully failed.

Now in a freefall, the pilots wrestled to control the craft and ease their landing.

Luke looked out the holes to see that the fighter jets, satisfied with the motion of the now plummeting C-130, quickly turned around to make their way back to home base. The assault was now over, but the pilots had yet to regain any semblance of control. In the windowless bay of the plane, all they could do was hope for the best as they continued falling. The plummet was even more nerve wracking since they were unable to see the distance to the ground.

After what seemed like an eternity, the plane shifted to a more stable fall and started to glide. The pilots had managed to regain some control, and now straightened the plane for a relatively calm landing.

Luke looked out of the damaged walls to see that they were quickly approaching the surface of the ocean. The plane bounced off the water's surface a few times, as things looked like they would turn out ok.

The mood soured again however, as the nose of the plane clipped an unseen rock that jutted from the water. Within moments, the craft lost the remainder of its momentum as it skipped across the surface of the water. The metal walls screamed as it tumbled until with one loud smash, the side of the plane hit another rock and split.

As the portion of plane Luke was in flew through the air, the last thing he could see was the ground of the coast quickly approaching.

With one final crash, the segment landed on soil, and Luke was knocked unconscious by the impact.

Chapter 20: Wasteland

The world slowly returned to Luke's eyes as he woke up from the knockout. He blinked as his blurred vision sharpened; the sun now glaring overhead as a heavy throbbing pain shot through his head. Luke clutched at the helmet and waited for the headache to dull, as he was unable to move or focus in his current state.

Eventually, the pain had subsided enough for him to concentrate, although he now realized his entire body ached from the crash. Luckily however, it seemed that he escaped from their situation relatively unharmed, with only minor scratches and bruises over his body.

Luke followed this self-check by peering around to make himself more acquainted with his surroundings.

Waves crashed against the beach he was now seated on. All along the shoreline, bodies were strewn in every which way of operatives that were not as lucky as himself. The assortment of debris mixed in with the corpses also told Luke why he woke up on sand. It appeared that the portion of the plane they crashed in had shattered upon its impact.

Luke's heart sank as he looked to his left. A short distance away, Sabrina lay in the sand motionless.

With a pained crawl, Luke made his way over and shook her shoulder. "Sabrina, Sabrina" he repeated, fearing the worst after seeing the results of the crash. Luke laid his head on her shoulder as she remained unresponsive, despair slowly creeping into his mind.

He lifted his head a moment later though when he thought he heard a subtle groan. Then, Sabrina blinked as a louder groan escaped her lips. Relief washed over Luke as he moved her onto her back, checking to make sure she wasn't seriously wounded.

It seemed her luck was similar to his own however, as she laid still and waited for the pains of the crash to dull.

Luke once again swept his gaze across the shoreline, and he realized that not everyone was dead. John and Emily were already seated and recovering further down the beach, with operatives slowly doing the same throughout the area.

Luke caught the attention of one operative that seemed to be even luckier than himself and beckoned him over, as this man was already standing and walking around.

"Check anyone not getting up on their own. If any of them are still alive, check them over for serious wounds and help them if possible."

The operative answered Luke's command with a salute, as he turned down the beach and began checking motionless bodies.

Now remembering that this wasn't friendly territory, Luke turned his gaze past the beach and to the land beyond. What he saw from here was something that could have only been pulled from nightmares.

Dilapidated houses lined streets filled with abandoned cars in the coastal town. Although the skies were clear and the sun shined overhead, it looked like dusk had already settled beyond the sand of the beach. Almost as if the corruption had infected the air itself... The corruption that also infected everything in sight.

This area reminded Luke of the island, as he took note of the armored grayish bark that plated the trees rooted between rows of houses. The grass along the sidewalks and yards shined against the low light. In addition, no motion could be spotted in the wind as grass stood in defiance to the natural order.

Luke continued looking around and saw that bushes and flowers turned into the same bloodthirsty, thorn ridden monstrosities that attacked them on the island before. Apparently the specific species of the plant life did not matter for what form they took when corrupted, only the general category.

Bushes all became blood draining balls of thorns; flowers gained the recognizable center spike that acted as an infected grappling hook.

John and Emily made their way over to Luke and Sabrina as Luke finished his visual sweep of the village. There was no immediate threat nearby, so they could gather their bearings and prepare for what to do next in relative safety.

"How do you feel?," Luke asked Sabrina as she started to sit up.

"Well, my head is killing me. But I guess things could have been worse. Let me try to see where we landed," she finished her statement as she pulled a map and GPS out from a large pocket on the inside of her coat. Coordinates showed up on the screen as she compared them to the detailed map in front of her, before pointing to a portion of coast on the eastern edge of Japan.

"It looks like we crashed just outside of the coastal city of Choshi. Not accounting for hostiles or other obstacles, it would take us a little over 24 hours to reach Tokyo on foot. We will also be slowed down a bit by the fact that we will now have to carry our supplies the entire distance."

Luke nodded to her statement as he looked off towards the city while thinking.

"Maybe we can find something to make travel a bit easier. The streets look to be too cluttered for a car to pass through, but a few wagons or something similar would make it far quicker and easier to transport what we need."

As the group of friends tried to plan their next course of action, the operative finished his sweep of the beach. Luke counted twenty personnel recovered and approaching their location. A mere fraction of the initial assault force, but far better than Luke initially expected when he awoke to the scene of bodies.

Luke directed the operatives to gather what they could find of the supply crates and weapons that survived the crash, as he pulled four of the operatives and Emily to join him in going to the town and searching for something wheeled to ease their travels.

Everyone except Luke assigned to the small search party grabbed a Dawnbringer rifle. Luke instead pulled out the Banshee's controller crystal and tossed it in the air.

In a puff of black smoke, the spirit appeared in the air before everyone. Luke picked up the crystal from the ground and holstered it as he commanded the Banshee to stay quiet and protect the group. As before, his only answer from the calm spirit was its cold piercing stare. Which was plenty for him, as he felt as if the Banshee was truly bonded to him. Luke had no way to explain it, but it seemed like he could even understand the spirit without speaking now.

The party made their way up the beach towards the town as everyone else busied themselves gathering what undamaged supplies they could find. Luke led the group up a small hill to the nearby road; on his right was Emily, as the Banshee took up his left. The four operatives he pulled filed in behind these three, rifles at the ready in case an assault came.

Luke motioned for everyone to head towards the houses nearby, since someone's yard or garage could possibly have what they were looking for.

The group strolled from house to house in the barren town, quietly searching for anything that could fit their purpose. Unfortunately, nothing was even remotely close to the kind of object they were looking for.

The occasional garage had tools in it, while others were used as storage space for old children's toys and discarded decorations related to various holidays.

The group thought that they had hit the jackpot when a garage door opened to reveal a trailer, however it was only a boat trailer. The open center and angled walls of it were designed specifically to

196

hold the rounded shape of a boat's hull. This shape would make it near impossible to fit their supplies on it without an extensive time investment to rebuild it. A time investment they could not afford, given their already heavily delayed mission.

The party made their way through the streets once more, passing a few gas stations along the way. Luke had really wished the streets were clear as he viewed the pumps and blockade of abandoned cars. Being able to just drive off to Tokyo would have made this journey so much easier.

As the six of them continued deeper into town, what looked like a small home improvement store started to fill their vision. If anywhere had what they needed, it would be there.

Luke quietly motioned the new direction and the party set off. While it seemed like the town was abandoned long before the corruption spread here, they had to be careful just in case. The last thing they needed was for their small group to be swarmed by a veritable army of creatures. The Banshee could move quick, but not that quick, and they would surely be overwhelmed within moments.

Once they got closer to the store, Luke sighed quietly as he noticed barricades in front of the doors. Wooden boards were nailed hurriedly along the windows to seal them off as well. These would take time to clear, so they decided to check the back of the store first. Maybe there would be a lumber yard they could enter from more easily, or perhaps a few wagons or wheelbarrows would be stored outside for sale.

Luck seemed to be on their side; for as soon as the group turned the corner of the building, they discovered a flatbed trailer. It was only large enough to carry maybe four of the crates in a single stack. If they doubled up the crates, it could probably handle the weight of eight containers instead. However, this smaller trailer was a benefit, seeing as they would still have to haul the trailer itself without a vehicle. A smaller trailer meant less starting weight, and even with wheels a full 24 hours of travel time would surely exhaust the operatives before they ever reached Tokyo.

When the group neared the trailer, Luke swore he could hear a thud sound in the distance. Curiosity took over, and they did a sweep around the far side of the store to see if they missed something. They had not run into any corrupted yet, but that might have just been blind luck.

As the party returned to the front of the store without finding anything, the thud came through again. Albeit this time it was much louder, and Luke had a realization as he swung his head quickly to the left.

The reason they had not seen any corrupted yet was because of the town's emergency protocols. The home improvement store was barricaded because that was where everyone gathered during a crisis. As Luke squinted his eyes and looked more closely at the store front, he could see the empty shadowed eyes of hundreds of corrupted.

"Get back to the beach! Now!" He yelled, as a dagger-like claw from one of the creatures shattered a window. The boards would hold off the creatures for the party to get a head start, but not nearly long enough to keep them safe.

Luke looked up and watched as the Banshee quickly flew past his head and down the road to the beach. He began cursing to himself as realization struck for what he had just done. With the broad nature of his command, he had also accidentally sent their best weapon away.

The group sprinted as Luke pulled his radio out from his belt, hoping that Sabrina's wasn't damaged in the crash as he keyed the microphone.

"Sabrina it's Luke come in!" He managed mid sprint. Moments later Sabrina's voice could be heard over the radio as a hint of worry could be heard in her tone.

"Luke what is it? We thought something happened when the Banshee came back without you all. Is everything ok?"

As she finished her statement, Luke keyed his microphone once more to reply. "We found the corrupted, prepare everyone for an attack! I accidentally sent the Banshee ahead and there's hundreds of them coming!"

As Luke finished this statement he holstered the radio. The group made their way across the parking lot. When they started running along the neighborhood sidewalk once more, a crash could be heard behind them. The corrupted had broken free from their barriers.

With how quick the monsters were able to move, the group had a slim chance at making it back to the beach.

Shrieks could be heard in the distance behind them as the corrupted tracked their prey fervently. Gear shifting could be heard behind Luke as the rear-guard operatives readied their Dawnbringer rifles; the sounds of the swarm now growing even closer.

The party had made it roughly one block towards the beach, with three or four more to go. Luke looked back just as the massive wave of teeth and claws rounded the corner where the parking lot was located. At this pace, they wouldn't even make it halfway before they were overwhelmed.

Emily must have had the same thought, as she held up a closed fist for a moment before pushing Luke to keep running.

Luke was confused by this, however he quickly understood what she did when he looked over his shoulder again. Lewis' words from the briefing ran through his mind once more.

Luke was to be protected at all costs.

When the four operatives in the rear guard spun on their heels and readied their rifles, he realized her command was for them to hold the line. Within moments, screams could be heard from the first few corrupted as the operatives opened fire.

One by one creatures fell, but the firing line simply did not have enough people in it and was quickly overrun. Luke looked over his shoulder once more as screams of the operatives filled the air; blood splattering as limbs were torn free. The defensive personnel were quickly mutilated as if the mass of hostiles was a biological sawblade.

However, this gave Luke and Emily the time they needed to create some distance.

The corrupted began to give chase again, and by the time the two survivors had reached the final road that ran along the beach, the army was only a few short paces behind them. As one of the creatures reached out with its dagger-like talons, the pair jumped across the last strip of land before the hill and rolled down the terrain to the sand of the coastline.

Luke noticed mid fall that Sabrina had heeded his warning well, for the remaining operatives had now formed a full-sized firing squad. Rifles were at the ready and began to open fire the moment the corrupted came into view.

"Attack the corrupted!" Luke yelled as he pointed in the general direction of where he came from. His command replied was to with a shriek from the Banshee as it promptly dove towards the mass.

Bodies from the creatures began to pile up as the flurry of crystals fired dropped them one by one. The Banshee had made its way to the mob as well and began swooping and tearing through the creatures. It was much faster than them, and the few that tried to fight back missed their mark repeatedly. Blackened blood sprayed and oozed in every direction as the Banshee returned the favor for the deaths of the rear guard; tearing limb from limb towards the middle of the pack while crystals dropped anything in the front.

The corrupted could no longer gain any ground as their numbers dwindled rapidly, and within a few moments the firing had stopped.

The only thing standing now in the pile of purified bodies and eviscerated corpses was the Banshee, which hovered calmly to Luke's side as he kneeled on the ground to catch his breath.

"We found... a trailer," Luke managed through labored breathes as he stopped to recover. His body had still been sore from the crash, which made the run take a greater toll on his muscles than normal. After all, they were still in the middle of repairing from prior injuries.

Sabrina and John helped Luke and Emily back to their feet as Luke finally recovered enough to finish his statement.

"We found a trailer around the back of a home improvement store. Large enough to carry four crates, eight if double stacked. The townsfolk must have barricaded themselves inside the store when the Phantom Hawk arrived though, because the building was sealed shut and filled with creatures. We lost four operatives as they held the line for our retreat, but I think that attack was the majority of the corrupted in the area."

Luke looked around now to count sixteen operatives remaining and sighed. They had made virtually no progress so far and were already down one fifth of the troops that survived the crash.

About halfway down the beach was a pile of crates, nine in total still secured shut. A tenth one sat open next to the stack, which contained the rifles the operatives were now carrying. Two of the crates were labelled as food, while another two contained a supply of water. Four of the remaining containers had supplies for setting up a camp, and the last one was marked as ammunition.

Given the depleted number of people left, this would be plenty of supplies. At least for the next couple days. They might have to ration things cautiously later, but tonight everyone needed as much energy as they could obtain in order to recover from the crash.

"Set up camp on the road at the top of the hill. It will give us a better vantage point for the evening. Tonight, we will rest and recover from the crash, tomorrow we load up the trailer and head for the Phantom Hawk."

The operatives then shouldered their firearms and set to work unloading the crates containing tables, tents, and other base camp supplies at the top of the hill.

The sun was now beginning its descent into night, and soon they wouldn't be able to see anything. Even if they weren't injured, a low light start to their journey assured disaster if they came across any more creatures. They could use the night to recover and set out at sunrise the next day.

As the four friends made their way up the hill to the camp being built, Luke took another look around the town.

While the search party had cautiously avoided the flowers on their way out, it had seemed that none of the spike wielding plants faced the road and sidewalks they sprinted down on their retreat. They had lucked out, for in their hurried state no one was aware of the booby traps strewn about.

As Luke took a closer look at the grass, he realized why it stood so rigid against the wind. Each individual blade of grass was now a literal blade; razor sharp and stiffened in its corrupted state. A look down at his boots made him realize that he was lucky he had not tripped on the way back, for cuts now crossed every which way in the thick material of his footwear. One stumble and he would have looked like he went five rounds with a blender.

The first structure to be finished was a tent top covering a fold out table. With this completed Sabrina walked over and laid the map out.

"I believe that we can avoid most of the remaining larger cities between here and Tokyo if we take this route." With pen in hand, she drew a line down a path of roads which would surely speed their journey along. Less corrupted meant less losses before Tokyo, as well as hopefully less cars blocking their path. The trailer would be difficult enough to transport as is without having to weave between cars and blockades the entire way.

Over the next hour the sun made its way behind the horizon. With dusk settled in, the remainder of the camp had been set up and was ready for their period of rest.

A few of the operatives worked together to cook a warm meal. Luke grabbed a plate full of the delicious smelling food before sitting down with his friends nearby. Not much discussion was had around the table other than what was necessary to plan the start of their trip tomorrow. Mostly because everyone was still worn out from the day's excitement.

With dinner finished and the sun fully set, darkness took over and the first group of operatives had been assigned watch. Luke commanded the Banshee to assist the watch as well, seeing as the spirit itself did not need to rest like the human members of the contingent.

With everything in place, Luke made his way to his tent. He had expected John to join him and was surprised when, instead, Sabrina walked over.

"John said he would join the operatives in case things went south overnight, so you're stuck with me."

Sabrina finished her statement with a tired smile as Luke lifted the flap of the tent, returning her gesture.

Since the tents were specially made to reflect any corruption, the pair were able to kick off their boots and lay down a little more comfortably. Luke removed his utility belt, but the remainder of their clothes remained on in case they needed to react quickly to an assault in the night.

Once Luke laid down on his back, Sabrina unexpectantly laid on his shoulder. Her head rested against his chest as their breathing calmed down. Luke proceeded to kiss the top of her head as he stroked her hair for a moment, the motion slowing before coming to a stop as his mind slipped from thoughts of the day to the feeling of exhaustion which now fully spread through his body.

His thoughts faded off into the abyss as the exhaustion won over, and the pair slipped into a deep and restful sleep.

Chapter 21: The Journey

Luke awoke just as the sun peered over the horizon, daylight slowly spreading across the camp. He shook Sabrina awake and laughed at the tangled mess her hair had become during the night.

In reply, she groggily rolled her eyes at him and flopped back down, while he slid his boots and helmet back on and stepped out into the morning air. As some of the operatives from the last watch were already preparing breakfast, Luke crossed the camp to the smell of sausage and eggs.

"Good morning," Luke stated to the operatives. They returned his greeting in kind while he grabbed some of the prepared food. The night's rest worked like a miracle drug, and his body felt renewed from its pains the day before.

With food in hand, he made his way over to the command table and map just as Sabrina stepped out of the tent, her hair in a much better state. Or at least, Luke had assumed, given that he could only see some of it flow down from beneath the helmet she wore.

"Theres's food ready," Luke stated with a smile as she sleepily waved to him in acknowledgement. Sabrina then hungrily walked in the direction of the tantalizing smell.

"You two have a good night?" John asked with a wink as he came to Luke's side with his own food.

Luke cleared his mouth and answered John's implicative joke a little more seriously than he intended. "I slept like a rock to be honest. Between yesterday's crash and almost becoming food myself, I was exhausted. Today should be better I would think though. At the very least, it isn't like we can crash again."

"Ain't that the truth," John returned as Sabrina joined the pair. Emily was off in the distance waking the remaining operatives up and directing everyone to eat and then pack up the camp, it would seem she wasted no time getting back to business.

Sabrina tapped Luke's shoulder to grab his attention as she swallowed the mouthful of food she had. "Oh, by the way, I forgot to mention something in the heat of the moment yesterday. We found a long-range radio and were able to get into contact with Adam. Headquarters is aware of our predicament and will attempt to send us a resupply. This time by sea to avoid another air assault on us."

"Oh, that's great news actually," Luke replied. A sigh of relief escaped his lips as hope was renewed that they would have enough personnel in Tokyo when the time came.

Once Emily had finished her rounds and joined the other three, they went over the plan for the morning once more, before Sabrina packed away her navigational tools to make room for the operatives to pack up this area as well.

Around the time the clearing filled with a warm orange light, the camp had finally been packed away in its crates, and everything was ready to be transported. The plan was simple; two operatives each would carry crates the few blocks to the four-wheeled trailer they had spotted the day before. John and Emily would assist now that they did not have enough people for all the crates due to the losses they took the day prior. In the meantime, Sabrina and Luke would act as a caravan guard in case an attack came during the short trip. The Banshee, which had just now hovered back over to Luke with no camp to guard, would be plenty defense for them against any stragglers that were left behind by the army of corrupted.

Once the trailer was loaded, half the operatives would pull it while the other half acted as a vanguard. Trading places throughout the day to prevent exhaustion from setting in.

With the crates lifted, Sabrina and Luke split to the sides of the encumbered group as they started their journey into the dusk shaded town. Luke made sure to alert everyone of the hazard the grass posed, and suggested they stick to the main road to avoid any run ins with the bushes or flowers that also laid in wait. The last thing they needed was to lose more people to such an easily avoided threat.

The walk through the neighborhood blocks was mostly uneventful. Although, the pile of flesh that used to be four of their operatives had started to rot as they came upon the location where they held the line of defense.

Luke noted a swarm of flies around the stench, which were corrupted just like the rest of the environment. Their wings clicked from their hardened, new shape, and the sound continued as their elongated bodies dove down into the meal.

They looked more like armored dragonflies now, with the addition of a large set of blade-like jaws they used to cut up the rotting tissue into more manageable pieces. Luke pointed them out to Sabrina so that she could take notes on anything important just in case these became a future threat. For now, though, this swarm seemed content with simply enjoying the meal left behind from the previous day.

With the swarm of razorflies avoided, the party continued their way to the open parking lot. A few corrupted wandered about seemingly lost, but they were easily handled by the Banshee as Luke commanded it to clear the way. With a few quick swoops, what was once a major threat to them become piles of eviscerated goo, and the Banshee returned once more to Luke's side.

The group then made their way through the parking lot and around the home improvement store. They then finally set their sights on the trailer waiting on the other side.

One by one the operatives unloaded the crates from their arms. A base level of four crates was laid down, followed by another four crates stacked neatly on top. John helped one of the taller operatives heave the ninth crate onto the peak of the stack, seeing as he stood probably a foot above most of the rest of the group in height.

With the trailer fully loaded, eight of the operatives took to the sides and back of it as the remaining eight unshouldered their rifles and stood a short distance nearby.

John took to the back of the trailer to help the rear guard as Luke, Emily, and Sabrina made their way to the front of the group. Luke did one quick check to make sure everyone was ready, before he waved everyone onward back to the road.

As the caravan made its way down the main road of the town, it was clear that the townsfolk all made it to their emergency shelter on time. Or at least, on time to them. They had no way of knowing that the building would provide them with no protection against the Phantom Hawk's aura. An aura that turned their shelter into a cage while they painfully transformed into corrupted.

Luke shuddered at the thought and quickly shook it from his head to refocus on looking out for any threats nearby. Since the townsfolk had made it to their shelter though, no more corrupted lay in wait for the remainder of the walk. The expedition had easily made it the rest of the way through the town and onto a mostly open stretch of road just outside.

With the ocean to their right, the group travelled northwest. Since the road ahead was devoid of anything but the occasional car, Luke spent most of his time staring off in the direction of the ocean. They would lose sight of it by the time they reached the next town, so he wanted to take in as much of its mystical wonder as he could right now.

The natural beauty entranced him, and he momentarily forgot about the struggles they had faced. The struggles that they would also face in the coming battle ahead. His mind wandered back to a simpler time, a time when he would stress about tests. Not because they were difficult for him, but more because he spent so much time on his side project that the knowledge he was supposed to obtain on the material was lost to him until the moment the papers were handed out.

He wondered what he would do once the Phantom Hawk was taken care of. Would he return to school next year and try to retake the classes he had neglected? Doing so in order to graduate just a semester late? Or would this be his life now? Part of a secret organization that hunted the paranormal. Either option was okay with him, although the life more in tune with his passion would easily be his choice if given the opportunity.

A few hours passed as the group made their way down the dull road. The operatives had already switched off on pushing the cart a few times, and a town could be seen coming into view in the distance.

Sabrina noted this as Tonosho, and pointed out a route across the river that would make sure they avoided the more populated portions of the town. Even with the promise of reinforcements in Tokyo, they would prefer to avoid any major conflicts along the way. Not only because of the time they lost crashing so far away, but also to prevent any unnecessary loss of life in a disadvantaged battleground.

When their turn off to the alternate route approached, Luke signaled the caravan to stop. A crate was opened, and water was rationed out. Everyone sat against either the trailer or the nearby rocks to rest their legs.

With no interruptions, they had made excellent time on their trip so far. At this rate, they would reach Katori sometime in the late afternoon. Which would mean another two or three days of travel before they reached Tokyo. They easily had the supplies for the journey though. Furthermore, as crates were emptied, they could be abandoned to lighten the overall load of the trailer. This would accelerate their progress slightly towards the second half of the trip.

With everyone rested, the next set of operatives took control of the cart as they went about on their detour. After the party had crossed the river, hope swelled in Luke as they came across what looked to be the ultimate blessing.

Abandoned on the side of the road was a small pickup truck, and on the tail end of it was something Luke had never once thought he would be so happy to see.

The shining metal ball shape of a tow hitch.

As the group neared the vehicle, Luke signaled for the caravan to stop. With Emily on his right and the Banshee to his left, he cautiously made his way to the driver's side door and tested the handle. In the hurried retreat from the vehicle, it had been left unlocked.

Once Luke opened the door and peered inside, however, his mood rapidly dropped. While the truck was left unlocked, the keys looked like they had been taken with the previous owner. The empty ignition slot seemingly mocked him as he accepted that they would have to continue their slow progress on foot.

When he shut the door and moved to return to the group though, his foot kicked something that made a metallic jingle. Luke recognized this sound all too well, and as he looked down at the ground, the shining teeth of an abandoned set of keys lay on the road.

Luke signaled for them to bring the trailer over and hook it up as he picked up the keys from the ground. Filled with excitement, he swung the driver's side door back open and seated himself. With a twist of the keys in the ignition, the truck came to life around him. He looked at the dash and saw that it had at least half a tank of gas left in it. Which was plenty for their journey considering the lack of traffic they would face.

Once the trailer was properly hooked up, the operatives all moved their rifles into their hands and promptly filled both the bed of the truck as well as the sides if the trailer with their bodies. They would have to drive a little slow so that no one would fall off the trailer, but the vehicle would still speed up their trip considerably.

Sabrina jumped into the passenger seat as John and Emily took to the back seats of the truck. With everyone now loaded in, Luke shifted the vehicle to drive and pressed the gas pedal. The truck carried the party forward down the road at a much quicker rate.

Even with the controlled speed to ensure no one would be kicked from the trailer, they felt as if they were speeding along rapidly to their destination. In ten to fifteen minutes, they had already reached Katori. This portion of the trip would have easily been the rest of the day's journey on foot.

As they passed the town, corrupted could be seen wandering the streets. Some of the closer ones looked up towards the sound of the truck. However, given the speed they were moving at, and the distance already created, the creatures deemed a chase impossible. So, they instead returned to their search for an easier prey.

While they continued down the road, Sabrina pulled her map and GPS back out. She went through a few mental calculations as she charted their route, before finally speaking up.

"With the pace we are moving now, we could reach Funabashi by the early afternoon. If we can find a clear area to set up camp, we can rest for the night there and be in Tokyo the following morning."

As she folded up the map and pocketed her tools once more, Emily spoke up. "Perfect! We are going to make excellent time then! Although with how crowded the area once was, we are highly likely to be interrupted by more than a few wandering corrupted. The watch will need to be well aware of their surroundings, and the perimeter must also be set up prior to the campsite in order to prevent any unseen ambushes."

Luke nodded to show his understanding of her statement as he continued down the road.

John followed suit, as he peered out of the window. Occasionally, he looked back at the operatives to make sure everyone was still safely secured inside the bed or on the trailer as they travelled. He had quickly taken on the role of Alpha wolf; constantly worrying about and protecting his pack of men and women.

Luke grinned at this thought, as a few weeks ago John would have been frozen in fear at the thought of what they were doing. Now though, he was the rock the rest of the operatives would need in their current situation.

Sure enough, Sabrina's estimate was correct. As the sun slowly made its descent towards the horizon, the truck had passed a sign marking the outskirts of Funabashi. Unfortunately, Emily was also correct, and the streets were filled with corrupted roaming about.

Luke pointed out a fairly clear parking lot outside of a large store nearby, and promptly took an exit from their road to make a beeline for it. The corrupted were a lot sparser in this area; probably since it was not a residential portion of the city.

As the truck made its way and pulled into the center of the parking lot, however, nearby creatures shrieked and began to make their way to the newly discovered prey.

The Banshee, which had easily kept up with the trucks slower speed, was the first to attack at Luke's command. As it flew to meet the corrupted swarming the truck, the operatives all leapt from their seats and opened fire as well. Crystalline ammunition now flew in every direction as the Banshee began to tear its way through the crowd. Once Luke and his friends jumped out of the truck's cab, Luke saw that the area was not as underpopulated as they had hoped. A few hundred corrupted now swarmed the parking lot from every side, a storm of duskshot being fired out as the Banshee's claws ripped apart body after body.

Even as the edges of the parking lot filled up with corpses, more of the creatures replaced the fallen. The wave of corrupted seemed endless. Shrieks filled the air as the creatures slowly closed the distance between themselves and the truck.

John jumped into the trailer and ripped open the ammunition crate as he started to hand out fresh rounds to the operatives around him; for their own supplies were surely dwindling. Emily and Sabrina each pulled out their own Dawnbringer rifles and joined in the defense, the hailstorm of crystals easily hitting their marks as the mass of creatures closed in on the truck.

When more than half the parking lot was filled with piles of purified corpses, the numbers of the corrupted seemed to finally thin out. The following minutes felt like hours since the creatures were almost within clawing distance of the operatives. However, one by one the remaining monsters were dropped, and silence filled the air once more.

Luke panned his gaze across the perimeter to make sure nothing was left standing as he called his Banshee back over. He then directed the operatives to clear out the closer fallen bodies to make room for a camp. John took eight of the operatives himself to set up a perimeter watch, and the remaining eight started to unload the camp crates from the truck while they set up tents.

While the camp was slowly set up, a few corrupted wandered close enough to attempt an attack on the party. John's perimeter was more than enough for these stragglers however, and within the hour the site was fully built. A few of the operatives moved a food and water crate into a large dining tent away from the corrupted air so they could start to prepare the evening meal, while the remainder were set to the task of piling up corpses to clear the parking lot out once more.

With how the swarm had arrived, they currently had nowhere to drive the truck out the following morning. In addition to this, no one would feel comfortable in their tents if the creatures were just outside of the walls. Even though a purified corpse had never been resurrected before, no one wanted to take the chance.

The sun began its descent into the horizon itself as the light of day dimmed at an increasing rate. Luke realized that his eyes were now adjusted to the constant dusk-like state of the air around them, and wondered how he would adjust once the corruption was no longer a factor. For once the aura had been cleared, hopefully bright light would once again fill the island nation.

With dinner finished, the operatives on clean up duty as well as the cooks dug into their meals. Emily, Sabrina, and Luke all joined them inside the dining tent. The occasional comment was shared, but otherwise everyone focused on filling their hungry stomachs.

Once this set of operatives had their fill, they quickly relieved John and the other half of the party from perimeter duty so that they could get some rest and nourishment as well. The corrupted still occasionally assaulted the camp, so the constant focus had taken its toll on the perimeter patrol's-tired minds.

With the remaining sunlight, John led his newly fed half of the operatives to continue cleaning up any remaining nearby bodies. Once the sun had fully set, he dismissed them to go get some rest and be ready for a midnight shift. He himself then joined Luke, Sabrina, and Emily at the command tent. Sabrina had already laid the map out across the table once more, as the group had begun to plan the next day's operation.

Sabrina was the first to speak. "From what we know, the Phantom Hawk has chosen its perch above the skyscrapers of the city. Assuming it keeps to this post, it would be best if we set up our forward camp right outside of its range tomorrow. We wouldn't want to be on the defense against the spirit in its own territory, and this would give us a fallback location in case we need to regroup. Where we currently reside has already been called in to Adam, and once we finalize our forward base's location I can pass the coordinates on for that as well. The reinforcements will then be shipped out and will take the bay to rendezvous with us sometime tomorrow afternoon."

Luke nodded as he replied. "Sounds good, go ahead and radio in the coordinates so they can ship out as soon as possible. Looks like we almost made it to our final battle."

As Luke stated this, he looked around the campsite at the filled tents and perimeter patrol. The patrol which had still dealt with the occasional corrupted; but was now comfortably in control of the situation.

He continued, "What's more, we made it with minimal casualties. Not including the crash itself of course, but that was entirely out of our control."

Emily nodded as John tried to contain a yawn from escaping his lips. He was clearly tired from today's exertion. They all were in fact, and with their plans set for the next day John was the first to say his goodnight and leave for one of the nearby tents.

As Sabrina moved to the long-distance radio to relay the coordinates for tomorrow's base, Emily followed suit and left for her own tent and a night of rest. Luke waited for Sabrina to make sure that headquarters needed no other confirmations from them, then the two of them finally made their way to the final tent closest to the truck.

Once they entered, helmets and boots were removed; the two of them returning to the cuddled-up position they had shared the night before. Luke wrapped his arm around Sabrina this time, holding her close as the two of them drifted off to sleep. Thoughts of tomorrow faded away as sleep invaded their minds.

A few hours later though, Luke's eyes shot open as a roar could be heard approaching in the distance. Followed by another and another, as the ground started to shake. One word filled his ears as he heard one of the men on the perimeter yell, "abominations!"

Chapter 22: Onslaught

Luke and Sabrina quickly shot up out of bed as the man repeated his warning. Monstrous footsteps could be heard outside as they quickly threw on their helmets and boots, flying out of the tent flap to turn in the direction of the disturbance.

At the edge of the parking lot, five abominations were lit up by a floodlight the perimeter used to improve their nighttime vision. The front one let out a roar as it smashed through a pile of corpses, sending pieces of purified bodies flying in every direction.

Luke quickly commanded his Banshee to attack, however it was on the other side of the perimeter and could not close the distance before the abominations reached the camp's edge. Bursts of duskshot were fired into the first creature, which slowed it down slightly. Unfortunately, it was too late for the guardsman closest to it.

With an overhead swing of its massive arms, the monster quickly brought them down onto the operative. A scream was quickly interrupted with the sound of bones crunching as his form exploded from the force. What was even more horrifying, is that their proximity to the Phantom Hawk seemed to have a much stronger influence on flesh.

The moment the man's remains split from the protective layer of clothing, corruption had already started to spread. Before any of the severed limbs could hit the ground, they quickly exploded in bone spikes, which shredded away any remaining tatters of cloth.

As if filled with magnets, the semi-transformed gore quickly pulled back together. The shattered bones and torn muscle reformed into a dark red mass the size of a large dog. The arms and legs of the body quickly snapped down as the creature stood on all fours, with hands and feet quickly reshaping into long bony talons similar to a hawk's own claws. In the front of the newly formed torso, the man's heart erupted out of the flesh and split apart, revealing a single large blood-filled eye in its center.

As the first abomination fell from the extended barrage of shots, the new creature lunged at another member of the perimeter and pierced their flesh with its talons. The woman screamed as the creature sank its claws in, before it promptly pulled its limbs in all four directions.

The operative's cries were again cut short as their body was ripped to pieces in a cloud of viscera, which again reformed into another of the nightmarish beasts. The Banshee finished off its targeted abomination, just as Luke redirected it to take out these new and more agile threats.

Once the third abomination barreled through the perimeter, two more operatives fell to its strength. During their reformation once more into beasts, Emily quickly lunged at them with her blade drawn.

Before they could even finalize their new forms, she slashed straight through the rematerializing forms. Flesh and tissue quickly collapsed into harmless piles on the ground as her crystalline blade purified the corruption within. She then quickly swung her rifle up into her free arm and unloaded into the back of the third abomination, dropping it before it could do any more damage.

The fourth abomination was luckily felled before it could do any major damage to the party, and the sleeping operatives were now fully armed and reinforced the perimeter with their own rifles.

Everyone turned to the final abomination and let loose a storm of crystals as it smashed through two more operatives. Luke redirected the Banshee to instead take out these forming beasts to make sure the spirit didn't get caught in the line of fire. The last thing they needed was their trump card to be cleansed so close to the final battle.

With the beasts destroyed before they could become a threat, the final abomination now stumbled forward. It roared in its death throes, as it finally collapsed... right on top of the truck.

Luke winced as he watched their vehicle flatten under the weight of the massive creature. Even if they were able to move the monstrosity, there was no way the truck would function now. The entire hood was caved in; pieces of the engine block now smashed on the ground below.

Not only had they lost more than a third of their remaining operatives, but they would have to undertake the last stretch of the journey on foot.

Once the air calmed after the battle, John checked to make sure the remaining ten operatives were uninjured. Emily joined him as Sabrina and Luke looked over the map once more.

With the truck, they would have been able to reach the forward camp within an hour and had everything set up to receive the reinforcements well before they arrived. Now though, the trip would take them almost the entire day on foot. An entire day through an area swarming with corrupted, and who knew how many more abominations.

To make matters worse, Emily came back with an ammunition count: They had roughly 200 rounds left in the crate. Assuming they were lucky and no other corrupted approached tonight, that would leave the remaining operatives with enough ammo for one last large swarm before they ran out.

Not only had they lost their vehicle and a large portion of their fighting force, but now the journey the following day had to take on a more covert role. They had to avoid any large conflict at all costs, or they would never make it to the rendezvous point.

As Sabrina folded the map back up, John set to re-assigning who was on what shift of watch. Five would be stationed for the next couple of hours, to be then relieved by John and the remaining five. Luke made sure to command the Banshee to once more join the perimeter, and anyone not on watch returned to their tents to try to get some more sleep. With the mood now soured and adrenaline pumping through everyone's veins, no one expected to fall asleep easily.

The camp settled nonetheless though, and Luke once more dreamed with Sabrina close against his chest.

The morning light struck Luke's tent and warmed the interior, which promptly woke him up. Thoughts of the previous night whirled in his brain as he woke Sabrina up once more and pulled on his boots and helmet. After seeing what happened to the operatives the night prior, he made sure his helmet was extra secured against his head. A chill crept up his spine as he imagined how that kind of transformation would feel if he was still alive during it.

Shortly after Luke left the flaps of his tent, he instructed a nearby man and woman to prepare as much of the remaining food as they could. With the loss of the truck as well as a large portion of their force, there was no way they would be able to bring a large quantity of supplies with them. This would be the last meal they eat before the rendezvous point, so they might as well make it a hearty one.

As the personnel busied themselves cooking breakfast, Luke took note of the night's destruction with the light of the sun now rising into the sky.

The truck was definitely useless at this point, as even the cab had collapsed under the weight of the fallen abomination. When Luke's gaze moved down to the trailer, he noticed one of the wheels had popped in the sudden change of force as well. Even if they had no casualties in the assault, they would still be unable to take the supplies any real distance.

A gore filled scene filled the area around the tents, as the fallen operatives remains laid strewn across the parking lot.

Luke shook his head at the unfortunate events as he entered the dining tent. With everyone now seated and eating their fill, he joined his friends to fill his own belly.

Silence filled the air as everyone ate; with now even the more junior operatives sitting in silence after witnessing the events last night. The morale was definitely shaken, hanging on in tatters as everyone went through the motions of a typical morning.

Once the first set of operatives filled up, they quickly left to relieve the current watch so they could also feast. The air was no different with this second group however, as the deaths had taken their toll on everyone.

Luke ordered a few of the living party members to bring the remaining crates into the dining tent and away from the infectious corruption that was now thick in the air. "Everyone fill your pockets and uniforms with as much ammunition and water as you can safely carry," he stated. To which the remaining supply dwindled quickly from the crates.

With the ammunition crate fully emptied and the water supply close to it, Luke continued his speech.

"We have lost a lot of good men and women over the past few days. But don't let this take your sight away from our objective. Our mission will be slowed... and we will have to take a more covert route now, but our goal is the same. If you keep your heads clear, then before the sun sets, we will be at our forward camp and ready to assault the Phantom Hawk. Reinforcements are on their way and will meet us at this location. All is not lost, so don't fall to despair!"

The news of reinforcements seemed to lighten the mood a bit, as the operatives now moved with slightly renewed motivation in their preparations to leave. Sabrina alerted Adam to the prior night's events over the long-range radio, before the group abandoned both it and the camp. Making their way across the parking lot and towards the exit Luke had taken the day before.

This time though, they were stuck on foot.

The party quietly made their way back onto the highway as this was deemed the safest location to be. With the majority of the corrupted wandering the streets below, Luke hoped that they would be more drawn to looking for prey within the buildings of the city rather than the abandoned cars on the highway. While the group walked on, they spotted corrupted scattered along the streets as far as the eye could see. None had taken notice of them though, which was a blessing in this cursed land.

They travelled in mostly silence throughout the morning; their breaks taken only when they had to wait for a larger group of corrupted to pass by. When water was ingested, they made sure to keep it tucked inside their clothing so that the thickening corruption in the air didn't taint it.

The corruption now closely resembled smog, as the daylight steadily dimmed more the closer they got to the Phantom Hawk's nest. There was still plenty of light to see, but the aura around them felt heavy and unnatural. They were surrounded by an unseen enemy in addition to the physical corrupted nearby, and even the smallest tear in their protection could spell doom for any individual member.

While the group could have completed the journey by early afternoon before, the covert nature of their mission now slowed them down considerably. The survivors nonetheless were making good time, and Sabrina pulled out the map to check their progress once the sun was firmly seated high overhead.

"At this rate, we only have a few more hours until we reach the designated location," she whispered in order to not alert any unseen corrupted. Her finger ran along the remainder of the path in front of them to further her point.

Luke nodded to this as Emily and John moved to join the rest of the group once more. The extra weight on everyone was tiring, and upon learning of the short distance remaining more than a few of the operatives opted to discard the majority of their remaining water supplies. After all, if the reinforcements got intercepted by another air strike, then the mission would be doomed regardless.

With weary bodies, the troop stood up at Luke's command, and promptly returned to their trek.

While the early hours of the afternoon drained on, the group managed to successfully sneak their way along to their objective. The rendezvous point was now less than a twenty-minute walk away; although the distance felt much longer now that the buildings had begun to crowd the road more tightly. This joining of housing and road led to a lot more necessary pauses to avoid passing corrupted.

Step by step they cautiously toiled on, until Luke heard a strange noise a short distance behind them. As he turned around, his eyes locked with the shadow filled sockets of a corrupted staring right at him. Emily quickly lifted her rifle and fired off a round into the creature's chest, but it was too late.

Before the duskshot could connect, the monster let out a shriek and alerted everything in the area to their location.

"Run!" Luke screamed, as everyone began to sprint down the road now. "Protect us!" he directed shortly after to the Banshee, which started to circle the group in a perimeter roughly twenty feet out.

The silence around them quickly disappeared as swarms of corrupted started filing out from behind buildings in every direction. The group ran onward, firing a barrage of crystals into the mob that now blocked the road in front of them. As bodies fell to the ground, everyone quickly leapt over them and continued their frantic sprint.

One of the operatives clipped their boot against a body in their efforts and was sent tumbling to the ground. Before the rest of the party could react, the swarm quickly engulfed him. His screams filled the air before they were drowned out by the blood filling his throat as he was torn apart.

222

"Don't stop! Run!" Luke shouted as a few of the operatives faltered to help their fallen comrade. Luke knew however that they would not be able to fight their way out of this one. If you stopped, you were dead. Hell, even if you didn't stop you might still be dead; as another group of corrupted sprinted out of the woodwork in front of them.

This time, the pack was felled by the Banshee as it made its rounds to the front. The survivors continued onward, rapidly closing the distance between them and the rendezvous point. Luke prayed that the reinforcements had already arrived, because if they weren't ready and waiting, then the party would be swarmed regardless.

Luke's lungs gasped for air as his legs burned from the exertion, but he knew he could not slow down right now. Just as he reminded himself that they were getting close, the swarm had caught up to a few straggling operatives. Screams filled the air as claws sliced into their backs, promptly causing them to collapse as their spines were severed. The partially paralyzed agents were then torn apart, as a distant **dink** could be heard in the air.

Luke wondered what this noise could have been, but his thoughts were quickly answered when a massive explosion landed behind the group. Corrupted were either thrown in all directions or ripped apart as they were struck by the attack. The distant **dink** could be heard repeatedly, as explosions continued to tear apart the swarm behind them.

Once the group made their final turn before the goal destination, Luke laughed in relief as he saw what was causing the commotion.

The reinforcements had indeed already arrived, and a camp was already set up. What looked like hundreds of soldiers were now sprinting to the party's location, Dawnbringer rifles in hand. As Luke looked left, he saw deep in the bay was a Japanese destroyer. The artillery cannon let loose another round, which quickly tore away at more of the swarm.

The soldiers stopped as they formed a massive firing line, big enough to stretch across the entire pathway. An opening was left in the middle to which Luke dove through, followed shortly after by the remaining survivors of their mission. After tumbling for a moment, he looked back to see what devastation really meant.

The army opened fire, and a wave of duskshot flew into the massive swarm that had now reached numbers in the thousands. An unending barrage of crystals followed this initial wave, as the destroyer let loose missiles in addition to the artillery fire; now that the survivors were safe. Explosions ripped throughout the main body of the corrupted, while the firing line dropped everything in the front. By the time Luke had finally caught his breath, next to nothing remained of the swarm of corrupted.

Silence filled the air for only a few moments however, as a booming screech then filled the area. Luke's stomach dropped as he looked up and finally saw their target after all this time.

With another screech, the Phantom Hawk spread its skeletal wings; shadows oozing off like curtains as it dove from its vantage point above the skyscrapers. Luke slammed his hands against his helmet in an attempt to cover his ears as the Phantom Hawk let loose another cry. Moments later, the massive bird spirit slammed into the destroyer floating in the bay.

Debris and explosions followed suit as the demigod crashed into the water. Its wing had instantly destroyed the ship, which was now quickly sinking in two pieces to a watery grave. A massive wave rose from the water as the Phantom Hawk submerged, followed by another wave as the spirit swiftly exited the bay. One after the other, the waves crashed against the shore. Sending a spray of water over the forward camp that had been set up a decent distance away from the water's edge.

Luckily, it seemed the Phantom Hawk did not consider the base an immediate threat though, as it returned to its post above the skyscrapers in the distance with a final, triumphant cry.

Luke was helped up by a man wearing the same outfit as his operatives, complete with the riot style helmet. A Japanese flag was hastily sewn onto his shoulder though, and as Luke looked around he spotted both Japan's as well as South Korea's flags across the shoulders of the troops.

It had seemed that the organization had thrown the reinforcements together by making use of both what remained of Japan's military, as well as a portion of South Korea's. This made sense, as one of the forces would have gladly accepted the aid in retaking their homeland. The other was probably concerned that they would be the next to fall if things we not contained.

"It looks like you have all had quite the journey," a commanding officer stated with a grin as he approached Luke. "You could say that again," Luke replied. His answer was rushed through labored breathes though, since he was still trying to recover from their mad sprint to safety.

When he finally looked around, Luke spotted only four surviving operatives left. Emily and Sabrina were nearby recovering from their escape, and John was being led to a medical tent. A large gash ran down his left arm; but judging by his reaction to it he had already purified the burning pain of corruption from within.

A shift of his torn sleeve showed a handful of the crystalline ammunition being clutched against the wound, and Luke mentally commended him on his quick thinking.

Luke laughed again to himself as relief fully washed through his body. Their invasion force was shot down by a greedy military, and they had crossed an apocalyptic wasteland on the ground.

Realization interrupted Luke's thoughts as he remembered the Banshee was still out. With a quick sweep of his arm, he pulled the crystal back out from its holster and recalled the spirit. The reinforcements had not opened fire on it yet, but he didn't want to take the chance.

Their nervous gazes in its direction told him that they had been informed of the spirit's existence; but seeing it up close was a different matter entirely. With the spirit's crystal safely stowed back on his belt, he gave one final look around to his surviving members.

They had made it; the journey was complete.

Chapter 23: Preparation

Luke joined the commanding officer of the joint assault force by a large command table under a fully enclosed tent. Representatives of both military forces flanked him, as a representative for the organization stood close by as well.

Emily and Sabrina had left to check on John in the medical tent, which left Luke to help plan the attack with the foreign officers alone.

"From our current position, we will lead the troops to the base of the skyscrapers here," the commander stated as he pointed at the tabletop layout of the city on the command table. He had a thick accent to his English, but Luke was able to understand him, nonetheless.

As Luke nodded along to this statement, the man continued.

"From this point, we will clear the area of any corrupted, before then luring the Phantom Hawk down from its post with explosive fire. Once it has begun its dive, the troops will split into twenty squads spread at these locations to minimize casualties while we open fire." The commander promptly moved a few small figures into a makeshift circle, symbolizing the shift in formation on the battlefield.

"From this position, our forces should be able to sufficiently weaken it with the ammunition your organization has provided us. Once the spirit has been weakened, your Banshee will then be used in a more even battle to wound it to the point of capture. I was also told you have a means to capture the spirit, yes?"

Luke nodded at the statement thrown his direction as he threw back the edge of his coat and pulled out the primed, empty controller crystal.

The commander nodded in confirmation as he finished stating their plan of attack. "Good, once the Banshee has been let loose on the Phantom Hawk, any remaining forces will reinforce your position. They will get you within striking range so you may capture the spirit."

The commander continued. "As we have come to understand that your organization specializes in dealing with this kind of threat, we have agreed to allow your operative to fly in with a helicopter upon capture. Once he arrives, he can safely remove this Phantom Hawk from our region."

"If no one has any issues with the plan, then we will begin the assault in the morning. The Phantom Hawk does not currently seem to consider us a threat, so we can use this time to rest and prepare. There is no telling how long it will take to complete our objective, so the more daylight available to us, the better."

With no one voicing concerns, the meeting abruptly ended. As the evening was drawing closer, Luke felt a grumble in his stomach to let him know he was in fact famished from the day's events.

Upon leaving the command tent, Luke hastily made his way to the dining one. It seemed that the reinforcements were thoroughly informed as to the nature of the corruption; for everything was safe inside the semi-gloss looking walls he had come to recognize as the adaptation of his clothing's crystalline barrier.

With a flick of his arm, Luke entered the dining tent and made a beeline straight for where the smell of food was.

Given the militaristic nature of the reinforcements, Luke was not surprised when the food in front of him was a few degrees lower in quality than the cuisine the organization provided. Still though, his hunger consumed him, and he would have eaten anything set before him at this time.

Once he had a tray of food made up and some water to go along with it, he walked his way back through the massive tent. While looking around for an open table, Luke noted that the tent could easily fit a hundred soldiers. It was closer to the size of a large house than it was to something you would take camping with you, which made sense given the size of the reinforcement force that was brought along.

As Luke walked down the lines of tables, he soon spotted Emily and Sabrina eating their own meals amid a group of soldiers. A space was available by them however, so Luke quickly veered to the side and joined them.

"So, how's John doing?," Luke inquired as he sat his tray down beside Sabrina before seating himself.

Emily, being the first to swallow her food, was the one to respond. "He's doing fine. They have him stitched up and resting in the medical tent. Unfortunately, though, his injury was deep enough that he won't be able to join us in the assault."

Luke nodded, relieved that his friend had made it out alive and semi-well. "That's good to hear. He deserves the rest anyway, the bond he built with our operatives has probably taken its toll on him with how many we have lost the last few days. He has been noticeably quieter, so I think he needs some time to process things anyway."

"And what about you Luke? How are you holding up?" Sabrina asked to add on to the subject.

Luke looked towards the ceiling of the tent for a moment deep in contemplation as he repeated the question to himself. How was he holding up? In the heat of the moment all he could think about was getting everyone to this location. The losses and destruction were moved to the back of his mind in the process. But now that he had a moment to think, it all came rushing back to the front. Things had not gone to plan at any step of the journey, but overall, they made it here.

"I guess I'm fine. I've been more worried with succeeding than anything else, so we will see how I feel when this is all said and done."

Sabrina nodded as she laid her head on his shoulder for a moment. This small gesture comforted him greatly, and he stroked her hair. A moment later she sat back upright though, as she continued to devour the food in front of her.

Luke gave out a short laugh, "I'm glad to see I'm not the only one starving."

Sabrina replied with a nod, her mouth full of another bite of food, as Luke began to work through his own supply. Eventually the group finished eating, and Luke left to explore the rest of the camp while Emily and Sabrina stayed behind to banter over recent happenings.

Compared to their expedition's camps, this one easily dwarfed them in size. Upon leaving the dining tent Luke spotted the command tent he had recently used straight ahead. As he looked left, a large medical tent stood against the stark cityscape. In the distance, Luke identified the road they had recently made their escape from death on.

Between the road and medical tent, barricades were now set up. At least fifty soldiers guarded the perimeter from any future corrupted attacks.

Luke paused for a moment, and decided to make his way to the medical tent before he continued his stroll. Although he had received an update from the girls, it would be a good idea to check on John's condition himself.

Moving the entrance flap of the medical tent, Luke was greeted with the sight of two rows of beds lining the walls. Most of them were empty since the reinforcements had just recently arrived. There was no reason to treat injuries in their landing when they were able to secure the area so easily.

A few of the beds had the remaining operatives from their mission seated upon them; a cautionary checkup more than anything else. Just to ensure that they were healthy and ready to go for tomorrow's assault.

As Luke's gaze wandered deeper into the tent, he spotted a bandaged John towards the back. He seemed to be asleep, but Luke wanted to check on him, nonetheless.

Luke approached his wounded friend, to which John's eyes lazily flicked open at the new presence. A tired grin crossed his face as he gave an exhausted salute with his good arm.

Luke rolled his eyes at the gesture before he spoke up. "Congratulations, you have successfully avoided the Phantom Hawk mission now. How are you feeling?"

John nodded before he opened his mouth to reply. "Honestly, I was going to try to still make it. The medical staff here insist that I rest instead though, and the number of painkillers they have me on would make me completely useless anyway. Not that I mind of course, I can't feel a thing."

John finished his statement with a small wiggle in the bed, which drew a laugh from Luke. "Well, regardless I'm glad you're ok. I was worried for a moment when I saw your wounded arm after we arrived. Good thinking to use the ammo as a barrier from the corruption."

Luke paused for a moment, before he decided to wrap up the talk. "Anyway, I will let you get your rest, wish us luck on tomorrow's attack."

John replied with a simple thumbs up as he closed his heavy eyelids once more. Luke assumed the painkillers had left him in a sort of daze, so he turned to exit the medical tent and resumed his exploration.

Once he returned to the open air, Luke turned right and walked past the dining tent towards the remainder of the secured area.

The sun had finally begun its descent onto the horizon, and soon it would be too dark to see anything in any level of detail.

As Luke walked, he looked up to the sky and realized that although it was devoid of any clouds, the thick aura from the Phantom Hawk had easily choked out most of the light. In any other circumstance, one would think that the sun was blocked by the foreboding presence of thick clouds preparing for a thunderstorm.

Beyond the dining tent stood another tent equally as large. This one seemed to contain the various supplies needed for their assault.

As Luke crossed in front of it, he took a moment to peer inside. Lines of opened-crystal reinforced crates sat along the walls with hastily made signs above the various contents. Everything from ammunition to excess outfits and Dawnbringer rifles filled the space; piles of back up crates also sat between the open containers.

Onward Luke continued as he reached the tents intended for sleeping in. On his right, a series of large barracks style tents were lined up. Luke made his way down the line and focused his attention more on the smaller tents to his left; probably intended for the officers of the assault force. The first of these was labelled as Luke's, followed by one each for the commander and officers that had joined the force. Towards the end of the row was one designated for Emily and Sabrina, with a final tent for the organization's representative Luke saw earlier.

When Luke finished his walk through the sleeping area, he noted that this side of the camp matched the direction the survivors escaped from. Another mass of soldiers patrolled a barricade here as well, although the occasional corrupted chanced an attack from this direction.

They were easily dropped by the sheer defensive force ahead of them, and the bodies were added to a burn pit outside of camp to be safely removed from existence. Luke thought this was an unnecessary step as the purified bodies had never been resurrected.

It would, however, make cleaning up the city that much easier. Once they managed to remove the Phantom Hawk, at least.

With the sun now set and the camp lit up by rows of lanterns, Luke made his way into his personal tent. No doubt they would be awake before sunrise to prepare for the assault, so Luke wanted to make sure he got plenty of rest before the big day.

As he entered, Sabrina herself was also preparing to sleep.

"Oh? Decided you didn't want to stay with Emily?", Luke asked jokingly. Making sure she saw his wink in the process.

"I mean I can leave if that's what you prefer," she replied with a grin. To which Luke simply shook his head no and proceeded to remove his own boots and helmet.

A small table stood to the side of the tent with a set of chairs and some water in case he needed a drink during the night. It wasn't the most lavish sleeping conditions, but it was far more spacious than the barricades looked.

Luke continued to prepare for bed as he took off his coat and laid it across the back of one of the chairs. He then removed his belt and draped it over the coat, before laying down to join Sabrina on the provided mattress.

As his body hit the bed, Luke let out a groan. Although it was not much, the relatively luxurious sleeping conditions were years better than the sleeping bags set upon a hard ground.

"Oh my god I feel like a queen," Sabrina remarked as she also hit the bed. "Just leave me here" she continued, which was followed with a wide stretch as she allowed her limbs to fall outstretched across the entire space.

"I just might if you don't fold your arms down because holy shit do you need a shower," Luke stated with a laugh.

"The same could be said to you," she replied with a jokingly annoyed tone before continuing. "Trust me, I had looked around for some showers the moment we arrived. However, it seems that with how short they expected their time here to be, they opted not to bring any."

"Well, hopefully we won't be here much longer either now. In the morning we take on the Phantom Hawk, and hopefully by the afternoon we are on our way back home, with all this destruction behind us." As Luke finished his statement, he pulled Sabrina close to achieve a more comfortable sleeping position.

"Mhm," she replied as a yawn escaped her lips. With a gentle motion she raised her head to softly plant a kiss on Luke's lips before snuggling back against his chest.

He smiled and returned the kiss, before wrapping his arms tightly around her and drifting off to sleep.

Chapter 24: The Phantom Hawk

Luke awoke to the sounds of the troops throughout the camp making their preparations for the assault. With a yawn and a stretch, he noticed that Sabrina had already left the tent. Luke got out of bed and strapped his belt back on, before throwing his coat over his shoulders. With his boots and helmet slid on shortly after, he exited the tent ready for the day.

A culmination of all their efforts over the last few weeks summed up in one large assault on the demigod that threatened everything.

With this on his mind, he made his way through the dark morning air and into the dining tent for breakfast.

After filling his tray, Luke found Emily and Sabrina seated at a nearby table and subsequently joined them. Sabrina was midway through her meal talking with Emily. Emily had already finished her food and was casually tossing her crystalline dagger in the air; The blade flipping end over end as she participated in the discussion.

Once Luke took a seat, Emily caught her dagger as the two of them turned their attention his way.

"Well, we have received our assignments for the mission, and let me tell you do they sound boring as hell," Emily stated to Luke.

"Oh yea? And what would that be?" Luke asked as he watched the weapon continue its acrobatics.

"I am to continue as your personal guard until the moment where the Phantom Hawk is captured. From there, I will take the controller crystal to Adam, before joining in up cleaning up any remaining corrupted. Which would be a lot more fun if not for the fact that apparently you yourself will be on standby during the primary assault."

Luke laughed and shook his head at her eagerness to fight. "Knowing our luck, you will probably get ample opportunities to join in the battle."

Luke began to dig into his food after his reply, leaving Sabrina open to relay her own given role in the upcoming assault.

"Emily thinks her role is dull, but at least she gets to see some action. I've been chosen to take a more observational role a safe distance away from the battlefield. Since I have the most experience studying the effects of your crystals, I will be giving you the clear to enter the fight once the Phantom Hawk has been sufficiently weakened for your Banshee."

Luke was relieved to hear this, as he had felt like the two of them were growing ever closer over the last few weeks. If Sabrina was on the battlefield in a dire situation, then that would be a distraction Luke could not afford. He knew she was more than capable of handling herself, but the initial force sounded like a suicide mission, and Luke had feared she would have been a part of it.

"All officers and commanding personnel report to the command tent for final briefing for the assault."

Luke tilted his ear to the previously unnoticed intercom system wired throughout the camp. He quickly shoveled the last few bites of the meal into his mouth as he stood up, nodding his temporary farewell to the ladies.

"Good luck," they both managed in unison, with Emily quickly reacting with a rushed "Jinx!" to Sabrina.

The last image he had inside the tent was of Sabrina rolling her eyes as Emily's proud smile spread widely across her face.

Luke was waved over to the command table the moment he entered the tent. With a nod, he quickly joined the circle around the table and observed the pieces upon it. They had been reset into their original positions to be used as a visual aid while the assault progressed.

As the Commander went through the motions of explaining how the troops would be organized, he assigned a squad to each of the various officers that flooded the room. Luke realized he was mainly

236

here to learn the general assignments given out. This information did not seem too important to him, but this was the first *military* mission he would be on, so what did he know?

As the assignments were continued, the intercom outside blared a more general message: "All troops make your final preparations for the assault. Join formation in fifteen minutes."

The message was followed by what Luke assumed was Japanese and Korean, each relay repeating itself to the troops in their various tongues.

When the officers were all finally assigned their units and the strategy from the day prior was relayed to them, they left the room to begin briefing the infantry on their roles. This had left Luke in the tent with the four men he had met with the day before.

The Commander turned to face Luke as the focus of the entire room shifted to him. "Are you ready for your big moment? Everything will ultimately come down to you, Mr. Connor."

Luke nodded as both his mind and heart raced. They were mere moments away from the assault, and Luke was starting to feel the stress overtake him; his hands shaking in anticipation. He tightened his fists and set his jaw though, reminding himself that he could not lose focus now. The world depended on what they accomplished here today, and he would not be the cause of their failure.

Luke exited the tent and made his way to where the formation was lining up. With a look around, he was taken aback by the sheer force that was now in front of him.

Hundreds of soldiers were positioned in neat rows, stretching back like a modern-day version of a medieval army. Officers patrolled the front of the formation, barking out orders and instructions to their men; ensuring everyone knew their role when chaos broke out.

A look beyond the group was a wide-open concrete field that would serve as their battleground. What were once streets lined with houses and other various structures now laid pulverized into oblivion by the Phantom Hawk's takeover of the city. Apparently, it had not taken a purely hands off approach once it claimed the island after all. The spirit probably left this clearing under the skyscrapers to better see any approaching threats from the safety of its nest.

While Luke stood at the edge of the camp, he spotted Sabrina in a makeshift tower a short distance away. He waved to her, and she returned the action as Emily walked behind Luke and tapped him on the shoulder.

"You ready? The moment has arrived," she stated with a grin on her face. Emily was clearly looking forward to some action, which made Luke laugh at her eagerness to face such a massive threat. It would seem that she was completely at home on the battlefield. This probably played a huge role in her extensive abilities as an operative.

"Ready as I'll ever be," Luke stated in reply as he noticed that the assault force was now readying to march.

The battle was about to begin.

With a loud command, the army had begun to move towards the clearing near the Phantom Hawk's roost. Luke watched as they moved in unison, and with every step taken they had kept their formation perfectly. He was in awe at the display of discipline as he and Emily began to walk down as well.

Slowly, as the sunlight basked the area in its muted glow, the force made its way further from camp.

Eventually, they made their way to the middle of the clearing. Luke and Emily stopped as well, now halfway between the main force and the camp behind their backs. This would give enough distance to not be caught in the initial conflict, while also leaving Luke close enough to join when the time was right.

In the distance, a new command could be heard as the army stopped. One of the troops swung his Dawnbringer rifle to the side as he kneeled down and shouldered an unknown variant of rocket launcher.

During this, Luke reached for his Banshee's crystal and promptly threw it straight up in the air. With a puff of shadowy smoke, the Banshee materialized overhead. Luke caught the crystal as it fell back down to him, and he quickly holstered it. Luke then commanded the spirit to stand by, which it obeyed as it floated down to wait by his left side.

Emily joined him on his right, moving her own rifle into her hands as she prepared to defend their post; on the off chance that something went awry.

As one of the officers sliced the air with his arm, a rocket shot from the launcher. It collided with the top edge of one of the immense buildings, where it exploded. Debris rained down as windows shattered and framework collapsed inward on itself.

While the rocket launcher was reloaded and prepared for another shot, the Phantom Hawk shot up into the air from behind the buildings. Its large skeletal wings unfurled with the sun as its backdrop. The shadows dripping from its form acted as a curtain to darken the sky as it let out a cry. A second rocket was then fired into another building to disturb its nest and provoke it more, which was answered by a cacophony of shrieks from all directions.

The Phantom Hawk hovered high overhead as thousands of corrupted poured out from between the various buildings that enveloped the clearing. The officers could be seen giving commands as the formation rearranged into a defensive stance; with rows of rifles pointing in all directions towards the mass of creatures.

With another cry from the Phantom Hawk, all hell broke loose as the corrupted began a mad sprint towards the phalanx.

Crystalline ammunition rained down in all directions as the two armies engaged in battle. Corrupted after corrupted fell to the barrage as they continued a crazed sprint towards their prey. When the outer rim of the formation reloaded, they stepped back into the phalanx to allow the next wave of soldiers to let loose their own gunfire.

Purified corpses dropped to the ground dozens at the time as the creatures were ripped through relentlessly. Hundreds of the beasts fell as the assault was thinned by the sheer force the combined army displayed.

Luke grinned as he watched his weapons perform admirably, but it was quickly wiped from his face as the Phantom Hawk let out another cry.

A series of roars shook the area as close to a hundred abominations joined in the mass to reinforce their troops. The monstrosities towered above their fellow corrupted; shoving them aside or outright stomping them as they made the way towards their targets in a berserker's rage.

The phalanx stood their ground, dropping as many of this combined assault that they could. Eventually though, an abomination had reached the group and barreled straight through the center of the phalanx; Breaking it apart as soldiers were sent flying in every direction to be subsequently ripped apart by the corrupted.

The abomination fell soon after, but the damage had already been done. Luke recognized the danger that was to come as the fallen corpses took in the Phantom Hawk's corrupted aura from their newly exposed flesh. One by one, fallen soldiers began shattering and reshaping into the alien-like quadrupeds Luke had recently discovered on their journey.

"Help them!" Luke commanded the Banshee. He then watched as the spirit flew off to take care of this hellish new threat.

The army was now split up into smaller pockets, surrounded on all sides by corrupted, abominations, and the alien-like beasts. If they fell now, there was no way that the Banshee would be able to take on an unharmed Phantom Hawk.

Luke's spectral summon began to make its rounds ripping through the newly formed beasts, as the army returned to clearing out the main assault. The more corrupted that were removed from the theater of war, the more ground the soldiers were able to regain.

With the Banshee clearing out the remainder of its own hostiles, it instantly detoured to join the main force. With evasive maneuvers to dodge the duskshot at its back, it began the arduous task of dropping the abominations spread throughout the swarm with deadly precision.

Luke watched as one by one the abominations fell amidst the waves of smaller creatures. Each time one of the monstrosities fell, they crushed their fellow forces--making the troops' job slightly easier. The initial battle seemed to have been won, as only a few hundred corrupted had remained.

That was the moment, however, that the Phantom Hawk decided to join the fray...

With the threat of the ground forces taking everyone's full focus, no one saw as the Phantom Hawk folded its wings in and began to dive. It promptly smashed full force into one of the smaller phalanxes in the clearing. Dust and debris kicked up in every direction as the Phantom Hawk shot back up out of its cloud of destruction.

Moments later, vision cleared up as a newly created force of the four-legged flesh beasts began to leap from the dust; all targeting the various groups scattered throughout the area.

One by one soldiers were ripped apart and reformed into further reinforcements for this threat, as the Phantom Hawk made another swoop. It again crashed down into a group of defenders, spawning more of the horrid beasts to further overwhelm those that still survived.

Luke's stomach dropped as the perimeter from this side of camp broke away and ran past him in an attempt to reinforce the dwindling number of soldiers. This battle had quickly turned to the Phantom Hawks favor, and Luke now realized the extent of the spirit's intelligence as it turned the tide of war instantaneously.

This was the demigod's plan all along. It wanted to lure them into the clearing so it could strike with its own flanking force. Then while the battle ensued, it would strike next for the killing blow.

With the struggles of the battle continuing, the Banshee joined in dropping the newly created beasts while the few hundred remaining corrupted started to finally close the last stretch of distance between themselves and the remaining troops. Luke counted only maybe a hundred left of their assault force, spread unevenly between five phalanxes.

A short distance away from the battlefield, a large shipping container was dropped unnoticed via helicopter.

Luke watched as one by one the remaining force was broken. The Banshee did all it could, but it was not enough. For every four-legged beast it dropped, another five rose from the bodies of newly fallen soldiers to reinforce the enemy.

Despair began to well up inside him, as the battle had seemed lost. The final troops were quickly snuffed out, which left them with only whoever still guarded the camp.

As the Banshee flew up to a vantage point in defiance at the army of corrupted and beasts in front of it. It let out a massive shriek in preparation to reengage.

The battle cry was quickly stifled though, as a massive leg pierced through the spirit's form. The Banshee froze for a moment, before melting into a shadowy pool and dissipating entirely.

Luke looked down as his controller crystal for the specter shattered; their final weapon now destroyed.

When he returned his gaze to where the Banshee once hovered, a colossal spider had taken its place. Eight green-flamed eyes peered around as its fangs dripped with a similar energy to the Phantom Hawk's wings: Tendrils of thick green shadows dripped from its teeth, while an aura of green enveloped the rest of its massive figure. A large metallic harness could also be seen latched around the center of its form, with a small army of spiderlings flanking its position.

The Broodmother had arrived.

Chapter 25: Downfall

The Phantom Hawk let out a cry and leapt into the air as the Broodmother matched it with its own piercing shriek.

Sabrina joined Luke and Emily with a rifle in hand, and the trio watched as the two armies clashed anew. Spiderlings were ripped apart by a barrage of claws as they returned attacks on the four-legged beasts and corrupted.

While the corrupted were decimating the spider's numbers, the spiderlings venom gave them an edge. For whenever a corrupted or one of the beasts fell to a spiderlings venom, it reformed into an explosive cocoon and birthed more reinforcements for the Broodmother; the force of the explosions sending corrupted flying in every direction each time. The closer ones were less lucky, flying in the form of limbs rather than injured bodies.

The Phantom Hawk flew high above the skyscrapers as the Broodmother promptly skittered across the battlefield to follow, spearing portions of the corrupted army on its legs as it travelled.

The friends watched as the giant spider spirit leapt from building to building, forming an intricate array of webs as the Phantom Hawk swooped down to assault its equal. The Broodmother was just as agile however, and managed to jump aside each time the Phantom Hawk's corrupted claws attempted to sink in.

In a defiant act against their defeat, Luke began to sprint along the outskirts of the battlefield and towards where the two titans clashed. Sabrina and Emily followed, firing off rounds into any creatures that broke off from the main conflict to halt the party.

While the two forces seemed to be at equal strength, the spiderlings had the benefit of replenishing their own numbers. So, while the corrupted numbers dwindled, the spiders had held their ground firmly. Since a constant supply of newly formed cocoons exploded to renew their ranks.

As the trio approached the edge of the buildings, the two demigods seemed to be at a stalemate. While the Broodmother continued weaving its massive web, the Phantom Hawk dove and lunged at it repeatedly. It avoided the array of traps well; however, the bird spirit was also unsuccessful in its own assault.

Eventually though, the Phantom Hawk was able to hit its mark. After a missed dive, it quickly rolled in the air to reposition as it sunk its claws into the Broodmother. The majority of the damage from the talons was blocked though, for they struck the main body of the spider's controller harness. The assault destroyed the mechanism, and it promptly shattered and fell away useless to the ground below.

With this momentary advantage the newly freed Broodmother had, it lashed out with a leg and shattered one of the Phantom Hawk's wings. The bird spirit let out a cry in pain as it tumbled straight into the array of webs laid out before it. When the caustic webbing burned into its body, the Phantom Hawk flailed in every direction in an attempt to break free.

As the Broodmother made the final leap to catch up to its quarry, the hawk was able to free itself. A momentary victory--as it quickly began to freefall towards the ground below.

When it came crashing down into the debris, a massive cloud of dust was kicked up from the impact. Luke began a mad sprint to the location of the spectral bird's fall from destructive grace, with the primed controller crystal in his hand.

Once the dust had partially cleared and the shadowed outline of the Phantom Hawk came into vision, Luke pulled back his arm and threw the crystal with all his might. As the dust cloud fully dispersed, the crystal connected with the injured body of the demigod.

With a final cry, the Phantom Hawk exploded into a massive cloud of shadowy energy, which was quickly sucked into the crystal.

"We have the Phantom Hawk!" Luke yelled into his radio as he ran over and dove to grab the crystal.

Already, the effects of the spirit's removal could be seen. For corrupted instantly began falling, purified, to the ground across the entire battlefield. Just as Luke got back up, the spiderlings began to make short work of the bodies. They bit the corpses one by one, turning them all into a massive field of cocoons.

Swiveling back in the direction of the camp, Luke began a desperate sprint to relative safety with the crystal clutched close to his body.

With the Phantom Hawk gone, the sky had begun to return to normal. The thick heavy cloud of corruption cleared quickly; flooding the battlefield in renewed sunlight as the trio made their mad dash around the army of spiderlings.

When the threat of the corrupted was fully taken care of, the spiderlings began to lunge at the escaping friends. Sabrina and Emily rapidly fired off round after round into the fleshy spiders as they closed distance with the party.

Once he reached their original vantage point, Luke saw a small helicopter flying towards the camp--beginning its descent. The spiderlings were getting close however, and the three of them would soon be overrun.

Closing in on the camp itself now, Luke saw the remaining contingent of troops had formed a firing line relatively close by. Within minutes, they were safe behind the soldiers as a defensive barrage flew into the swarm of reformed flesh and tissue that made up the spiderling's bodies. One by one they dropped as Luke continued his dash, focused entirely on where the helicopter was now landing.

Adam could be seen piloting the aircraft as Luke closed the distance. Just as he touched down on the ground, Luke tossed the Phantom Hawk's crystal the remaining distance between the two.

Adam's arm shot up as he caught the crystal in his grip. "A plane is waiting at the airport for you, you need to leave now!" He yelled over the sound of the helicopter's blades. Following this message, he began his ascent back into the air.

A small squad of soldiers flanked the Commander as he intercepted Luke once he removed the crystal. With a hurried gesture and a shove to his back, they directed Luke towards the far side of the camp.

While the group ran, screams could be heard from behind as the spiderlings finally clashed with the wall of soldiers. The camp would soon be lost.

As they weaved between the tents, Luke spotted a row of military vehicles that had once been used to transport the camp supplies sitting in the distance. The Commander and a few of his troops filled in the first vehicle, while the trio of friends jumped into the second. John was already positioned inside of it, and he waved them on into their seats. The third truck behind them then quickly filled with the remaining squad members, and the convoy began to move out for the airport.

Now in safe retreat, Luke sat back against his seat to catch his breath. They had caught the Phantom Hawk, but what about the now released Broodmother? Although it was contained to the island for now, this surely wasn't the outcome their reinforcements wanted.

But even with the country still lost to this new spirit, they had ultimately succeeded in their objective. The corrupted influence was now removed from Earth... and for the most part humanity could recover.

Luke's relief was cut short though, as he turned his gaze back to the battleground. The Broodmother had now landed back amongst its minions in the heart of the clearing. The massive spider-like spirit let out a ghastly triumphant shriek at its victory, with the spiderlings repeating the gesture across the entire clearing.

Luke then watched as the spirit stood up on its hind legs and shot its four front legs forward into a singular spot in the air. With his jaw dropped, Luke tapped Sabrina's arm to get her attention directed towards the Broodmother.

The giant spiritual arachnid began to spread its airborne legs in four directions as it let out another shriek. Then, reality itself ripped... as the Broodmother opened a massive portal. On the other side of the portal, an apocalyptic wasteland of a world could be seen.

The party sat stunned as they watched hordes of spirits now flood out into the landscape, spreading in every direction. As the convoy sped off towards the airport, the party had now realized that they had failed. The Phantom Hawk was not the biggest threat after all.

The initial portal into their realm, the one that the military had taken over in an attempt to weaponize the spirits... it was created by the Broodmother.

Once they reached the tarmac of the airport's runways, the convoy hurriedly stopped at a relatively small plane. Its engines began to warm up as they loaded single file into its body. Moments later the door shut, and the vehicle began the process of initiating liftoff. With no other air traffic nearby, as well as no surviving air traffic controllers, the plane was quick to launch into the air.

Luke sat back as they ascended into the sky, with thoughts of this new conflict filling his mind as the party began their long journey back home.

While the spirits spread their way across this new land from the portal, the party made their way to South Korea. From here, they separated from their military escort and boarded a plane set for Los Angeles.

During the long flight, the group of friends sat in silence as they processed the world they now lived in. Exhaustion took over the members at various points though, and they each renewed their bodies with rest.

Everyone except John, who spent the majority of the flight staring out of the window; already freshly rested, but also tormented by the thoughts of the portal and invasion they had witnessed.

Upon landing in California, no car could be seen to ferry them back to their underground base. Luckily, Emily had known the way to headquarters, and the group managed to rent a car to make their way back home. News of the portal had already flooded the various news stations, and every screen around them now lit up with reporters commenting on humanities fall. The radio inside the vehicle also iterated the same narrative, so the group opted to turn it off and sit in silence for the trip back. They did not need a reminder of the events they had witnessed firsthand.

As they travelled, everyone except Emily realized that the headquarters was deep in the woods of western Colorado. Back road after back road they drove, eventually making their way to a hidden narrow path. The same path that led to the inconspicuous hunting cabin they had all become so familiar with.

Relief washed over them as they exited the car and made their way for the secret base below. The apocalypse was a worry for another day. For now, they were finally home and could get some relaxation in.

When the group made their way down the hidden staircase though, something was amiss.

The command room was empty, which Luke had never seen before. He thought for a moment that the organization had sent the majority of its members to fight the Phantom Hawk, but he had not recognized any faces in the large reinforcement force they received.

Except for the one representative, who Luke now realized was oddly missing once they captured the Phantom Hawk.

They may have left to confront the new threat of the Broodmother, Luke thought to himself. Because the majority of the supply of controller crystals and weaponry was now missing from its crates as well.

He was told the controller crystals did not work though. So why would they take them?

A cough sputtered from behind one of the abandoned desks as the four friends went to investigate.

When they turned the corner, Adam could be seen propped up against the table. Blood now flowed freely from a wound on his head; joined by a rapid flow from his chest where two bullet holes could be seen. The group frantically attempted to help their comrade, but his skin was already turning pale from the blood loss.

"Lewis... lied." Adam managed to cough out as blood now flowed from between his lips. He laid his head back against the table as he met Luke's eyes with his own dying gaze.

"The crystals... work. Take... what you can. Escape," Adam's final word drifted off as his life finally drained away.

The group mourned the loss of their newer friend, but realization had now struck Luke. Lewis did not want to stop the Phantom Hawk, he wanted to use it. But to what end? And more importantly, how would he control it? The crystal was clearly linked to Luke alone. This was the exact kind of scenario he created the fail-safe for; to prevent someone from stealing and using captured spirits against their owners.

The group made their way to the open air outside as they buried their friend. A few words were spoken, before they made their way back underground.

"Stock up on crystals, we will probably have need of them soon," Luke stated to the rest of the party as he grabbed six of them himself. They each also grabbed a backpack, to which they stuffed with food and water supplies to last them in the coming days.

John had the mindset to also grab a few simple camping supplies. Since the party had not expected to have to leave so suddenly, they drained most of the car's gas in their hurried trip back.

Once everyone had stocked up, they made their way back up to the surface. With a final nod to Adam's grave, the party began their journey into the woods beyond.

An unknown world would be waiting for them, but they had the tools to fight it.

Chapter 26: The Truth

Alarms blared at the secret paranormal facility below Area 51. Gunshots rang out as agents fought back against the unknown force of black-clothed operatives storming the once pristine halls.

The halls now filled with pools of blood from operatives and agents alike as the two sides met in combat. Given the secretive nature of the facility however, they were ill prepared for a frontal assault. Slowly, the operatives made increasing progress through the facility as more agents fell.

Squad leaders directed their men and women into the various doors throughout the hall. Researchers were being captured from within the observation rooms and forced to unlock the doors to the various captive spirits cells.

One by one, operatives stormed the rooms, clearing out any minions within using their Dawnbringer rifles. As each room was cleared, the spirits contained within were promptly captured into crystals wielded by the operatives. Class B spirits were captured mostly by the squad leaders, while lower classifications were given off to their subordinates.

As the operatives demolished their way through the base, the facility was slowly emptied of its prisoners. Many of the remaining agents had taken up post outside the Director's office; one final defiant act against the invaders. However, they were quickly outnumbered and one by one fell to the ground in a spray of blood and bullets.

The door slammed open as the operatives breached the Director's office. Two agents stationed inside the room were quickly taken care of, while the Director stared coldly towards these faceless intruders.

"The Broodmother has opened a new portal in Japan, and spirits have now invaded the world." The Director started, leaning back in his chair as he finished his statement. "The world as you know it is lost, therefore your assault here is now meaningless."

Once Director Johnson finished his statement, the operatives cleared to the side. Lewis then casually strolled into the newly opened space within the room.

"No matter to us," he stated as he pulled out a handgun from his suit jacket. With one shot fired, Lewis promptly executed the Director. A simple hand signal followed, directing the operatives to begin dragging the dead bodies of the military personnel from the room. Once the area was cleared of the mess of combat, Lewis casually sat down in the Director's chair.

"Secure the rest of the base," he casually stated with a wave of his hand. The remaining operatives quickly filed out to resume the cleanup of their carnage. Thus, leaving Lewis completely alone in the office.

With a spin of the office chair, he faced the desk laid before him. Lewis then grinned as he set his elbows on the desk; his hands lining his now fully bearded chin.

Everything had gone according to plan.

Lewis procured the Phantom Hawk's crystal from his pocket and set it on the desktop before him. The red lights still flickered across the object's surface, but that mattered little. Time was now on their side, and with the army of spirits the Duskwatchers Organization obtained... they would be unstoppable.

Furthermore, the Phantom Hawk was now his to control.

Lewis thought back to the previous mission's setup. While Luke slept, Lewis had an operative sneak into his room and replace the primed crystal Luke had on his table with a new one. A crystal that was primed and bonded to Lewis himself. With the simply lie that the rest of the crystals had been destroyed, Luke had no choice but to use the one he thought he had primed. Unknowingly delivering Lewis his greatest weapon.

The invasion force was also hand-picked from some of the organization's newer members. Ones that had no idea as to the group's true purpose. This allowed Lewis to relieve their numbers of any who might act in defiance once his plan to assault the secret facility was laid bare.

The Duskwatchers Organization had never fought for humanities protection against the paranormal. In fact, every decision made over the last few hundred years had a singular goal in mind. They would lead humanity into a new age. One where the organization had all the power and would direct humanity as it saw fit.

Every decision and every bit of research up to this point was to achieve this singular goal. Even this very research facility was built upon long forgotten knowledge they had discovered. The knowledge to encourage the Broodmother into opening a portal deep within its walls. One that they knew the military in its infinite greed would attempt to weaponize.

Ultimately this lust for power led them to progress the organization's own knowledge far more rapidly than they could achieve on their own. With operatives planted in place among the staff, they had been fed every last bit of knowledge obtained in the study of the spirits. And with the idea planted in the Directors mind to let loose the Broodmother, things would be set in motion to create the world they had longed for.

A world where nations were thrown into chaos by the invading spirits. A world where the general public was ill prepared to defend itself, and would have to quickly turn to the organization's leaders if they had any hope of survival.

All the organization was missing was the final key: A way to capture and control the spirits. So, when word reached them of a college student working his way through the invention of a device to prove the existence of ghosts, they knew where to find this key.

Using the excuse of removing the Phantom Hawk, they had directed the boy into molding the one weapon they needed to enact their plan. Even the collar of the Phantom Hawk was intended to break upon its release. As this gave them the motive they needed to manipulate their way into Luke's mind. Which in turn, got them the controller crystal technology they needed to finally take their seats of power.

"Sir, we have fully secured the facility," an operative stated as he entered the room.

Lewis looked up from his thoughts and acknowledged the man. "Good, initiate phase two of our plan, and begin making preparations to move out."

With a salute, the operative left the room. Offers would now be sent out to the world's leaders. An offer with a simple message; accept our takeover... or fall to the upcoming onslaught.

Lewis leaned back in the chair and grinned once more, success heightening his mood as one last thought spread throughout his mind.

The world would soon be under his control.

www.ingramcontent.com/pod-product-compliance
Lightning Source LLC
Chambersburg PA
CBHW021156010826
48971CB00014B/2187